Blue River

by

Michael Frederick

WEST GEORGIA REGIONAL LIBRARY SYSTEM
Neva Lomason Memorial Library

Novels by author:

White Shoulders

Ledges

The Paper Man

Missouri Madness

Shy Ann

Summer of '02

Autumn Letters

Places

This book is a work of fiction and represents no actual persons living or dead in any way whatsoever.

September, 2007/1st printing/5,000 copies
Copyright 2007
all rights reserved

Thanks, Tony, for your art.
Cover Design by Anthony Conrad

Dedicated to Ryan Lee Saunders

FOREWORD

I am the only one in the world who could tell you this story, and I'm not even a real person. I'm Eddie's mind, referred to as "Fast Eddie" at times. As Eddie got older, he began questioning things, slowing down, ignoring me more and more. I did not like this "Slow Eddie" at all.

Yes, only I can tell you what really happened, because I was there and Eddie wasn't — most of the time. In this early part of the twenty-first century, more people like Eddie will find a better way to live. These people are evolving so that others living "in their head" can stay on this planet a bit longer.

Mind Games

My name is Fast Eddie. How a brilliant mind like me got mixed up with this cartoon family is a mystery! Edward Lesley Dense — the name given to the body that houses me — came into this world in 1960 with a full head of orange hair just like his parents and his older sister, Sara. And like his sister, Eddie was born on the third floor of the Methodist Hospital in Council Bluffs, Iowa. Eddie came out of his mother's womb ass first, or "ass-backwards."

Right from the beginning I set baby Eddie apart as "different" from the rest of his family. Mr. and Mrs. Dense realized that their second (and last) child would be unique because I caused little Eddie to be left-handed. Mommy Dense would offer her baby a spoon, and I made his tiny left hand reach for it every time. "He's an artist!" Mommy Dense would proclaim to his proud father, completely oblivious to my role in the matter.

Now, I realize I'm *only* Eddie's mind — something intangible — yet I know that lefties are wired differently and are forced into doing things backwards in a right-handed world that's been very ill for a long time. Making Eddie a lefty was key to my being able to control and manipulate him from the beginning.

Eddie's parents were drunken hippies from the 40s and 50s. Sara called them "drippies." Mr. and Mrs. Dense loved to drink alcohol and never really wanted to give it up. Eddie's mom and dad had a bizarre sense of humor; long before they ever had kids, they loved to get drunk on Saturday mornings and roar with laughter watching cartoons on their black-and-white Zenith television. Their names were even cartoonish. Ichabod Martin Dense, nicknamed "Ike," was Eddie's father. When I. M. Dense married Mary Ellen Stahl, she became M. E. Dense. In fact, Ike and Mary admitted to both of their kids that each had been conceived during a Saturday morning cartoon drunk.

Ike and Mary had children late in life — in their late thirties when parenting couldn't change them as much. First came Sara Opal in 1957, then Edward Lesley three years later. S. O. Dense and E. L. Dense made their family of four a complete set of orange-haired characters who were just plain different.

It was no wonder Sara became a raging alcoholic at twelve years old and nearly died twice after mixing vodka with her mother's antidepressant pills. But Sara was strong; she conquered her alcoholism and willed her body to abstain from it after her second near-fatal episode. Only Eddie managed to escape alcoholism altogether because I gave him an aversion to the taste of alcohol. I knew right away that I could never let alcohol wrest control of Eddie from me.

Physically, Eddie favored his father. His orange hair was fine and wispy, and his porcelain white face had freckles all over it on either side of his nose, just like his old man. But unlike the other three sets of green eyes in his family, Eddie had clear cornflower-blue eyes that blinked lazily, as if his eyelids were too close to his eyeballs and rubbed against them when he blinked. Also like his dad, Eddie inherited giant protruding Dense teeth that could never be concealed behind his thin red lips that neither scowled nor smiled. (The flat appearance of his mouth was probably Eddie's most remarkable feature.) But what I caused Eddie to be most bothered about were his teeth, which was another trait he shared with Ike: Whenever they pronounced words with Ss and Ts, they would lisp them so that specks of spit would fly out from those Dense gaps between their upper front teeth. Ike was too old to care, but Eddie secretly wanted braces — except they were expensive and Eddie was terrified of going to the dentist. So Eddie lived with his spitting lisp and learned to talk by barely opening his mouth, almost like a ventriloquist. Because I made him so self-conscious about his teeth, Eddie didn't smile or talk much as he got older.

But it was those flat Dense lips that gave Eddie a pathetic look of grim determination. It was as if Eddie's mouth told the world that he would amount to something one day . . . somehow.

FIKSHEN

Eddie was fifteen and Sara eighteen in the summer of 1975 when their parents separated. Ike had slapped Mary during some stupid argument right after closing their bar at two in the morning.

It took Mary two weeks to move out of their house and find a new place for her kids and her to live. Sara was more upset about their parents' separation than Eddie was, for she was starting college at Creighton University in Omaha in the fall and didn't like all this "drama" going on when she was determined to get all As in college and make something of herself.

In reality, Mary Dense was usually the one to be physical with her husband, often throwing glasses and beer bottles at him after he verbally insulted her. Most times it was something Ike had said earlier in the day, such as, "You don't have a clue;" "Don't be so stupid, Dense;" or, "You're a real mental giant, aren't ya?" Or sometimes Ike would purposely tilt the jukebox during a certain song Mary had played, like "Stand by Your Man"or "Send Me the Pillow that You Dream On."

But not until closing would Mary jump Ike about what he'd said or done earlier. Usually they'd been drinking all through the day when she'd let him really have it after closing. "Don't you EVER call me STUPID, Dense, in front of the customers!" she would rail as the smirking Ike unplugged the red neon "IKE & MARY'S" sign in the bar's front window. If Ike said anything moronic then — like, "Okay, stupid" — she'd let fly with a beer mug or a twelve-ounce pilsner glass in his direction, purposely missing Ike and the front window. She just wanted to scare him and make a point that she was not to be hassled.

Eddie couldn't recall his dad ever getting violent with his mother until this recent episode which had caused his mother to move them out of their modest three-bedroom house on the north side of Council Bluffs. The Dense children never heard their father's side of the story, yet both Sara and Eddie knew that their father had to be pushed pretty far by their mother for him to lose his temper that way.

During this transition period, Mary didn't work at the bar. She withdrew three thousand dollars from their joint checking account and found a two-bedroom stucco cottage to rent temporarily outside the city limits to the south, close to Lake Manawa State Park, a stone's throw from I-29 which runs along the east bank of the Missouri River.

Panoramic hills were farther to the east, yet the area was so flat around them that a small private airport was a short distance from their cottage. The airport was bordered by an elevated gravel road with very deep ditches on either side of it; and adjacent to the airport on the opposite side of the gravel road was an unlandscaped mobile home park housing a single row of mismatched trailers. The only thing these trailers had in common were the silver-colored propane tanks about the size of a hippopotamus which stretched in a perfect row behind each unit and along the gravel road. To live in this part of Council Bluffs meant that you didn't care about any sense of order or have much pride in your neighborhood.

The temporary Dense cottage was next door to a furniture and mobile home dealer, House Furniture, whose smooth-talking namesake owned the trailer park. Mary Dense had told her kids when they moved into the small cottage that she put a thousand dollars down on a new mobile home that would be delivered in a month.

Eddie and I watched our new home being delivered the day it arrived. Eddie walked along the giant transport truck as it slowly moved to the end of the dirt lane to deposit the brand-new trailer house in the vacant lot Mary had pointed out to her kids one day as they drove along the gravel road. Eddie could see right away that their new home was the longest one in the park; it was white with charcoal black trim. As the truck positioned our dwelling in line with the rest of the units in the park, Eddie got close enough to read the Michigan manufacturer's lettering plated on the back of the home: FIKSHEN. Right then I planted the idea in Eddie's mind that one day he would write about his new home. I made Eddie creative in that way, molding him into a writer with a different way of looking at things. Like the time his seventh grade English teacher had printed in bold letters on the blackboard, "What is fiction?" Nearly everyone in his class turned in a similar answer: "Something like a novel; a story that's not true." But the answer I gave Eddie was different: "Fiction stands for Feelings I Chose To Ignore One Night." Yes, Eddie was different and I made him that way.

As the long trailer was being jacked up and carefully set onto concrete blocks in line with its propane tank, I hinted to Eddie that his first novel would begin here. And I quickly convinced him that this could never be a real home — because it was FIKSHEN.

A week later the Dense family, minus Daddy Dense, moved into their new home. Each had his or her own bedroom. Sara's room was at the front facing the dirt lane and next to the only bathroom, which was right across from the back door — the only door they could use because the front door in the living room did not have any steps to it. Mr. House said he'd have to "order it special."

Eddie's room was tiny, down from the bathroom and off the narrow hallway that was paneled with artificial walnut-like particle board. Eddie's room was the smallest of the three bedrooms. The new queen-size bed, its mattress wrapped in plastic, and his new dresser made of particle board took up more than half the floor space. His room had a lone window that looked out to a late-model, small green trailer with dirty white trim some eight feet away from FIKSHEN. The two units shared a septic tank, which was right below Eddie's window.

As Eddie removed the plastic covering his mattress, he heard strident voices outside his window. On his knees and careful not to let his black tennis shoe bottoms touch the new mattress, he peered out between the stiff brown linen curtains, whereupon he could see two dark figures. The whites of their big brown eyes were staring at him from behind a screened bedroom window inside the green trailer. Eddie ducked back, a bit startled by his gawking neighbors.

I told Eddie to forget about his nosy neighbors and go check out the rest of our new dwelling. I was curious to see what this place was all about and how I could use it to my advantage. As Eddie passed through the kitchen, he saw Mr. House giving his mother and Sara a walk-through inspection. Eager to make a good impression on his new tenants, he went through each room of FIKSHEN with them to ensure everything was to their liking and working properly, such as making sure the refrigerator was on and set to the right temperature. Mr. House was particularly attentive to the newly separated mother of two, but Mary's disdain for men would not allow her to be romanced by any slick-talking, egotistical old man who believed he was God's gift to women.

The floor of the mobile home was a slick and shiny vinyl, a vanilla-caramel color with gold flecks forming an obscure pattern. Mr. House's dress shoes were shiny and slick too, a glaring butterscotch color of expensive-looking leather. The new landlord, who appeared to be in his sixties, was tall and thin and sharply dressed in a brown suit with a string tie. His red-veined eyes were hidden by dark sunglasses that matched his shoes.

Eddie and I went ahead of the tour into the expansive living room that was furnished with a large Zenith color television, a chocolate brown fold-down sofa, and a gold-colored high-back rocking recliner. There were two full-length mirrors that gave the illusion of more space and some semblance of modern design.

When Eddie went into his mother's bedroom, we saw that it was about the size of Sara's room, but it had more closet space. Unlike the other bedrooms, it had a king-size bed and a long mirrored dresser that Mr. House knew his tenant would like.

Outside his mother's window, Eddie again saw those two faces that he had seen from his bedroom window. They were black boys. The tall, skinny one appeared to be Eddie's age; the other boy was seven or eight years old. Both boys had tall afros that were neatly shaped and made them appear much taller than they were. They were standing on their property line not far from the Dense propane tank. Weeds grew tall around their property line and gave the green trailer a shabby appearance compared to the brand new FIKSHEN. Eddie and I heard the boys whispering words that were carried through his mother's bedroom window by the prairie winds blowing steady and ruffling the curtains markedly, but we couldn't make out any of their words.

When Eddie tried to exit out the front door of FIKSHEN, Mr. House warned him that there wasn't a step outside; that's when the landlord repeated to Mrs. Dense that he'd "special order" a step for the front door.

Outside, Eddie saw our neighbors pointing at a small plane landing on the runway of the private airfield across the double-ditched gravel road. The older boy waved and smiled at Eddie and then looked down at his little brother as if warning him to be friendly. Eddie stepped over to the weed line. I didn't know it at the time, but these two boys would lead Eddie to the beginning of the end of my running his life. I never saw it coming.

"My name's Eddie."

"I'm Dave. This is my brother, Charles," the older boy grinned with the whitest teeth Eddie had ever seen.

"How long have you lived here?" Eddie asked Dave.

"This'll be our third summer here," Dave smiled back.

"You like living here?" Eddie inquired.

Dave shrugged his shoulders and scratched his bare knee through a big hole in his faded jeans. It was clear right away that he had light coming from his brown eyes. I know now that it was "that light" that was the beginning of Eddie's quest to get rid of me.

"It stinks here when it gets hot," little Charles blurted, which caused his brother to laugh hard without sound even though his thin body convulsed from head to toe.

Dave explained, "When it gets hot the septic tank stinks like crazy. You'll see," he smiled while pointing over to the exposed black waste hoses coming from each trailer.

"Now it'll just stink more," Charles complained.

Dave slapped the back of his brother's head and told him to keep still, fearing his cynicism would drive away a potential new friend. Then Charles sucker-punched his taller brother in the stomach before running for his life. Dave stayed put after feigning chase, and his body language appeared to apologize for his brother's remark. "How many are in yer family?" he asked Eddie.

"My mom and my sister. My dad doesn't live with us."

"That's the same number as in our place, 'cept I have a brother. Ya wanna shoot some hoop?" Dave gestured with a one-hand shot.

A beige trailer forty feet on the other side of Dave's trailer had a dirt lot, and at the edge of the lane was a sturdy basketball hoop with a mud-stained backboard and a new white net. Dave's neighbor, a truck driver with a wife and five kids, made the thing solid and the rim was exactly ten feet off the ground. Just before they knocked on the door of that trailer, Dave told Eddie that the trucker had played on a championship team in '63 and that he never had time to play now but has a new ball. One of their kids opened the door and handed Dave the ball.

The dirt lot under the basket was uneven and made dribbling difficult for Eddie, but not so for Dave Armstrong. Eddie's neighbor was a natural with a basketball; his long fingers and smooth fluid shot hit nothing but net from any distance. "Shoot till ya miss," Dave smiled, which meant Eddie rebounded most of the time. Eddie managed to make two in a row three times, but Dave made six, seven, then nine in a row from twenty feet out.

"You play at school?" Eddie asked. He was surprised when Dave shook his head no without explaining.

When Dave's mother called out from her trailer that dinner was ready, Eddie kept shooting for twenty minutes until Dave returned with Charles. Dave kept coaxing his brother to shoot by feeding him the ball, but the scowling boy just bounced it right back to him.

Eddie left to eat when Sara drove up in their mother's Gremlin with Mary on the front passenger seat. On the way to a nearby restaurant, Sara asked about the two boys and commented that they might be the only black people living in the area. That's when Eddie and I started looking around trailer row to see if she was right. Dave had referred to it as "trailer row" while shooting baskets. I tried to tell Eddie then that a friend like Dave in an all-white neighborhood might get him in trouble at a mostly all-white school. I was running Eddie in those days, and that's how I liked it.

There is a River

Charles was right. The shared septic tank did stink bad when the weather was hot. Oftentimes Eddie would have to crank shut his bedroom window and forego the air that kept him from feeling claustrophobic. Dave told his new friend that he did the same thing because he'd rather breathe old air than old crap anytime.

One August afternoon, Eddie made his way gingerly across the two-by-four plank Dave had positioned across the ditch so they could still access the road when rain flooded it. The ditch on the far side of the road was narrow enough that the boys could easily leap across it if it were flooded and access the manicured grass of the airfield. Dave often went over to the airfield and would sit with his back against a large fluorescent aluminum box that served as a landing marker for the pilots. He liked to go to this isolated place to smoke his mother's cigarettes while watching the gliding twin-engine planes landing day and night. This particular day Eddie found his friend crouched behind the landing box where he was smoking. "I wondered what you did out here," Eddie smiled as he crouched down next to Dave.

"My mom won't let me smoke inside around Charles. She says it's a bad influence on him. But, man . . . she smokes all day 'round that kid."

Dave offered Eddie one of the cigarettes, but Eddie shook his head no, adding, "They make me dizzy."

Dave laughed, his body convulsing, as he explained, "Maybe that's why I smoke 'em. Life is dizzy, man, that's for sure."

"Where is your dad?" Eddie asked.

Dave shrugged his thin, broad shoulders saying, "Who knows. Last letter we got from him he was on some oil rig off the coast of Louisiana."

"How'd you end up here with your mom?" Eddie asked.

"My dad hated it here." Dave laughed as he told Eddie his father said that Iowa and Nebraska are full of bull crap and cold-ass winters.

"You gonna go out for basketball?" Eddie changed the subject.

"No way, man. I ain't runnin' up and down the court with these skinny-ass legs. I'm gonna fly outta this place one day and get me a good job down south where it don't snow and blow cold air right through me." Just then a landing plane caught their attention as it touched down about a hundred yards off. Its clean white body with green trim captivated Dave as Eddie watched him follow its landing with wondrous awe until it vanished down the runway.

After an awkward silence Dave told Eddie he was taking his brother hunting for night crawlers by the river and asked Eddie if he wanted to "go with."

"No, I better not. My dad's coming over to see our new place, and he might stay awhile after supper."

"There's this old man at a bait shop who pays me a buck a dozen for night crawlers. I take a coffee can, a fork, and a flashlight, and I can dig up a hundred of 'em in an hour. Gots to make me some money so I can buy me a half-gallon of chocolate chip ice cream. I love chocolate chip ice cream," Dave laughed.

"We've got chocolate chip ice cream. You want some?"

"Hell, yeah!" Dave got to this feet and they headed for FIKSHEN.

The weeds around the Dense trailer were catching up to the weeds around the Armstrong trailer. Mr. House still hadn't "special ordered" a step for the front door like he said he would.

Mary said she didn't care if he ever ordered it because she didn't want people using the front door and tracking in mud.

Nobody was home so they ate ice cream in the living room. All Eddie had to offer to drink was Tang on ice. Eddie's guest was humble and really quiet; he appeared impressed by the new mobile home that was more than twice the size of his place. Dave was used to clutter in his trailer. To Dave Armstrong FIKSHEN was nice. His body language became solemn and respectful of the new space and new smells as he sat on the sofa with his host eating ice cream much more slowly than he would at home. "This place is huge," Dave remarked while looking around FIKSHEN with the same light in his brown eyes Eddie and I had seen when we first met him. "Even your color TV is huge — twice the size of our little black-and-white," Dave laughed.

Dave's body showed joy like no other person Eddie or I had ever seen. Even the way he ate ice cream was alive with a palpable joy in every bite that was sent between his thick brown lips — lips which never hid for long those perfect white teeth that beamed with his light.

"Where you from, Eddie?"

"Here. My parents split up but they still work together at a bar they own here in Council Bluffs."

"Why'd they split?"

"My dad slapped my mom and she moved out."

"But they still work together?"

"Yeah. My mom owns half the bar with him."

"And he's comin' over for supper?"

"Yeah. He's sorry he slapped her, but my mom won't live with him after that happened."

"That's one thing my dad never did. He never got violent with my mom. But he abused her other ways by gamblin' and sleepin' with other women. My dad used to always tell me 'there is a river.' He calls it 'Blue River' — a river of crystal blue water like ya see in that Hamm's beer commercial. He said the water is so crystal clear . . . but just out of our reach," Dave gestured with his long arm. "He says that when he's drivin' he can see it through his windshield. But he says that the trick is to know that you're already there. See, our minds trick us to think we aren't there, that we have to suffer and keep searching for it. My dad says it's a fearful thing."

"Why is that fearful?" Eddie blinked lazily.

"'Cause if it's a thing you don't have, it means yer not okay where you are. Yer afraid," Dave winked and took a sip of his Tang.

"Did your dad reach this Blue River?"

"He told me that's why he left us. He said he could never get there around my mom. She told him he was just runnin' away from havin' to grow up to be a man and face his family responsibilities."

"Did you ever tell him that?"

"Didn't have to. My mom told him every day till he left."

When they finished their Tang, Dave politely rinsed his bowl and spoon and glass in the sink, which made Eddie do the same.

"Thanks for the ice cream and Tang. It was good. I'll have to give you some of mine after I get those night crawlers."

About Sara

It seemed to Eddie that all Sara did while growing up was read and do her homework in her room with her door closed. Very rarely would she talk with members of her family. Like her mother, Sara had thick orange hair and wore it short. Like any girl with orange hair, she had to be careful what colors she wore. Once she dyed her hair an auburn shade that really looked good on her, except she abhorred her tell-tale roots that in her opinion made her look specious and cheap. Although not strikingly beautiful, she was a pleasant-looking girl. She didn't inherit the same male Dense choppers that Eddie had; her teeth were small and not bucked. But she was a lot like Eddie was before he met Dave. The Dense eldest child always resented the fact that her parents owned a bar and contributed to the alcoholism she had conquered and which was so prevalent in the area. She thought her parents were "weak parasites living off other weak people."

When Sara was fifteen and still living in the old neighborhood in Council Bluffs, she had a neighbor boy who became a big part of her life. Larry Diamond was seventeen and became Sara's first boyfriend — of sorts. Larry smoked, rode a motorcycle, drank beer, never studied, and could get loud like her father. Funny how Larry was so similar to Ike.

When Sara turned sixteen, her mother let her babysit the three Diamond girls. Larry, their only brother, was a senior at the same school Sara attended as a sophomore. Redheaded Larry was considered one of the rough guys to stay clear of if you were male or female. He was already a man with rugged good looks who dressed like a Hells Angel at school. He either drove his black '57 Chevy or 350 Scrambler to school.

Mrs. Diamond, twice divorced, tended bar just a few blocks from their little house. Sara would come over around six or seven in the evening on Friday and Saturday after Mrs. D. fed her kids and then left for work. The Diamond girls were always cleaning the kitchen when Sara showed up to watch them. Larry was never there for the evening meal, and Sara was always petrified when he did come home late before his mother got off work at two in the morning, as Sara's parents did.

Sara's fear of Larry began months before she began babysitting his sisters. One day Sara had been standing at the end of a long lunch line at school when Larry walked by her with a Marlboro riding behind one ear and said to her, "You don't have to wait in line, ya know." Then he walked away in his old jeans, t-shirt and loafers with no socks, confident she would follow him out to his car in the school parking lot. His magnetism did pull at her until he was out of her view. She had seen so many girls in her school with good intentions to graduate, and along came a guy like Larry and motherhood happens nine months later. That's what Sara was afraid of — Larry's power to change and control her future when she was so determined to do something special with her life. And yet she kept thinking about what she'd say if he ever asked her again. But he didn't. Larry had plenty of girls, and Sara was the kind of girl who could never be with a guy who was unfaithful.

One day Sara was walking down her street on her way to babysit the Diamond girls when she saw Larry coming toward her on his motorcycle. He stopped his bike beside her and told her to get on. It was on that very short ride to the Diamond house that Sara Dense fell for the guy. She was drawn to a combination of things — the power of the machine, Larry's funny confidence, and his hard stomach muscles that she held onto for dear life when he accelerated.

After that ride to his house, Larry started hanging around his place more when Sara babysat his sisters. One night Larry returned home with his mother after she closed the bar and walked Sara home. Not a word was spoken between them until they reached the Dense back porch. "How come you won't go to lunch with me?" he asked with his unlit cigarette between his lips.

"I don't want to sit in a smoky car," she stated firmly after turning to face him at the bottom of the porch steps.

"What if I don't smoke?"

He made her smile bashfully. "Maybe," she laughed and went inside.

The next Monday at school Sara had lunch in Larry's car at Fred's Drive-in not far from school. Larry didn't smoke and Sara didn't complain when he loudly played his Led Zeppelin tape during their entire lunch period without saying a word to each other.

Some weeks later, when Sara was going to lunch with Larry three times a week, she cynically told him he played the music too loud and that any conversation would be a welcome change. He was polite and accommodating, but he admitted to being "uptight" because he wanted to smoke. He said it would loosen him up to talk.

"Well, go ahead and smoke. But keep it outside your window and blow your smoke that way . . . please."

Larry smoked discreetly, just as she wanted him to — the same way she made Ike smoke around her.

"What do you want to talk about?" he asked.

"What do you want to do with your life when you get out of school?"

"I don't know. Plans don't mean much to me. I always thought I'd end up in the Army, but I got a couple felonies on my record and I hear they won't take me now."

"Felonies? For what?"

"I sawed off some parking meters in Omaha."

"Both times?"

"No. The other one was for punchin' a cop in Council Bluffs. He pulled me over on my bike and wanted to look inside my saddlebags. I told him he ain't touchin' anything on my bike. So when he reached for my stuff I pushed him away and things got outta hand."

"Did you go to jail?"

"For a night. My mom bailed me out."

"What did she say?"

"Not much when I told her I had a couple parking meters in my saddlebags," Larry sniggered with his smoke.

Sara stopped asking Larry about his past and curtailed her lunches with him. But Larry started coming by to Sara's place and taking her for walks to the river. Sara would read her books while Larry smoked and drank beer. They started fooling around then, but Sara never let Larry go "all the way" with her. That was something she realized early on could ruin her chance to live her life on her terms. Sara Dense would never allow anyone to control her future.

Larry dropped out of school in the spring of his senior year. He told Sara he couldn't graduate with his class anyway because he was four credits shy and would have to return next fall. "No way I'm going back," he told Sara. "I'm gettin' a job instead of this B.S."

And Sara would not preach to Larry, for he was her emotional protector. As long as Larry Diamond was her friend, she had his protection from her own emotions. No man was going to get into her head and force her to sabotage her future, and Larry Diamond was not part of her future. If Sara were beautiful, Larry wouldn't be her friend. They both knew that, except Larry didn't want to really get to the bottom of his feelings.

"Why do you ask me that B.S.?" Larry would protest to Sara's indignant smile after telling him he wouldn't be her friend if she were beautiful. "To me yer a beautiful girl," he'd snap. "The big reason I like you is because yer smart — book-wise — and I'm not. It makes me feel good to be around a smart girl. And to me that's beautiful."

Sara would only laugh, even though she knew it was true. She also knew of the easy girls he'd bring home to his bedroom and sneak out the next morning before she came over to help him with his math and English homework.

Yes, Larry was perfect for Sara . . . while it lasted.

The last time Sara heard from Larry after he dropped out of school was the Christmas before they moved into FIKSHEN. He had sent her a tape from California. It was music hits from the '70s, and highlighted on the tape was the song "How Could I Let You Get Away," sung by the Spinners. To Larry it was their breakup song. Sara cherished it as one of her prized possessions, wrapping it in plastic and saving it with her collection of family photos.

Eddie's Light

That early fall Ike bought Sara a new white Gremlin for her commute to college in Omaha. Dave and Eddie walked together the two-and-a-half miles to their high school. They walked fast, so it took them about forty minutes. Time flew by because they joked and talked about silly things the whole way. There were only three African American students in their school, and Dave was the only male.

During nearly every early morning trek to school, the same white upperclassmen boys would drive past them in their red Mustang, honking at them and shouting bad things. "Nigger lover!" "You black bastard!" I really caused Eddie to bristle about those racial slurs, but they didn't seem to bother Dave too much. He would always laugh at them and say something funny to his friend: "Now you know why I walk so fast;" or "If they stop, I'm runnin' like one fast nigger." I gave Eddie the idea to walk on the side of the road facing oncoming traffic on their way to and from school. That way their backs weren't to the passing cars.

Dave and Eddie had four class periods together: English, algebra, study hall, and P.E. They sat across the aisle from each other at the back of the classroom in English and algebra. Eddie got good grades in English and Dave was much better at math. They would help each other by sneaking answers to each other. They made up a system when they had a quiz. If it was multiple choice, first one would signal the question number by showing fingers on an open hand on their desktop. If the question was number seven, the one who needed help would pat an open hand once and then put two fingers out. Then came the number of the multiple-choice answer from the one who knew it. In algebra class they were caught by the teacher and both failed the quiz, so they stopped cheating and did their homework together at night. They studied together in Eddie's room because Mary Dense worked nights and Mrs. Armstrong was home every night.

Just before Thanksgiving, late one weekend night while Eddie was on his bed and I was helping him compose a short story for an English assignment, he heard a tapping on his bedroom window. It was Dave, and it was freezing cold outside. Dave asked if he could come over.

They sat on Eddie's bed as Dave told him he couldn't sleep because his mom had a man in her bedroom. This was the first time Eddie had seen his affable friend sad. Eddie noticed that Dave's eyes were glazed with a murky film that revealed only brown. They talked in a low whisper so as not to wake Sara. Eddie didn't talk much that night; he just listened closely to his friend.

"Look, man, I'm not sayin' it's a bad thing or she shouldn't be bringin' a man over. I know it's her home an' she's been alone for a long time. And that's just part of life. But on some kind of deep level it bothers me. It's almost like she's betrayin' my dad and me and Charles. Man, I tried to figure out what that was all about, and all I could come up with is that it's a human thing — somethin' boys feel about their mother. When I saw yer light on I had to get outta there. When I got outside freezin' my ass off, I was mad at her for bringin' some man into my house and wakin' me up. It's cold, man. Real cold."

Eddie didn't know what to say. Yet Dave's problem was bringing up issues I'd planted in Eddie's mind about his own mother. He felt safe to voice them now. "I know what you mean. It's like you don't want any man around, because you know you are part of your father."

"Yeah," Dave whispered in agreement. "It's like you don't want any man besides yer dad tellin' you what to do."

"Did that ever happen to you?" Eddie whispered.

"Yeah, once. My mom had this boyfriend. He sold insurance to her. And he started stayin' over and always tellin' me and Charles that we could help our mother keep the place clean. Charles told the guy to kiss his ass, so the guy pushed Charles down. I was scared 'cause the guy was big. I knew he'd kick my skinny butt if I did anything. So the next time he was over, it was pretty hot out and I put my half-gallon of chocolate chip ice cream on the front seat of his new Cadillac."

Eddie laughed with Dave. "What happened?"

"It melted. You know how hot it gets here in the summer. Well, it was really hot — and so was that guy when he found a big puddle of chocolate chip ice cream covering his new front seat. He got so mad he never came over again. And that was the last time he ever saw my mom."

Since Dave didn't want to return home until his mother's guest left, they fell asleep on Eddie's bed.

The next morning Sara was surprised to see Dave and Eddie eating cereal together at the kitchen table, and she quickly put her robe on over her pajamas. During breakfast, Sara enjoyed Dave's company and thought he was a well-mannered kid, telling her brother later that Dave's eyes shine brighter than any eyes she'd ever seen.

"I know!" Eddie agreed. "But what does that mean? How come our eyes don't shine the same light?"

Sara told her curious brother that she'd read about such light in novels by D. H. Lawrence and said, "He's alive with life. He's conscious — living in the present moment — so he sees everything. Things that we don't notice."

"Like what things?"

"Like nature. He sees plants and animals as living things. Everything is alive to him, and it's all such a wonder to him. Some people are wired that way. They are the lucky ones. He's filled with joy, and love is in his heart."

"He laughs at things that happen to him that I would never laugh at."

"Exactly! He's special. You can learn from a guy like that. People like him don't judge or label every person they meet. If I were you, I'd ask him how he does that — because it's a real gift," Sara smiled.

Stolen Brother

In late March when the grip of winter was letting up some, little Charles went to the river with a friend right after school. Charles wasn't supposed to go anywhere without first asking his mother — especially to the river. Around dusk Mrs. Armstrong told Dave to find his brother and bring him home. Eddie went looking for Charles when Dave asked him to help with the search.

They followed the muddy tracks made by the two boys, footprints that were headed on the same route Dave used whenever he took Charles hunting for night crawlers with him. Within about ten minutes, Dave's shortcut took them to a huge sewer pipe that was dry and which led to the east bank of the ice-covered Missouri River. There they made out two sets of tracks close together that went out onto the river. Soon Dave saw a spot some twenty yards out on the ice that was broken clear through. Eddie could feel Dave's horrific terror at the thought of his brother falling in and being trapped under the ice. This terror made Dave's mouth tremble; his voice cracked when he uttered to Eddie, "They fell in. My brother's been stolen by God."

Eddie stopped Dave from going out onto the ice by pointing to cracks around the pair of footprints and shouting, "It's too dangerous!"

Dave stood staring at the spot his brother and friend appeared to have fallen in, his face heartsick and dotted with salty tears on his cheeks and eyelashes. "How do I tell my mother?" he cried.

"It's not for sure that's what happened," Eddie's voice faltered.

"Not sure? Look, man! There's his tracks! They stop out there and don't come back!" he cried out while pointing with a trembling finger that nearly made Eddie vomit.

That was a terrible night for Dave and his mother — and I tormented Eddie to no end about it. A county sheriff squad car and a fire-rescue vehicle were parked outside the green Armstrong trailer for some time. From his closed bedroom window, Eddie could hear the plaintive cries of his friend's hysterical mother for hours. "My baby is gone! Lord, why take my baby from me? Oh, God! NO!"

Later, when Dave's grandmother arrived, it became absolute madness. The sounds of grief pouring from the Armstrong trailer were nearly unbearable to Eddie, and I so weakened him by magnifying the tragedy that his legs shook terribly when he tried to stand or walk.

Sara stayed up with her brother until their mother came home after closing the bar. Mary sat on their sofa between her kids. Eddie's legs were shaking so fast that his mother placed her hand on his knee to calm him. For a couple hours the Dense family stayed up listening for news about the missing boys on a local radio station. Eddie told Sara and his mother that Dave only knew that Charles's friend was a classmate of his who lived near the stucco house they'd lived in by House Furniture.

Alone in his room after four in the morning, Eddie could not sleep; he got out his notebook and began writing about the terrible tragedy. It was a short story titled "Stolen Brother." Eddie knew that he'd never let Dave read it or turn it in for credit in their English class. This tragic moment marked the beginning of his life as a writer.

He wrote about how this was the first time that death had touched his life; how he could never imagine how his friend would ever get over this terrible loss of his brother. He wrote:

There was a knot, a twisting kind of coiling snake in my belly that I thought was changing my insides forever. It was the same feeling I experienced in a smaller way when I knew my parents didn't love each other the way I wanted them to. Except now, this knot burns. I'm on fire with fear and this overwhelming feeling of dread that makes me fear my own death.

I wanted to go over and see my friend when I heard him comforting his mother with such tender pleas for mercy from God — for God to help his mother now. But my legs wouldn't move. I was stuck with my fear of what I would see when I saw my friend with his mother. I was not up to being close to such things that I've only seen on TV.

How will Dave and his poor mother ever get through this kind of loss? Will I ever see and hear my friend's beautiful laugh again? Even now I am selfishly afraid for myself when I think of how I will be when I see them again. It's my mind telling me these awful things I will see. I want to control my mind, but I can't. This voice in my head has stolen me just as God has stolen Dave's brother. Yes, my world is all so dark now because of these thoughts about tomorrow and the terrible grief I will see.

For sixteen agonizing days and interminable nights, there was no sign of the missing boys; the river had not broken up or thawed, so divers were not able to search for them.

Mrs. Armstrong was heavily sedated. She was placed on a prescribed medication that somehow inhibited her ability to cry.

Every night Eddie left his bedroom light on in case his friend ever needed to talk. But Dave never came over. Eddie knew that Dave was smoking in his trailer because he could smell the smoke coming in through the cracks of his bedroom window.

Nineteen days after the boys had gone missing, divers found the bloated bodies of Charles and his friend several miles downstream on the Nebraska side of the river. The awful news was delivered to Mrs. Armstrong by a red-faced Omaha detective.

Shortly after the detective left, Dave headed for FIKSHEN. He stood at the bottom of the steps without a coat on and told Eddie they'd found the boys' bodies twelve and fifteen miles down river. Eddie was numb, standing in his open doorway not knowing what to say. "I'm sorry, Dave," was the only pitiful phrase he managed to utter.

Dave looked so tired; he could barely hold his head up. He just nodded and told Eddie in a soft voice that it was a relief to finally know.

"How's your mom?" Eddie asked.

"She's really devastated. My grandma's with her. It's been a real nightmare. I better get back home. I'm supposed to call my dad and let him know they found Charles, and let him know the funeral is Tuesday."

"What church?"

"My grandma's church in Council Bluffs."

"I'll go with ya on Tuesday."

"Okay. See ya, man."

Three Bad Drives

Eddie missed school Tuesday so he could ride with Dave to his brother's funeral. Dave wore his worn black suit with a white shirt and wide black tie. Eddie wore his best dress slacks that were gold colored with his only white shirt and a blue tie.

Five of them rode together in Dave's grandmother's big yellow Bonneville. Grandma drove with Mrs. Armstrong in the front passenger seat. Dave sat in the middle on the backseat with Eddie to his left and his father to his right, directly behind Mrs. Armstrong. Mr. Armstrong was tall and skinny, and both of his sons resembled him in the face. He was quiet and smoked with his window cracked open.

Not a word was spoken in that big car during the twenty-minute drive to the church. Eddie's neck itched badly from his buttoned collar and the dry, hot air that circulated through the car. And he had to go to the bathroom. For the longest time Eddie thought he was going to crap his pants in that luxury car. He was too afraid to ask the blue-haired driver to stop at a gas station, so he had to hold it until he could waddle into the church's bathroom like a penguin in dress shoes.

At the service Eddie sat in the front row with Dave and his father. Mrs. Armstrong and her mother sat across the aisle on the pew closest to the boy's closed coffin. There were perhaps twenty other people there in the little church. The African American minister was short and thin, and he spoke directly to Mrs. Armstrong with tender compassion in his powerful voice as he tried his best to comfort her over the loss of her son. "God's will is not for us to know. Each human being has no idea when his or her time is up on this earth. And just as I feel young Charles has left us too soon, I also know he is now in the hands of a merciful God, the Creator of heaven and earth. And He is the only one who will ever know when we will see Charles again."

Eddie could see and hear that the minister was reaching the women across the aisle by the way they nodded and pursed their lips when moved emotionally. There were dabbings at tears with white tissues, and those pathetic signs and outbursts of grief that bothered Dave more than anyone. There were times when Mrs. Armstrong groaned out such pain that Eddie could feel his friend's body shuddering from each maternal sound that filled the air — a commingling of grief and loss combined with the memories shared only between the son and his mother.

The drive to the cemetery was clouded with vicious carping and bickering between Dave's parents. Their vituperative words became more heated with each passing insult while they followed the black hearse carrying their son's body. Dave's grandma was so upset by their arguing that she came close to rear-ending the hearse at a stop sign. "Watch it, Grandma," Dave warned her just in time.

To Dave's relief, the Bonneville's squealing tires had also stopped the bitter words that had given him a pounding headache. There was a moment when Dave told Eddie with his brown eyes that he was sorry he had to listen to his parents' family drama.

It was the third drive back home that was the worst.

"When's the last time you even called your sons?" Mrs. Armstrong pointed accusingly at her ex-husband. *You* was spoken with such enmity that it was as if Dave's mother were the devil incarnate.

Eddie could see the bulging Adam's apple of Mr. Armstrong bobbing in his throat when he lashed back at his ex-wife, "You got no right to disrespect me in front of my son! Especially at a time like this."

Mr. Armstrong's scowling mouth was fixed on his face all the way to trailer row where he got out and slammed the door shut. Before he got behind the wheel of his rusted green Olds, he motioned for his son to come over to him. Eddie was relieved to be tramping home in the mud on his way to FIKSHEN, but he managed to overhear Dave's father telling his son to come down to Louisiana when he graduated from high school. "And I will get you platform work on an oil rig. You hear me? Platform work pays $22.50 an hour. You hear that?"

Dave nodded sheepishly. His father hugged him goodbye and drove away, sliding and fish-tailing down the muddy lane until he reached the main road.

Atlas Brothers

Springtime in the Midwest was turbulent, especially for Dave Armstrong. Although I did everything I could to tear down Eddie's self-esteem whenever I could, I convinced him to order the Charles Atlas isometric physical fitness course. Dave was in Eddie's room after school when Eddie opened the manilla envelope from "the world's strongest man."

"Wasn't Atlas some mythical dude who held the world on his shoulders?" Dave asked while inspecting the program.

"I think so."

The sophomores pored over the three pages of twenty-one "special exercises" explained and diagramed for each muscle group. These were two skinny boys not at all interested in building up their muscles for school athletics; they were just wanting to do something — anything — that would help them move further away from the death of young Charles.

There was the slightest hint of a competitive spirit as they performed the exercises in numerical order. Neither one wanted the other to become "Atlas Junior" while he remained the same, so they were consistent in working out together every day. Behind Eddie's closed bedroom door they would face each other, clasping one hand down on the other hand and pressing to flex resistance from each biceps. "It says to breathe," Eddie pointed out to Dave, who was clenching so hard while holding his breath it looked like his face would implode.

After a few minutes of several repetitions, they moved to their wrists and fingers. Dave's humorous quips busted Eddie's concentration into laughter. "Our fingers'll be so strong, we'll be able to walk to school on our hands like gorillas." As they squatted up and down fifty times Dave blurted out, "Your legs are like toothpicks, man."

"Just breathe, man," Eddie laughed.

The twenty-first and final exercise was for the neck. They lay on their backs on Eddie's bed with their necks resting on the edge of the bed, then they raised their heads up and down fifty times. When finished, they let their heavy heads hang over the bed and talked, breathing hard from their first run-through of the exercise regimen.

"Man, that's quite a deal. How often does it say yer s'posed to do this?" Dave asked.

"Every day."

"Should we do it right after school?"

"Yeah, and weekends anytime," Eddie said hoping his friend agreed. Then I made Eddie put his friend to the test. "Even if you don't do the exercises every day, I will."

"Hey, man, don't you worry 'bout me. I can do this as long as you can."

"Okay," Eddie smiled at the ceiling.

They sat up on the bed, the blood beating at their temples. "You think chicks'll dig us if we do this?" Dave asked.

"Maybe. It said in the magazine that the course will improve self-esteem and confidence."

"Chicks like that stuff! Man, we're gonna be chick magnets!" Dave laughed with Eddie.

The "Atlas Brothers," as they called themselves, were faithful to the routine. Every single day for six weeks they stayed with the program until summer break was getting close. Both agreed they were stronger and feeling better, especially during their walks to and from school. Since doing the routine, they noticed how slurs and insults from passing cars had diminished. When the insults did come, they both would scowl back at the passing idiots with a natural kind of raw strength they never dared to think they'd have. In time, the loud-mouthed pinheads drove right past them without a word or the usual horn blasts. The Atlas Brothers smiled smugly, knowing they were making real progress.

By summer, that time in the Midwest when energy levels can be harder to sustain, the Atlas Brothers diligently increased their isometric repetitions. Sometimes when Sara wasn't home they'd do their exercises in the living room. Never would they work out in Dave's trailer because his mother was in such a state of depression since losing her baby boy that she told Dave that she didn't think she'd live much longer.

One afternoon right after a workout, they decided to go for a walk in the rain. It was more like a heavy drizzle — the kind of rain that sprinkled from scudding clouds until bursts of sunshine appeared and stopped it all with incredible light. They walked at a quick pace on the elevated gravel road that bordered the airfield. Dave talked fast about his situation at home.

"My mom's gettin' worse every day, man. She smokes more and won't exercise a lick. All she eats is those TV dinners where the meat and vegetables taste like greasy rubber. There seems to be no end to her grief. She keeps sayin', 'It's not fair when a mother outlives her child.' I tell her, 'Life's not fair, Mom.' Then she'll cry all day and night in her room holding my brother's picture. I just don't see her livin' much longer like this, Eddie."

"Maybe you should get her to walk with ya . . ."

"No. I've asked her a hundred times and she won't do nothin'. It's a good thing we have our Atlas routine. It holds me together."

Dave was right. One August night, when relentless heat and humidity ruled the day and night, Mrs. Armstrong died in her sleep with a picture of Charles pressed to her heart. Dave found her that way and called an ambulance to pick her up. Not until the ambulance left with her body did he call his grandmother. She told Dave to call his father in Louisiana. She thought it best that he live with his father — to start his junior year in a new school and graduate down there.

But he didn't call his father. Eddie had knocked on Dave's door after his mother told him she'd just seen an ambulance drive away from Dave's place. He went over there right away in bare feet and wearing only cut-offs.

Eddie had only been inside the cramped green trailer a few times for brief visits when Dave invited him over. Dave was crying when he let Eddie in and told him the news as they stood in the cluttered, hot living room. "I knew it, man. She's gone. Dead in her sleep. Now my grandma says I got to live with my dad."

"I'm sorry, Dave. You've had the worst luck."

Just then Mary was at the Armstrong door wanting to know what happened. All three of them sat down in the hot trailer.

Dave really opened up to Mrs. Dense, telling her all about his father's sordid lifestyle and how he didn't want to live around him.

"Maybe you could stay with us," Eddie said to his friend while at the same time pleading with his eyes for his mother's approval.

"Eddie, I don't know. His father might not want Dave to live here."

"Mom, his dad might put him to work on an oil rig and he'll never graduate. Can't he finish school here?"

"Where would he sleep?" Mary asked her son.

"He can sleep in my room."

"Share the bed? You boys are too big for that bed."

"No, Mom, it's fine. Or I can sleep on the couch."

Mary was aware that her son was Dave's best friend and they did everything together, so the boys were hopeful when she told them they'd have to get Mr. Armstrong's approval first. But Dave dreaded calling his father with the disappointing news that he'd rather stay in Iowa. "Why should he care? He's never shown any interest in me before," Dave said to Eddie when Mary left his trailer.

Later that day Dave called his father and was thrown a curve when he was told to sell his mother's things along with the trailer; and when the trailer was sold he could pack his clothes, hop on a bus for Mobile, and his dad would find them a two-bedroom apartment.

"But, Dad, I want to stay in school here. Mrs. Dense said I could live with them if you say it's okay. I don't wanna go to school down there."

Was Dave ever surprised by his father's reply! "Well . . . I can't force ya to come down here. You're old enough to make your own decisions. Stay there . . . if that's what ya want."

Dave was torn between relief and an inexplicable feeling of rejection because his father didn't fight for him to come and be with him. It was that easy — one phone call and now he would be living with his best friend, and yet so alone without his brother and mother.

Dave stayed in the green trailer until Mr. House bought it for $2,200, and Dave agreed that he would have it empty and clean by the first of the month when school started. Eddie helped Dave dispose of most of the Armstrong furniture and his mother's things, and even some of his brother's things his mother was holding onto. Dave kept only a few pieces of his mother's jewelry, the TV and record player for Eddie's room, and some porcelain plates and silverware he gave to Mary.

Despite another sad funeral (this time without Mr. Armstrong) and the letting go of Dave's life in that green trailer, the Atlas Brothers remained faithful to their daily Atlas regimen. Dave told Eddie that the exercises combined with living in FIKSHEN were holding him together; and if not for those two things, he probably would have run away to California until his money ran out.

Black Shark

That fall Eddie's parents told him if he cleaned the bar on Sundays when it was closed, they'd pay him twenty-five bucks. Ike suggested bringing Dave along because when he was finished with the cleaning, they could play all the pool they wanted for two quarters if they stuffed bar rags into the pockets. "No drinkin', though. I could lose my license," I. M. Dense warned his son on the phone.

That Sunday Mary gave her son the bar's front door key and dropped the boys off at Ike & Mary's, telling them she'd pick them up at four — in six hours. On the way to the bar, Mary reminded her son to clean the bathrooms, which she knew that Eddie didn't like doing. Dave was more excited than Eddie because Eddie had done this Sunday job before and knew that the bar floor could be in bad shape after a busy Saturday night.

And it was. Peanut shells, muddy footprints, dirty bar napkins, and cigarette butts were everywhere.

"Wow!" Dave exclaimed while pointing to the solid pool table standing at the back of the bar. "My old man was called 'Black Shark' when he lived here. You're in trouble, Eddie Dense!"

"I gotta do the work first," Eddie grumbled while gauging the amount of debris on the tile floor.

"I'll help ya," Dave smiled.

First Dave helped Eddie put the eighteen bar stools upside down on top of the L-shaped mahogany bar. Then while Dave swept the floor with an eighteen-inch push broom, Eddie picked up the rubber floor mats behind the long bar and hosed them off in the back alley. When all was swept clean, including behind the bar and both restrooms, the roommates mopped the floor with thirty-two-ounce mop heads soaked in Mr. Clean and hot water. Several times the water in the wringered bucket turned black and had to be changed.

Eddie waxed the floor himself because they only had one applicator. Dave played the same two songs three times on the jukebox: Marvin Gaye songs "Grapevine" and "What's Goin' On." Dave danced by the jukebox while sipping on an iced 7-Up from a pilsner beer glass. Once the wax dried, Eddie buffed the floor with the electric double-bristled floor buffer. When the floor was done, they admired its shiny clean surface. Then Eddie quickly cleaned the tiny bathrooms while his helper hauled all the trash out into the alley dumpster.

The lone light above the pool table made the green felt come alive after Eddie stuffed clean bar rags into each pocket. He put in two quarters which paid for twenty-seven games of "last pocket," which meant you had to sink the eight ball in the same pocket in which you sank your last solid or striped ball.

Dave was also a "Black Shark." Like his father, Dave ran the table, rarely giving Eddie a shot. Eddie finally asked if he could break so he could at least get in one shot per game.

"Where'd you learn to shoot pool like that?"

"My dad would take me with him to these Omaha pool halls and bars when I was little. He taught me how to bank and shoot for shape — where to leave the cue ball."

"I know what 'shape' is," Eddie grumbled, then scratched on the break which made Dave burst into laughter.

For Dave, this Sunday in Ike & Mary's was about the best time he'd ever had in his life. Free pool, free music and pop, and all of it with his best friend who said he'd split the twenty-five bucks with him for helping out.

"Hey, Eddie, let's do this every Sunday."

Third Wheel

A couple months after moving into FIKSHEN, Dave turned seventeen; he got his driver's license and bought a '59 Buick for five hundred bucks. No more walking to school for the Atlas Brothers, except for one week when the Buick's starter went out.

I was able to really bother Eddie his junior year when he got acne just when he began to really get interested in girls. He also had begun writing his first novel. And Dave changed Eddie when Dave started dating his new neighbor Jenna, a seventeen-year-old Vietnamese girl who was a senior at their school. Jenna Lee, named for an American GI who had helped rescue her parents when fierce fighting broke out in their village in Vietnam, had moved into Dave's green trailer with her younger sister and their widowed mother. Jenna thought "Davey" was the sweetest and funniest guy she'd ever met.

Since Jenna's mother worked nights at the VA Hospital in Omaha, almost every night Davey was next door at Jenna's place. Now Eddie did his Atlas routine alone. I was able to crumble Eddie's self-esteem even further by telling him he's no Charles Atlas, that he's just a pimple-faced loser who's wasting time with these silly exercises. Of course, all Eddie had to do to believe me was look at himself in his dresser mirror while exercising and see all those festering sores on his face.

Yes, poor Eddie had acne and it was bad. He had pimples in a hundred places from his forehead to his chin. He'd pick incessantly at the little pimples at the corners of his flat mouth. Every time he talked or smiled, a pimple would crack open and keep him scowling and too embarrassed to even look at a girl in school.

Sweet Jenna tried to help Eddie by giving him some of her mother's makeup; however, it always washed away during a shower after P.E. Pick, pick, pick, all night long. Dave suggested he wear gloves to bed because he told Eddie that his constant face picking made him nervous and kept him from going to sleep.

Instead of closing their bedroom window on nights when the septic tank's fumes were bad, Dave liked it open all the time so he could hear the sweet music Jenna played on her harp in his old bedroom. Dave would lie against the wall under the cranked-open window after hushing Eddie so he could hear Jenna's music. Eddie was beside himself; his face itched in a hundred places as he wore brown cotton gloves, while I told him I hoped Jenna's harp strings would snap into the septic tank.

Eddie the teenager was clueless; he had no idea that his pimples were caused by the sugar in those little bottles of Coke his mother would bring him from the bar every night. Dave drank Coke too, yet his face didn't erupt like Eddie's did. Jenna was the one who told Dave to tell Eddie that the sugar in the pop was the cause of his acne. During one of those nightly harp concerts when the stench coming in the window was strong, Eddie kept his gloved hands under his thighs while I tormented him about his incurable geekiness.

"Jenna says the Coke is causin' your face to break out, Eddie. She drinks distilled water 'cause she says the tap water here is dangerous, loaded with chemicals from agriculture."

"She's Chinese. How does she know?" Eddie snapped.

"She's Vietnamese. Her family moved here when her father was killed by the Vietcong. She knows a ton of stuff about health. Her mother's a nutritionist at the VA Hospital. If I were you I'd lay off the pop and see if yer face clears up."

Eddie wouldn't admit it to himself — let alone to his friend — that he was jealous of Jenna. He was jealous because she was taking big chunks of their time together. And envious because Dave had a girlfriend and he didn't. He felt like a third wheel when around them — their constant petting, hand-holding, kissing, and sitting so close to each other while Eddie was beside himself and picking his face every chance he got. On their drives to school and back in Dave's car, Jenna would be right against her Davey with her hands all over him while the "Third Wheel" looked out the passenger window picking and rubbing and squeezing at a new pimple until it bled.

But Eddie really liked Jenna. She was so sweet, petite and cute, always smiling and laughing at every little thing said or seen. She had big brown eyes like Dave's. And even around those awful fumes between the trailers she'd smile at them because they reminded her of her homeland.

Deep down Eddie was aware that sweet little Jenna had truly helped diminish the losses Dave had experienced by giving him real love that Dave told Eddie would never have happened unless he'd had those losses. Jenna was teaching her boyfriend about incredible spiritual things. These were New Age things and words that the Atlas Brothers had never heard before. Words like meditation, consciousness, Being, presence, karma, and past lives. They were all so interesting to Dave and even Eddie. If she gave Dave one of her books to read, Eddie would often finish reading it before Dave did. That's when Eddie began paying attention to me and the things I was telling him — thanks to Jenna.

Dave picked up Jenna's spiritual teachings faster than Eddie because Dave saw that the more he understood her, the more he wanted to be with her — and it was likewise for Jenna.

Mornings before school Dave would jump out of bed early just so he could go over to the green trailer and pray with Jenna in front of a Vietnamese altar she made. There were candles, burning incense, a bowl filled with colorful stones and gems, and a rainbow-colored poster of an enlightened Buddha, all blended with the relaxing tones Jenna made with her harp that was varnished to a butterscotch-yellowish glow.

Eddie would lie there on his bed, the sweet incense mixing with the stench of the septic tank, as he listened to the sounds from that harp that never failed to make his face stop itching and the hairs on his legs tingle until he giggled himself awake. Yet amidst all these good things from his sweet neighbor, I kept bringing envy to his heart. These were dark waves of envy that made him feel lonely — like he was missing out on the best part of life that his best friend now had.

Winter passed and just before spring was supposed to arrive, one last winter storm blew into eastern Nebraska and western Iowa. Mary told Dave he could invite Jenna over for a dinner that she and Sara prepared. Even Ike was invited.

Eddie, Dave and Jenna ate on TV trays in the living room while watching *The Wizard of Oz*. It was the first time any of them had seen it in color. Jenna was captivated by the magical, colorful images. Outside it was freezing cold. Blowing snow from drifts pelted FIKSHEN with ferocity.

Eddie now knew that Jenna was right about the cause of his acne. For three days he had abstained from drinking any pop, and Eddie noticed that his face had dried and cleared up some. He loved Jenna for this because now he had real hope of finally having a clear complexion.

But now as Jenna and Dave sat close together on the Dense sofa, their aluminum TV trays touching while eating and watching *Oz,* again there were these loving glances between his friends. I again pelted Eddie with feelings of jealousy and envy that burned his neck as microbursts of freezing air blew through the shuddering storm windows close to his recliner. Eddie swallowed bite after bite knowing he was only a third wheel, the one who would be reduced to listening to me instead of a cherished lover. As the windows rattled and vibrated from the powerful wind blowing hard and constant from the north, I was able to talk to Eddie without letting up, getting my spiteful words to resonate between his ears until they were thoroughly chewed and dropped into his stomach. I made Eddie swallow all those negative thoughts, where they could sit and fester until digested and absorbed by every organ his blood would feed.

Yes, Edward Lesley Dense, I am your mind; it was me that made your hands want to pick your face raw. It wasn't Dave and Jenna or Coke that made your face look like a dartboard. It was me.

Since Jenna's mother worked weekends, Dave spent most of his free time inside his old home and had all but stopped doing the Atlas routine with his buddy. Dave's love interest had even tapered Eddie's doing the exercises to two or three times a week.

Since it was no fun to walk alone, Eddie kept up his role as a third wheel and rode with them in the old Buick; but Eddie missed the long walks to and from school, and his body felt it. On the other hand, Jenna was so incredibly interesting that Eddie felt compelled to be around them. She had keen social awareness and was eager to discuss her ideas. "It would be wonderful if schools taught communication skills instead of so much math. So many kids are fearful of making real connections with each other. It's like, wow, people; we're on this journey through life together at the exact same moment on this tiny speck in the universe. And all I get from most of my classmates is this incredibly fearful energy coming from their fear-filled minds."

Dave would nod and laugh in agreement, but mostly he was turned on from having her hands constantly on him. Eddie would ask her all kinds of things to try and provoke her. "What do you expect from them? They're only doing what they've been taught to do. How do you stop a busy mind from talking, anyway, Jenna?"

Jenna would just turn her brown, light-filled eyes to the third wheel and say with confidence, "Eddie, you stop it when you pay attention to what it is saying and how it is making you feel. For example, I can tell you are thinking right now while I am talking to you. You are thinking about what you will say to me before I am finished talking to you, right?"

Eddie smiled because I was giving him a couple things to say to her while she was talking.

"See? You noticed! That's good, Eddie," she laughed. She went on to tell him that "listening" should be taught in grade schools, especially in America.

"Why especially here?" Eddie asked with a tone of defensive patriotism.

"Because America is in the biggest rush. How can America lead when it doesn't listen to what is going on?"

"What is going on?" Eddie really wanted to know.

"It's like what Davey's father called 'Blue River' — this flowing river of consciousness that becomes polluted with negative energy like war and poverty, greed and withholding of love. My father also told me about something that was like Blue River. It is a kind of inner peace you can reach when you quiet that fearful voice in your head."

Since I'm that voice in Eddie's head, I resisted that Blue River baloney and let him know it right away when I put the first thought I could come up with between his ears and he spit it out to Jenna. "If everyone reached this Blue River place, the world would become overcrowded and then we'd all get wiped out by some virus or epidemic."

Jenna said nothing back to Eddie, yet Dave spoke for her when he said simply, "Resistance or surrender."

"That's right!" Jenna smiled and kissed the driver's neck.

"Resistance or surrender . . . what's that mean?" Eddie asked cynically, perturbed with their sappy affection.

"To resist, man, is negative in any form. And sweet surrender is letting those negative things pass right through ya."

Eddie was quiet. When he turned away and faced his window, I told him it was all a bunch of crap.

Somehow

In the late spring Sara, who appeared to have her life completely together, was carrying a 4.0 grade point average in college. By contrast, Dave's old Buick was falling apart — needing some part replaced every week, it seemed. One week when the Buick was in the shop, the three of them walked to school and back. Eddie enjoyed the walks.

On one of their afternoon walks home from school, an idiot in a carload of seniors barked at Jenna, "Slant-eyed gook!" It didn't bother Jenna at all; the remark seemed to pass right through her as she always preached "surrender" to Dave. But Dave glared at the passing creep who'd insulted his sweet Jenna. Eddie could see that his buddy needed to work on surrendering.

Dave stewed over the incident all the way home and surprised Eddie by asking if they could "Atlas" now. At first Eddie knew his pal was just wanting to let off some steam, except during their routine Eddie could see a palpable mission in Dave's eyes he'd never seen before. There was a seething anger in his stern brown eyes that never diminished even when their workout was over.

As they lay on their backs with their heads hanging over the edge of the bed, Jenna's harp music came in softly through the open window. Dave began to cry, sobbing with his big hands covering his face and his stomach convulsing with each sweet note.

"What's wrong?" Eddie asked softly with his head hanging inches away from his friend's.

Dave didn't answer for a while. It was as if he couldn't speak even if he wanted to. Then Dave sat up and blew his nose into a tissue Eddie gave him. Dave cleared his throat and managed, "Thanks, man. Somehow . . . I gotta kick that guy's ass."

"Aw, Dave, let it go. Surrender," Eddie smiled. Dave managed a chuckle at Eddie's implication.

Two days later Dave picked up his car on his lunch break.

Jenna and Eddie waited for their driver by the Buick in the school parking lot after school. Eddie noticed something was drawing a crowd at the back of the football field; senior boys were hustling toward an event that Eddie just knew was Dave's "somehow."

Jenna followed Eddie's dreaded footsteps to the football field, whereupon they saw a large circle of upperclassmen shouting like pent-up boys will do during a fight. The violence of the crowd scared Eddie and Jenna. The crowd yelled cuss words and hollered when a punch was thrown. Eddie likened the gathering to vultures lusting for blood.

Neither Eddie nor Jenna could see what was going on inside the taunting circle of vultures until they pressed through the crowd and saw Dave straddling a bigger kid's back — the same idiot who had insulted Jenna. Jenna's face became pale with shock as she watched her sweet boyfriend pummel the back of the guy's head with pounding fists that struck fast and furiously. The poor idiot had given up; yet Dave kept flailing away, which caused Eddie to force his way through the onlookers and wrap his arms around Dave's heaving chest. "Dave! Stop! It's Eddie! Stop now. It's over, Dave. Let's go home."

Dave got to his feet and was breathing hard, delirious with rage as he stood over the surrendered one who had dirt covering his wet face and who kept his trembling hands covering the back of his empty skull. The blood-thirsty group booed the end of the violence while Jenna pulled Dave away by his hand. As the trio walked away some idiot yelled, "Nigger lover," but they just kept on their path toward the car.

As they were trying to make their way off school grounds, they encountered Coach Randall who was headed their way. He was the varsity football coach and algebra teacher — a no-nonsense, muscular, middle-aged man. Dave's torn shirt and sweating face caught his attention.

"Armstrong! Come over here!" the man gestured with an index finger and one hand akimbo. The victorious fighter approached the coach with his friends. "What's going on here, Armstrong?"

Dave shrugged his shoulders then Eddie answered while pointing, "That guy called her a slant-eyed gook."

The coach's eyes softened a little bit when he looked at Jenna who was a good student in his algebra class. Then Coach Randall eyed the beaten guy who had played on his football team the previous fall. The loser was on his feet, obviously shamed in front of his disgusted peers who'd dispersed in a dozen directions. "So you taught him a lesson, Armstrong?" the coach smirked.

Dave remained quiet.

"The problem is you were fighting on school property. That's not the smartest place to fight. If I catch you fighting at school again, it's an automatic suspension." Dave nodded submissively and walked away with his friends when the coach told him, "Get outta here."

On their drive home after the fight, Dave pulled over a few blocks from home when he smelled something like burning rubber coming from his engine. He got out with his engine running and raised the hood to see if he could locate the source of the fumes.

Jenna's arms and legs were shuddering from the shock of seeing her Davey fighting as Eddie told her he'd never seen Dave this upset. He added, "It's like he lost his mind."

"No, Eddie. If he had lost his mind this would have never happened. It was his mind that took him over and made him go crazy."

Eddie really thought about what Jenna said and knew she was right, although Eddie was also filled with pride because of his friend's victory over one of those idiots who'd been pestering them for years.

In Jenna's green trailer she soaked Dave's swollen hands in Epsom salts at the kitchen sink while she massaged his tense neck and shoulders. Meanwhile, Eddie sat on Jenna's cushioned wicker sofa listening to her plea for Dave to realize that his violent actions hurt her a hundred times more than those "stupid words I let pass through me." She called the guy's remark "innocuous."

When Eddie went home to his room, he looked up "innocuous" in his pocket dictionary and repeated it to himself several times. Then Eddie wrote about the fight in his notebook that held his writings for his first novel. He titled it "Somehow" and wrote:

> *My friend had somehow managed to do something about his anger that I could never do. I would have run away because of fear of injury and fear of losing in front of so many. I blush to think how brave my friend Dave was compared to my cowardice.*
>
> *When his lightning fists were pounding away, hitting the guy with such fury, I could see the anger from losing Charles and his mother in every terrible blow. At least he got it out; at the very least he put his losses into action with those*

brown fists of fury that smacked back at this cruel, snarling world that has punched his heart so brutally.

Dave's girlfriend, Jenna, told me that his mind made him do this violence — that it had taken him over. But I say, "Good for that vengeful mind!" For I would have let my busy mind keep me awake at night tossing over the thousand things I did not do. At least now Dave knows he has taken action and will sleep in peace, while I will know I am a coward that way, and even one who runs and hides from unknown spiritual things that can somehow give such peace to any boy's busy mind.

Green is the Heart

One Saturday in the new summer, Jenna saw Eddie shooting baskets alone next door and invited him inside the green trailer. Dave had driven his stalling Buick to the repair shop. Jenna's mom was at work, so Jenna was watching her little sister.

Jenna loved Eddie for being such a good friend to Davey, and Eddie had matured enough to realize she was not keeping his best friend to herself. She was so sweet; she would always include Eddie in things like driving around, going to the DQ or the movies, and their walks to the river. When she would cook her Asian meals for her boyfriend, she would often invite Eddie to join them. Yes, Eddie loved Jenna too.

She had just finished her meditation and yoga that she did twice a day. On the clean trailer's floor was a beige-colored mat made of hemp with a green heart in the center about the size of a dinner plate.

"What's that?" Eddie asked, pointing to the green heart.

"Green is the heart," she smiled and went on to explain that when she meditates she imagines bathing her heart in a liquid green, coating her heart over and over because green is a healing color for the heart.

"What does it do for you when you do that?"

"I know that if I color my heart green every day, I have more compassion for others and myself," she smiled.

"That sounds . . . crazy," Eddie blinked lazily.

Jenna laughed and told Eddie, "I have to believe in my heart that it's true, or else it will be false and I'll become hardened to my life."

"So you sit on that green heart and paint your heart green while you meditate and listen to your music?"

Jenna nodded yes while giggling at the cute sound made by Eddie's lisp. Her laugh tickled him so that he burst into laughter and impulsively placed his hands on her frail shoulders. That's when Eddie got to really look deep into those clear brown eyes that had shards of white rays shooting out at him like some precious sparkling gem. He pressed their laughing shoulders together.

Now Eddie knew why his friend had fought that pinhead for insulting this delicate creature. While hugging her and laughing with her, he was free for the first time to relax with a girl. And he could now understand why Dave spent so much time with her. Yes, this was a ninety-eight-pound rare gem made of pure love, a valuable treasure Dave had found in the middle of nowhere. This was a rare find that could get his friend Dave to the Blue River Eddie yearned to know — a place she already knew.

Dave never really had to look for this rare gem. It had come to him after two terrible losses — losses that forced Eddie Dense to see the "destiny" Jenna often talked about. For if not for those terrible losses, Dave and Eddie may never have met Jenna.

After their laughing embrace Eddie asked Jenna if Dave was really supposed to lose his brother and his mother.

"Yea. They were his destiny," she answered with a peaceful countenance. "It's perfect," she smiled and laughed.

Later that night when Jenna and Dave were in the green trailer, Eddie wrote in his notebook that one of his future novels would be about "green is the heart." From that night on, every day and every night he would imagine his own healing green liquid painting his heart, bathing it in the color Jenna said would give him the compassion he needed in order to reach that place known as Blue River.

Beside the River

Summer was unusually springlike for western Iowa. Nights were cool and it was quite chilly by morning. Wet leaves and grasses close to the river's east bank were filled with song and the winged flush of human-startled birds when Eddie stepped into this isolated place by the Missouri. It had gotten cold the previous night, and Eddie had gotten up in the middle of the night to get a blanket. That's when he saw Dave wasn't home. Then he looked out at Dave's parking spot and saw that his car wasn't there either.

This spot by the river was not far from where Charles and his friend fell through the ice. Dave liked to come here at night with Jenna; it was their parking spot. He'd back his Buick up to the tree line and face that moving black monster that swallowed his only brother. Dave could never come here alone because his mind would show him memories of Charles that only Jenna could stop.

That's how Eddie knew to go to this place by the river. Dave told Eddie that he and Jenna would sit on the hood of his car and she would play her sweet music for Charles and his friend. Jenna said it would help heal Dave of his terrible loss.

Now it was ten in the morning and Dave had not returned home last night. They would always watch Saturday morning cartoons together in the bedroom with the door closed so as not to disturb Sara or Mary. The next day being Sunday, all three of them were supposed to clean the bar and play pool all day. This morning Eddie became concerned when Jenna's mother came over to ask Eddie if he'd seen her daughter.

Some one hundred yards down river from where he was standing, Eddie could see the black Buick backed into the tall grass, it's trunk partially open and holding Jenna's harp that was too big to fit in it completely. Closer and closer he stepped — into deep suctioning mud in places — until he could see that there was no sign of the couple sitting inside the car. He could see that all four windows were rolled up. Eddie thought they may be sleeping. When Eddie peered inside the passenger-side back window, he could see their embracing bodies and faces covered by a blanket on the backseat. Then he saw their clothes draped neatly over the front seat.

Eddie knocked on the glass to wake them, but they didn't move. "Hey, Dave! Jenna!" he yelled as he knocked louder. There was no movement. Adrenaline flooded Eddie's brain when he opened the back door and shook Dave's bare foot. Still nothing.

Eddie went around to the other back door but it was locked. He opened the driver's side front door and crawled on his knees on the front seat upon seeing that the ignition was on and the gas gauge on empty. He turned to the backseat in ghostly slow motion and lifted the blanket to see their heads. They appeared asleep yet there was no breathing coming from either of them.

"Dave! Wake up!" Eddie screamed. Then he touched their faces and knew that both of them were gone, yet both looked relaxed and at peace.

Eddie got out and stepped into the tall grassy weeds at the back of the car and clearly saw the harp partially sticking out of the trunk. Then he saw that the rusty exhaust pipe was covered by a tuft of grass that must have sent carbon monoxide back into the trunk and inside the car.

Eddie's teeth cut his dry lips that were trembling — along with the rest of his body — as he went over to dry-heave in the tall grass. His red head was a siren that drowned me out, since he couldn't even recall running back to FIKSHEN.

Upon reaching his back door he thought he'd better tell Jenna's mother — somehow — before calling the authorities.

Each dreaded step to the green trailer was a blur of confusion; all he saw was the basketball hoop next door that they had used year-round until the net was ragged and falling off in places.

Jenna's mother saw the ghostly terror in Eddie's eyes when she answered his light knock. He told her he'd found Dave and Jenna in Dave's car beside the river and that they must have fallen asleep with the engine running. Jenna's mother didn't understand.

"The trunk was open. They died," he choked and cried, unable to look at her.

Eddie stepped inside when Jenna's mother went to get her shoes. He called the police and told the operator what happened, explaining that they had better meet him at the trailer park so he could show them how to get to Dave's car.

It was hard to keep Jenna's distraught mother waiting for the police to arrive, especially since Jenna's sister was crying hysterically with her mother. Sara wasn't home, but Mary came to the back door when she heard them crying and asked her son what had happened.

"Dave and Jenna are dead. They got carbon monoxide poisoned," Eddie cried.

Mary was flabbergasted as she stepped outside in her robe and slippers and did her best to console the trio. It was awful. All I could tell Eddie was, "This can't be happening. Now Dave and Jenna. What kind of God would take these two young lives in such a big world?"

Everyone rode in the police car down the obscure road Dave would have taken to the river. Eddie stayed near the patrol car with Jenna's sister while Mary went with Jenna's mother and the officer. The officer wouldn't let Jenna's mother touch her daughter, explaining they'd have to examine the scene for evidence.

Later that horrible night, his bedroom window closed to once again shut out the grief emanating from the green trailer, Eddie scribbled in his notebook with a weak hand:

> *God has taken my only friends. Why? I have no desire to leave this room again unless I can run far away from this place. I have no strength to stand. Jenna's mother is devastated. I will never have children. What's the point, when a child can be taken and everything that matters be destroyed? I wish I had been with them last night, so I would not be here with this unbearable pain that I feel and see all around me. Jenna talked about "destiny" and accepting everything that happens in your life. I want no part of that. It's not what I want. I want God to leave me alone.*

Eddie's Boss

The loss of Dave and Jenna was the catalyst I needed to wrest full and final control of Eddie. I became Eddie's boss. Eddie went from being a better-than-average-student to barely graduating high school with enough credits. At his graduation I gave Eddie a new batch of pimples and lowered his self-esteem. Acne kept the girls away, which is what Eddie wanted back then. Ike and Mary gave Eddie a used white van for a graduation gift; it was the vehicle he told his folks he wanted to travel in while he wrote his first novel. Sara gave her brother a six-foot-by-three-foot white foam-rubber bed for his van so he'd be more comfortable during his travels.

No college for E. L. Dense, the name he would use on his first book. The young writer swore to me that he'd stay clear of structured learning — a merit system he'd nearly failed in. He told his family that more schooling would ruin his "voice" to tell a story his way. The truth is that Eddie didn't want to be around a bunch of new people as a lowly freshman. Eddie wanted the freedom to write his book without regimentation; he wanted total independence to do it his way.

I would be Eddie's voice. And that was okay with Eddie, partly because now he was way too introverted to listen to anyone else but me. I loved Eddie.

Three days after his graduation, Eddie said goodbye to Sara and his parents with the fifteen hundred dollars they gave him for starting his new life. He went south just like Dave had said he'd do that day he and Eddie watched the planes land.

Missouri was a moving blur to Eddie because I kept up a relentless diatribe about how he was on his own now and that he'd better get a job because money runs out pretty fast on the road with nothing coming in. So Missouri went pretty much unnoticed by him, except for the Ozarks where obscure little towns and villages appeared to be hiding their treasured secrets from E. L. Dense.

By the time Eddie was deep in the heart of rural Tennessee, he'd spent two nights in "Motel 4." He slept soundly on Sara's foam-rubber mattress laid out on the van's outdoor-carpeted cargo area. His mother's blankets kept him warm. No matter how cool it got by morning, though, he'd never turn on the van's heater if there was a chance he'd fall asleep like Jenna and Dave had. Lesson learned!

I kept economy in Eddie's head constantly; so in order to quiet me he wrote more and more on his novel.

Southern towns impressed him. He liked to write in cafes around friendly strangers then move on. He wrote:

> *I crossed this invisible line and I was in Dixie. Humidity and drooping trees were everywhere on these narrow roads cluttered with drab billboards, small businesses, and radio waves jammed with country music and Jesus.*
>
> *Southern people are very friendly and no doubt label me as a Yankee when I speak to them. History is important to these people. I ask them in these small Tennessee towns if there's any historical sites around, and there's always an old museum, courthouse, or some preserved home. It is so interesting to tour these off-the-beaten-path places where I can get lost and observe them like a writer.*
>
> *I've decided to title my first novel* Blue River *to honor my friends Dave and Jenna, who died young a year ago. They died near a river, yet that isn't what the title means. Jenna told me that there's a real yet invisible space in this*

world that only enlightened people reach. They see things perfectly. She said this only happens inside the body after quieting the mind, and that I would know it when I'm there . . . totally.

Dave's father called this place Blue River — a strip or patch of blue that's always there behind the windshield when traveling, and always unreachable to most. I asked Jenna if she could see this Blue River where we lived in Council Bluffs, Iowa. "Yes," she'd glow with this blazing light in her eyes.

"How did you get there?" I asked her.

She said it came to her when she was a little girl in Vietnam and she was walking down the road near this poor little village where she lived with her poor family. I don't recall her exact words, but I know she said that "all living things become less dense, sort of like the way a river appears on the surface when it's clear and flowing free with the natural rhythm of life."

I am so far from that kind of seeing — or "Being" as Jenna called it — because my mind is busy telling me to worry about my future every waking minute, it seems. My mind tells me to go to college, to get any job I can, and to find a "perfect girl for me." It's all so maddening. Writing and sleeping are the only things that shut it up, because I don't think about what I should write — I just write.

This living alone on the road is new to me, so it's too early to say whether I like it or not or for how long I can do it. It rained a bit last night when I was parked to spend the night on this store's parking lot. As I lay on my mattress listening to the raindrops pelting the roof of my van, this new feeling of aloneness crept into my bones and made me fear what I would do with my life. I knew this confusion was coming from a voice inside my head, yet I made no effort to stop it. Jenna told me once to focus on my breath. I do that, but I don't sustain it. I must find a way to stop my mind from running me, from telling me these fearful things that only leave me tired.

Day afer day E. L. Dense worked on *Blue River* without me. When he would come to a place on his page when he hesitated, I tried to come in and tell him what to write. But he caught me and dismissed my idea, and he waited for something to come.

Eddie drove all the way to Maine, then clear across the country to San Francisco. Along the way he had written in dozens of small-town cafes and truck stops after buying gas and oil for his van.

In a Marin County laundromat outside San Francisco, he found a "roommate wanted" ad while doing four loads of dirty clothes. He showed up at the address given in the ad wearing one of Dave's shirts — a gold-colored, nylon, short-sleeved shirt that fit him perfectly. When the door opened, Eddie had no idea that his life would be changed forever.

Lauren

Lauren Barnes was twenty-two. She was born and raised in Rio by her wealthy American parents. Her almond-shaped eyes were jade green; right from the start Eddie could see mystery in her eyes. He was captivated by her brown skin and thick, naturally curly, cinnamon brown-blonde hair that she wore wild and which fanned out a few inches below her shoulders.

Eddie had somehow found this five-foot-two-inch natural package of raw beauty without even looking. With her beaded pink and purple slippers, she fit right into this village of Fairfax surrounded by neighbors who were mostly young hippies with money and a liberalness Eddie never before had seen.

His new landlord was satisfied he could pay his four hundred dollars monthly rent for his bedroom and private bath in her four-bedroom home with two-and-a-half baths. Lauren never bothered to ask the Midwestern stranger for references. She told him he could park his van on her driveway, and he had kitchen access any time (as long as he bought his own groceries).

Lauren's father, Les Barnes, was in the commercial publishing business, of sorts, in San Francisco. He published colorful coupon booklets for expensive downtown restaurants, clothing stores, and gift shops. His daughter would proofread and edit his booklets that were popular throughout "The City." Since her father bought the Fairfax house for her, Lauren could live on the rent Eddie paid her since she had very few expenses. Her car was paid for and her father even paid her insurance a year in advance.

Within a couple days Lauren got Eddie a job detailing cars for a used car dealer less than five miles away in Greenbrae. This job gave E. L. Dense the peace of mind to write. Lauren would often see the young writer working on his novel at her patio table.

One day she asked him if she could read his first draft that he said was nearly finished. But Eddie wasn't ready for that because he was aware that his book needed editing. After a couple of months passed, Lauren again asked her roommate if she could read his finished book. She told him she wanted to "get a feel" for his voice. This time he gave in to those mystery eyes and handed her his stack of 265 pages torn from his notebook. He hoped Lauren was part of his destiny to become a writer and that her reading his work would manifest that.

Time and Pain

From that day on, every time he saw Lauren I made him anxious about asking her for feedback on his book. But Eddie was too shy to ask, since she appeared in no big rush to read it or report back to him what she thought of it.

While at work detailing cars, I gave Eddie an overwhelming sensation of being laughed at for having written too dull of a read for Lauren, which made him sick to his stomach. Though *Blue River* was a novel, it was drawn from people and things he knew while he lived in FIKSHEN. Dave, Jenna and he were the lead characters in the story. Although he wanted to avoid being autobiographical, he had to write about his life in Iowa. "What else could I write about?" he asked me.

Eddie was aware that no imagined story line or characters in his book could match the interest or impact that his three years living in FIKSHEN had on him. It was after the deaths of Darren and Jenny in *Blue River* that fiction took over the story line. The story was about loss — early loss — and how it can shape a life, until the lead character begins having incredible dreams that show him the way to reach that elusive space his neighbor Jenny discovered when living in a poor section of Omaha.

Darren Anderson, Jenny's boyfriend, was living with Eric Simple (a young writer) when Eric began having dreams. They were fun dreams where Eric was confronted with a dreamer's quick choice, and whatever he wanted this choice to be would happen. He'd turn a school exam or test into a perfect score; a mirror in front of his face revealed a clear complexion; and any obstacle that appeared in front of him would vanish in golden rays of particles and turn into whatever he wanted. The dreams were so perfect and the problems were all so easily handled!

And they were always positive choices — never once using greed and envy, lust or revenge for getting the desired change.

Eddie had had these kinds of dreams in his van during his trek across the country. Even though he took I-80 west right through Council Bluffs, he knew then that he could never stop and see his family. They would crush the dreams that he believed were bringing him closer to finishing his book and reaching his own Blue River. They would bait him with a job and free room and board. So, no, he would rather live with the guilt of driving past his family than risk losing his goal, because the people who loved him would never understand anyway.

Outside Grand Island, Nebraska — the magnet from home yet pulling at him — he wrote in a truck stop café:

> *I know I've done the right thing by plowing past all those familiar temptations that would only hold me back and stunt real growth. I've always let my family decide who I am and where I should be. If not for my parents splitting up, I would have never experienced those awful losses in FIKSHEN. Yet now I know for certain that FIKSHEN gave me* Blue River. *Now I must find one good reader who makes my pages real by "seeing them" and giving me the validation every writer must have to go on.*
>
> *Home has always brought time and pain; they are the same. I see this so clearly right after waking from these incredible dreams I've had on the road. Even during these dreams, some sensation deep within assures me that I am onto something wonderful and magical that can also happen for me during my waking hours. My old dreams at home were always fearful and confusing — a drab collection of fairy tales and*

impending doom about my future. Those dreams would wake me, and my day would be replete with lethargy and dread of the day before me. But not in these new dreams. Now I awaken with such unflinching hope and wonder and a "real knowing" that I am closing in on my own Blue River with every single breath I take.

Some weeks later when Eddie was in his room writing, Lauren knocked on his bedroom door. She was holding his manuscript pressed to her chest with both hands as if it were a valuable thing. "Eddie, I'm so sorry I've had your book for so long. I have had no time to read it, and I don't want to keep it unless I make time to read it." She handed him his unread story and told him how sorry she was.

Eddie managed to say, "No problem. It's okay." Yet when she left his room after softly closing his door behind her, I stabbed Eddie with that same old pain, perceived as rejection and caused by low self-esteem, and angry thoughts I know he wanted to hear: *Another waste of time. Time . . . she has no time. That's her problem. She blames time . . . What is time, Lauren? Please tell me. Could it be some imaginary way to keep you from helping me become a published writer? Why then, I ask, does your lack of time make me feel this pain that appears to be caused by your dismissal of my intent to share my writing with you?*

Because Eddie shared the kitchen with Lauren, she'd often feed him her vegetarian meals. That's how Eddie's face finally cleared up for good. The years of excoriation, rubbing his face raw, were over. Amazingly, his face had no scars from his bad habit. California sunshine had tanned him, and now his landlord was attracted to him. When she asked again if she could read *Blue River*, he answered with confidence, "Not now. I'm rewriting it." Eddie wasn't really rewriting his book; that was just my way of telling Lauren "you had your chance."

Difficult times were ahead for Eddie's ego with Lauren. She began bringing home boyfriends and sunbathing with them in her skimpy rust-colored bathing suit. Eddie would see his beautiful South American roommate with a boyfriend and would be jealous every single time. Lauren was oblivious to Eddie's attraction to her, until one night when she was alone on her patio having a glass of wine and Eddie came out to join her. She had him taste her wine to see if he wanted a glass, but he didn't like the taste of it. Then he asked Lauren if her father knew anyone who could publish his book.

"Self-publish?" she asked.

"Yeah, but I like to call it 'independent publishing.'"

"I'll ask him. Hey, I know! I'm going to meet him on his boat in Sausalito next Saturday night. Come with me and you can ask him."

The excitement of meeting Lauren's father and a lead to possibly getting his book published forced Eddie to try editing it; however, he had no clue what he was doing.

A couple days before his Saturday meeting with Lauren's father, Eddie was detailing a car when he remembered that Dave had one time given him an ad from a magazine for a vanity publishing company in New York. Eddie had saved the ad with it's toll-free number in the bill compartment of his wallet.

He called the company when he got home and found out they charge about five dollars per book for a 250-page title with a minimum of five thousand copies printed. That was way too much for Eddie. He recalled that Dave told him when he gave him the ad, "If I was a writer, I'd sell every copy myself door to door to businesses. I read about this guy in Canada who did that when he published his book. That's what I'd do if I was you. I'd be travelin' and sellin' my book and havin' a blast. To hell with publishers. They publish the same old stuff over and over. You got somethin' to say. Be a writer, Eddie. Don't wait for somebody else to tell you what to write or when to be a writer."

Eddie had only managed to save $2,500 detailing cars, including the money he had left when he got to Fairfax. There was nobody he could borrow from. His parents would only tell him to get a real job.

That weekend Eddie went with Lauren to visit her father on his yacht in Sausalito without much hope for his novel. Lauren introduced her father as Les. "Not short for Lesley; just Les," she told Eddie. Les was a silver-haired jovial man in his sixties who looked rich because he was rich. Les was a bit taller than Eddie and not a bit intimidating to be around, for he really listened with genuine respect to the young writer's desire to publish his first novel. "Be careful what you want, Eddie; you might get it," Les chuckled.

By the time they were ready to leave the boat, Eddie was flying high with the hope that Les said he could print his book at a cost of $1.25 per book if it was around 250 pages. The best part was that Les told Eddie he could pay half down for his five thousand copies and pay the balance from his sales as he sold them. Yes, it sure looked like Eddie had a golden opportunity to get what he wanted.

There's No "I" in "Mind"

Lauren helped Eddie get his pages camera ready for her father's printing press; and she read *Blue River* carefully, making editing changes here and there. Nearly one hundred hours later, she told her roommate, "It's ready."

Since Eddie was short about $300 for his half-down payment, Lauren gave her father the balance he needed. It would be about a month before all of Eddie's five thousand copies were printed and bound. Lauren had an artist friend design Eddie's front and back covers; plus Lauren wrote an impressive review about the book and had her father agree to use his name as the reviewer. The review read:

> *E. L. Dense's* Blue River *does not read like a first novel. The story is remarkably rich with interesting characters caught in the web of this new author's incredible imagination.*
>
> *I had never really been to most of the places in the story — until NOW. E. L. Dense has taken me there and made me see it more clearly than ever. I have no doubt that this title will be the beginning of a long career for this promising writer.*
>
> *Les Barnes*
> *Senior Editor/City Zine*
> *San Francisco, CA*

Right after Lauren showed Eddie her father's review, he began to prepare for the biggest venture of his life. Lauren didn't tell Eddie that she wrote the review, so Eddie believed that Les read his book and that's what he thought of it. Lauren had her reasons for not telling Eddie.

This was the period in Eddie's life I always feared — when he began to use me to remember things that Jenna told him. Jenna had made a point of letting Eddie know that "there's no 'I' in 'mind,'" and that he must observe what his mind tells him. She explained to Eddie that the more often he observed me, the more he would live in the present moment and prosper in all ways. Eddie started using me to show himself images of him selling his book with ease to strangers at five bucks a copy.

I still fought to maintain my control. I would conjure up old doubts and fears or give him a confusing list of the best pitches he should use when selling his book. But he was able to dismiss me and said he'd figure that all out by trial and error in the field.

Since reading *Blue River*, Lauren was confused about the author's resolution in the story line. Eddie's leading character was obviously Eddie, so she couldn't figure out how his character Eric reached his Blue River when Eddie the roommate seemed so far away from reaching the same state of consciousness she had personally seen so few people ever reach. One night she asked him about it. "Eddie, the things in your book I found most interesting were things I found hard to believe you experienced personally. I know it's a novel, but how do you know such things?"

"I don't know any of those things. I plan to know them when I'm living the life of a published writer. It's difficult to understand this right now, but I know such things are possible and are only reachable when my mind no longer runs my life. A friend once told me to publish my book this way to validate my writing. He's the one who first told me about Blue River. Another friend told me that most people never reach their Blue River unless they are close to dying or after terrible suffering. Selling my book will be difficult for me because nothing I've ever done has been such a risk for me. See, Lauren, to write about Blue River means I must reach it by investing myself totally — to risk failure. This is the only way for me . . . or I will end up working jobs that will kill me every day because my mind will tell me I'm a coward. It will keep me yearning for imagined things and regretting past inactions until I join the growing herd of other writers who gave up and justified it all by their lying minds. I won't do that. I'll die trying."

From that moment on, Lauren and Eddie became intimate best friends, spending more free time together. But Eddie's Midwest values wouldn't let him get over the fact that Lauren had other boyfriends, although he was too afraid to tell her how he felt. Instead, he wouldn't let Lauren get close to him emotionally or allow her body to send him waiting in the same line her other boyfriends were all too willing to wait in.

That part of Eddie Dense that didn't want to share her with other men was new to the free-spirited Lauren. And to her amazement, that exact character trait in Eddie made her want him even more.

Eddie's Ready

The day Les called and said that his books were bound and ready to pick up — all five thousand of them — was Eddie's last day detailing cars. Lauren said he could store his books in her garage for as long as he lived in her house. Other things had changed too. Eddie was now sleeping in Lauren's room a couple times a week, usually on the weekend. As far as Eddie knew, Lauren had stopped seeing the usual bunch of boyfriends; they suddenly had stopped coming over to see her.

I was able to tell Eddie that Lauren was way too beautiful and free-spirited to be trusted — that she probably was seeing them in other places away from her house in Fairfax. So Eddie didn't trust Lauren, despite the fact that she probably was the only person he ever met who believed in him enough to help him get his book published.

One hundred seventy cases of *Blue River* took Eddie three full loads in his van, and he stacked every case except five in Lauren's garage. Handling each thirty-pound case twice meant that he was exhausted by the time he'd finished loading and unloading some ten thousand pounds of product.

By 2:30 in the afternoon he had finished the task. Although he was tired, he was too excited to rest. "For a couple hours you could sell your book and test the waters. Take a shower and go!" I ordered Eddie.

Just then Eddie realized he hadn't even opened a case to see how his book looked, so he opened one of the five cases in his van and pulled out a copy. He stared at every detail on his front cover. "A novel by E. L. Dense" was printed in bold blue letters at the bottom of the mass-market-sized paperback — the likes of which could be found in book racks in retail outlets. A teal-blue, inch-wide winding river ran across the front cover left to right from both edges and matched the bolder title *Blue River* printed at the top.

When he flipped his book over to the back cover, the river was there in the right spot, which also ran across the entire back cover. Above the river was the centered review from Les. No typos. He liked the white background on both covers that gave the river a wintery look. On the spine he saw the same blue letters of the title and his name. Then he riffled through all 256 pages after seeing his dedication to Dave and Jenna. It looked good. He went inside to shower.

Lauren had given Eddie a new briefcase for his venture — a brown leathered case with a handle and a combination lock he set to open at 0531, Dave's birthday (May 31st).

During his shower and while he was getting dressed, I did my best to get Eddie to listen to me about what he was about to do. He let nothing in for long, observing and dismissing every thought just as Jenna would have wanted him to do.

Eddie filled his gift from Lauren with a dozen copies of *Blue River* and strolled down the hill to a small business section in the village of Fairfax. He went inside a little Italian restaurant he'd eaten in a few times and approached the manager, who was putting a clean red tablecloth on a table at a back booth. "Hi!" Eddie smiled.

The man recognized his customer after eyeing the sales case. "Hi. How are ya?"

"I'm selling this novel I wrote and published myself. It's only five bucks a copy. Could I show ya one?"

"Sure," the manager smiled and invited the author to sit down with him at the booth.

Eddie clicked open the two metal fasteners, opened his briefcase on the table, and handed his prospect a copy of his book, saying, "You're the first person to see it." The writer watched anxiously as his prospect scanned both covers, read the review, and riffled through the pages.

"Five dollars?"

"Yes!"

"I'll take two if you sign them. Sign one to Margaret and one to Jill."

Eddie was thrilled to sell two copies on his first call. He left after the man gave him ten bucks, shook his hand, and wished him good luck.

Outside, after his first sale — a double — Eddie felt ready. He had broken the ice and now knew he could sell his book. I tried to tell him to sell one book for six bucks and two books for ten since paperbacks were selling for $7.95 in most retail outlets we'd seen; but he dismissed my idea, telling me no because he's an unknown writer.

Door after business door, Eddie ducked in and exited as fast as he possibly could. In two lightning quick hours, Eddie sold all twelve books and had sixty bucks in his pocket. One prospect bought three copies in her beauty shop because Eddie learned to ask his prospects if they wanted any copies for friends or relatives signed to them.

There were lots of things the salesman learned in those first two hours. Many people didn't have five bucks on them. He learned to take checks, which gave him three additional sales. He learned that some prospects said no to anything any stranger was selling. And he learned that many people don't read for pleasure.

Lauren saw Eddie returning home toting his gift from her. He reminded her of her father when she was a little girl and saw her daddy returning home with that same powerful energy that determined salesmen have. She noticed that same twirling motion of his empty briefcase that her father used when he returned home after a good day in the field.

Inside her house, even though Eddie had a smile on his face, he had the same determined yet humble countenance of a salesman when he was happy for the moment; he knew he was lucky today and well aware that tomorrow could be different.

She had seen his cases of books taking up one of her two garage stalls, and she knew right then and there that *Blue River* was one good way of keeping him there. Yet she knew from experience that Eddie would run out of territory to work and would have to drive further and further from home to find new prospects until he would have to move on.

"Oh, God, what freedom," Eddie told himself several times a day over his first three weeks of selling his book in Marin County and the surrounding rural areas. He had driven as far north as Petaluma and worked the area for three days, knowing he was burning through territory faster than he'd imagined. All the while, Eddie was getting tuned up to pound the golden sidewalks of The City, where he knew his work was cut out for him because he would be calling on tough-skinned prospects. Yes, he knew San Francisco would reject him more, yet the massive number of small businesses could keep him selling there for months if he raked it clean and was able to sell consistently.

During his first two weeks in the Petaluma area, he sold about fifteen books per day. On the third week he increased his average to eighteen books a day with one day hitting twenty-three.

Now Eddie knew he was as ready as he could be for the big-time buyers and liars in the manswarm. Until his third week in the field, he had feared the mean giant that had money combined with a shorter fuse for the salesman. Both Eddie and I were looking forward to the challenge ahead on the other side of the Golden Gate Bridge.

Hot Walk, Cool Love

Day one in the manswarm. I convinced Eddie to park his van in a hilly residential area in the Russian Hill district. It drizzled all morning under a grayish-blue sky that showed promise of burning away to welcome the warm California sunshine all afternoon. The bustling territory was even tougher than I could have imagined for Eddie. He likened it to walking toward a beautiful woman that was out of his league and used to rejecting his kind with ease. Peopled by nationalities from all corners of the earth, these were indignant prospects who were less than receptive to his quick pitches to sell them his book.

Although five dollars wasn't much to shell out for these affluent business people, half of them acted like English was a language they'd never before heard. Cold, dark-eyed Asian men and women dismissed him quickly. Strapping Russians and Eastern Europeans told Eddie, "No, no . . . I don't buy book this way." And there were the British men and women who haughtily turned him down with brusque criticisms regarding selling a novel "in this particular and peculiar manner."

Despite massive rejection, Eddie would sell a book here and there while he allowed me to hound him about how difficult this territory was. That's how he fatigued — from listening to me go on and on about his poor sales ratio. Yet Eddie kept on in the constant Pacific breezes where he would walk fast between calls as if the pavement were too hot for his feet.

At lunchtime Eddie refused to eat and spend back the twenty bucks taken in from only four copies sold. Wasted time in businesses that kept him waiting without a pitch made him try a high-rise commercial building that was filled with lawyers and accounting firms, where attractive female secretaries and gay men sat alone in plush waiting areas answering busy phones.

Eddie used the stairway, moving higher and higher after pitching prospects fast. By the time he reached the top floor, his briefcase was only lightened by two books sold.

Again he hit the wet city sidewalks and sold only six more books in nearly four hours, for a grand total of twelve books sold for the day. His long walk to his van was slow, up enervating hills that really made him feel the growling hunger he had forced on his tired body.

It was getting dark by the time he returned home. Lauren warmed up chicken and broccoli she had baked for Eddie, which he devoured like a wolf after a long, arduous hunt for prey. She massaged his tense shoulders as he told her about his tough day in The City. Eddie and Lauren's favorite song, "Crystal Blue Persuasion" by Tommy James and the Shondels, played on the stereo and helped soothe away the tension I brought on Eddie by convincing him that his unmet expectations made him a failure.

After a hot bath Eddie took a nap on his bed and woke up three hours later with Lauren's legs wrapped around his legs. He listened to her soft breath at the back of his neck and realized that he now trusted her, that she had stopped seeing her other boyfriends. When I tried to suggest that she could be sneaking around to see them during the day, Eddie caught me and smiled because he knew he had paid attention to me and knew it was me. He thought how Jenna would be happy to know this.

For the first time, Eddie felt that his relationship with Lauren was some kind of cool love that was not pushing him to do anything. It was an easy kind of way to be with someone without the same dysfunctional expectations that he saw split up his parents.

Instead of getting up, Eddie went back to sleep and slept through the night — his body wracked from listening to me all day. It's not that I didn't want Eddie to succeed; I just wanted him to succeed with me, not by shutting me out and dismissing me every time I tried to talk to him.

The next day Eddie parked in the same spot downtown. It was pretty much the same story, except he managed to sell fifteen books. Again, Eddie's body was spent by the day's end from heavy rejection numbers. On his way back up the hill to his van he told me, *Shut up. I'm not giving up. Today was better than yesterday.* Just then from someplace inside Eddie came a calming voice that told him to "relax and enjoy the moment." I have no clue where that voice came from, but I know it wasn't me. I call that voice "Slow Eddie," his higher state of consciousness — and my enemy.

At home Lauren was right there again to feed Eddie and sustain him with positive words of encouragement. She reminded him that he was making more than twice as much money as he had been detailing cars, and that he was one of the fortunate few who was free to do his own thing. She added, "You're an artist in America, Eddie. Americans rarely support artists unless they're promoted by a corporation, like a publisher or distributor who has money to put you out there. And they take the biggest cut. I think if you explain to your prospects that you cut out the middleman, you might get more sales. Many of them will respect you because they started that way."

Lauren was right. The very next day Eddie sold twenty books in The City using Lauren's assertion that he had eliminated the middleman.

It must have been for at least two more weeks that Eddie hammered The City, averaging twenty books a day. By then he was ready to hit the smaller towns around the Bay Area, knowing that he made it through a tough territory and could not be stopped by them — or me — from selling his book.

After another month Eddie reimbursed Lauren the money he owed her, and he paid her father for the thousand books he'd sold since he started his direct-selling venture. Eddie figured he only owed Les for the next 1,500 books he'd sell, then the proceeds from the remaining 2,500 books in Lauren's garage would be all his. Eddie was happy; not only because of his sales, but also because he had begun his next novel. And he began writing down names and phone numbers of every person who bought a book from him. He would tell his buyers from now on that he planned to sell them his next book when he published it. Lauren had given him the idea after he'd sold his three hundredth book, telling him he had readers who would buy his next novel and that could be his motivation to write his next book.

He realized as his list of buyers was growing in his notebook that Lauren was good for him. That list had removed a ton of stress from his shoulders, diminishing the enormity and the uncertainty of his venture. It ended his beleaguered life as a one-time salesman without a business plan.

Circle of Doubt

Eddie plowed through Richmond, San Pablo, El Sobrante, Tara Hills, Pinole, Martinez, Benicia, and then up to Vallejo. He worked each town and small city as thoroughly as any salesman ever had.

After working Vallejo for a week, he felt comfortable with his sales, knowing he could average twenty books a day. All that week I brought up the idea that selling his book was taking all his energy, leaving no time to read and write and have quality time with Lauren. My broken record was, "They only buy your book because you are young, Eddie. They admire your gumption and drive to peddle your book. They give you five bucks because you ask for it. You surprise them, Eddie. But you're not a serious writer unless you write every day. You are just a good salesman, Eddie Dense. You wrote your book for me — to prove to me that you're a writer. They don't care what's on your pages, Eddie; it doesn't matter. You sell a book and go on to the next prospect without any intention at all of improving your writing skills. Instead, your focus is on selling your twenty books a day. I do that. You haven't stopped me, Eddie, from running your life. I just came to you from another direction."

On his drives to new territories and back again, Eddie lived in a circle of doubt he allowed me to give him. He rarely observed me doing this, despite all his Blue River baloney. Oh, he could keep me out during most of his selling time, but I was okay with that because he was selling each book with a means-to-an-end mentality. I loved what Eddie was doing.

Before long Eddie was working Oakland and south of there, in places like Alameda, San Leandro, Castro Valley, San Lorenzo, and then Hayward.

At home in Fairfax, Lauren could see the toll her boyfriend's selling was having on his personality. He rarely smiled. He'd become increasingly sullen and quiet, not talking unless pressed. The tension in his body was mounting, turning his muscles into a mass of knotted tissue and causing him to grow more and more anxious about each new day.

Sundays were the only day of the week Eddie didn't sell. That was the day Lauren would drive Eddie to the beach or into the country, to places where she could help him relax. She'd pack them a healthy lunch to save him money, and she'd always drive her car. Often he'd complain to her that he only had the same amount of money saved as when he was detailing cars, and how that was so discouraging because he'd worked so much harder selling his book.

"But you're living your dream, Eddie. Most writers never even finish a first novel, let alone see it in print. You have to stop beating yourself up, Eddie. Relax and enjoy what you've chosen to do with your life."

He knew she was right; that's why he needed Lauren. Sundays she would never fail to rebuild his spirit, and he'd have a break from the maddening circle of doubt I'd pound into him as the week wore on.

One evening when Eddie returned home from a tough day after selling only thirteen books, a familiar blue convertible was parked behind Lauren's car in her driveway. It was Jeff, one of her old boyfriends who tended bar at a local pub. Eddie didn't like Jeff, and not just because of his past relationship with Lauren. Ike always told his son that they could never hire a good bartender because "they're all a bunch of thieves."

Jeff was sitting on Lauren's patio having a glass of wine with her. They were laughing and having a great time. Lauren was wearing her bathing suit with a towel wrapped around her waist as if she'd been swimming. Playboy Jeff was in his bathing suit and t-shirt — his tanned legs stretched out on her patio table — when Lauren saw Eddie in her kitchen. She waved for Eddie to come out and join them.

Instead Eddie took a long shower. That's when I was able to plant images of Lauren and Jeff playing at the beach and making love on a blanket like he knew they had when they were dating. Lauren made the mistake of telling Eddie everything she did on her dates before Eddie was more than just her roommate.

Eddie did not want to go out onto the patio. He hoped Jeff was gone, but he wasn't. Lauren could tell from Eddie's bloodshot eyes that he'd had a stressful day when he sat down and joined them.

"You remember Jeff, Eddie?"

"Yeah. Hey, Jeff," Eddie shook his hand.

"Lauren tells me you're selling your novel to businesses," Jeff said trying to bait Eddie into a conversation.

"Yeah," Eddie forced a smile and added nothing.

Lauren picked up on Eddie's mood so decided not to tell him right then that she'd spent a couple hours over at Jeff's condo pool. "You hungry?" she smiled at Eddie.

Eddie nodded yes and sat there in a tired stupor until Jeff got the hint and left.

Eddie stayed outside until Lauren brought him a sandwich on a plate piled with cold veggies. "Aren't you hungry?" he asked.

"I ate at Jeff's. I went over there after he called and invited me over for some sun and chat."

Eddie kept quiet — only a cynical nod.

"You do know that Jeff and I are just good friends, don't you?"

Another nod.

"What are you thinking?" she smiled.

“Not much,” he smiled and chewed and kept his eyes averted from her stare.

“Do you think I fooled around with Jeff?”

“If it crossed my mind, is that a big deal?” Eddie got up and went inside, not wanting to hear what she and Jeff did. What bothered Eddie the most was that his mood was getting darker after every selling day. Several times a day I made him ask himself if he was doing something worthwhile or just wasting his time.

Yes, one giant circle of doubt was wrapped around Eddie Dense like one of Saturn’s rings. I tried to tell him that he always lived in doubt and fear about everything. Then he’d shut me up and eventually repeat the same pattern of looking for approval from exterior sources. That’s another thing I loved about Eddie.

Move or Quit

"You can't believe how much territory five thousand books gobbles up," Eddie explained to Lauren one night.

Eddie wasn't sure if he wanted to print another five thousand copies of *Blue River.* If he did he'd have to move to a new territory that would sustain him. His inventory was down to about five hundred copies in Lauren's garage. Lauren's father told him it would take four weeks to get the second printing back from the binder.

Eddie had already worked all the way down to Monterey and Carmel after working San Jose; he'd even worked up north to Santa Rosa and all the towns around the Russian River area. He estimated that Sacramento would use up most of his remaining product, and then he'd have to move. But to where?

Lauren wanted to go with Eddie as long as he stayed on the West Coast. She loved San Diego and told him she could rent out her house pretty fast if she were to go with him.

They agreed to move to the San Diego area. Eddie would go ahead of her until she found a tenant. "Why would you want to leave this place?" he asked Lauren.

"I've been here for six years. I'd like a change," she smiled.

"But what about after another year when my second printing is sold out? I don't know what I'll do then."

"That's fine. I'll get a year lease on the house and I can always move back in. Look, Eddie, I understand that you have to have new territory. And I know you'll have another book ready for all your readers. I'm not worried about it."

Yes, Eddie had to move or quit. If he quit after his first printing was sold out, I know that E. L. Dense would never finish a second novel. He hadn't been tested enough or hit bottom yet. A guy like Eddie has to hit bottom before reaching his Blue River; there is no other way for a guy like him. So Eddie ordered his second printing and got the same terms from Lauren's father at the same cost per book, even though the cost of paper had gone up seven percent. Les liked Eddie because he knew his daughter loved Eddie. And Les wasn't making any money off Eddie; he was just breaking even.

Eddie's bank account had never looked so good. This fact made him tell Lauren that he'd pay all of her moving expenses. They also agreed to share evenly their rent in San Diego. Lauren liked her boyfriend's sense of financial responsibility because she had a history of latching onto boyfriends who were good at freeloading off her.

Lauren was excited about going to San Diego with Eddie for another reason: Her best friend, Kim, lived in San Diego.

Until his second printing was ready, Eddie's selling days were filled with a new purpose that gave a bounce to his walk that I'd never seen before. Although he was having to drive further to find new prospects, he would return home energized instead of half-dead from me battering his brain about his future.

Now he was selling twenty-four books a day, because at the front of his pitch he would explain with incredible enthusiasm how he intended to sell them his next novel if they bought *Blue River.* He would proudly show each prospect his burgeoning list, explaining this was not a one-time sale.

By the time his second printing was ready, he was down to only sixty copies of *Blue River.* He rented a big U-Haul truck and loaded it with five thousand new books, his clothes, and most of Lauren's furniture (with Jeff's help). Lauren hadn't rented out her house yet, so she would stay in Fairfax until she did.

Their plan was simple: After Eddie found them a one-bedroom apartment and stored his books, he would fly back and haul the rest of Lauren's things in his van with Lauren following in her car, if she had found a renter for her house by then.

Boy, that Eddie was a trooper during his solo run in that U-Haul truck. He sold a dozen books at a time to truck stops, which really helped cover his fuel expenses.

After long phone conversations with Kim, Lauren wanted Eddie to find an apartment in the Pacific Beach area where Kim had an apartment. Kim already had a couple places lined up to show Eddie when he arrived — not to mention a free place to stay until he found an apartment.

Lasting First Impressions

Twenty-four-year-old Kim Louden was strikingly beautiful, if beauty is judged by looks alone. She was from San Francisco. She had long white-blonde hair and penetrating silverish-blue eyes that were wolflike — appearing to size you up, looking for a weakness. Her figure was perfect on her five-foot-eleven body that loved to party. What really scared Eddie about Kim when he first met her in front of her Pacific Beach apartment, some three blocks from the water's edge, was that she lived alone.

Most girls didn't really care much for Eddie right away. Even Lauren had admitted to him that she thought he looked like he'd make a good and quiet roommate because he was introverted and didn't seem the type to bring girls home.

When Kim first met Eddie, she hugged him as if she really liked him. That threw him; he didn't think people did things like that unless they really knew you. That's how Kim reminded him of Lauren. They were both such open and loving free spirits.

Within two hours Eddie found a one-bedroom apartment. Kim showed him two apartments close to hers, and Eddie signed a year-long lease when he saw the second one.

After unloading his books into a storage locker a few blocks from the new apartment, he unloaded Lauren's things into their new place with the help of one of Kim's neighbors.

Although he was exhausted, Kim talked Eddie into going to happy hour at a local pub she frequented on Garnet. Eddie was tired and amazed that his U-Haul was empty and that he already had a place to live. Plus he was having buffalo wings and sharing a pitcher of beer with beautiful Kim, who seemed to be the most popular person in the joint.

"So you were Lauren's roommate?" Kim asked coyly.

"Yeah, for a couple months before we dated."

"A couple months? Boy, that's a record for Lauren," she laughed. "Lauren told me she was your first."

"First what?"

Kim burst into laughter. "First what? You know first what, Mr. Dense."

Eddie didn't like her play on words with his name, yet he didn't make waves.

"Yeah, she was my first . . . roommate," Eddie smiled.

Kim's laugh was infectious yet masculine and demeaning, like some teasing bully. But that wasn't the only thing he didn't like about Kim.

After another pitcher they walked along the Pacific Beach boardwalk. The sun had vanished perhaps an hour earlier; it's blue-orange glow emanated behind them as all kinds of people strolled, jogged, and roller-skated past them from both directions. High tide was coming in fast and loud sixty yards off as Kim peppered her loud voice at her guest's ear. "It's cool Lauren will be living so close to me! We'll have a blast in Pacific Beach, Eddie! Do you surf?"

He shook his head no.

Then Kim got right up against his side, wrapped her long arm around his waist, and walked closely beside him as if they were lovers. "I can teach you how to body surf. Oh, there's a nude beach not far from here! We can all go. Talk about totally freeing!"

That's when I showed Eddie images of strange men gawking at Lauren's naked body on the beach, which reddened Eddie's face to match his hair as beautiful Kim rode his hip chatting about all the sights in San Diego she was going to show him.

"You have a boyfriend, Kim?"

"Not tonight!" she laughed and squeezed Eddie closer to her firm body. Then she went on and on about how she liked dating lots of guys, just as Lauren used to. "I want to play the field!

I'm like a guy that way. I like variety!" she laughed into his tired ear. "You would have to be a pretty strong man to put up with me, Eddie," she laughed.

Now and then whenever a guy would walk past them on the boardwalk, Kim would flirt with him by smiling and winking at him. But as soon as he was past them, she would make lewd comments to her companion. "Check out the caboose on that guy. He can surf on me anytime with that body. Yeah, baby, here's my number," she'd laugh into Eddie's ear.

Later that night Eddie called Lauren from Kim's apartment phone and told her all about the place he'd already found for them. He told Lauren that since she had found a tenant but needed a few days to clean her house, he'd work the Pacific Beach area and fly up to get her later in the week. Then Kim talked to Lauren while Eddie went to their new place to sleep.

Two days later the phone company turned on Lauren and Eddie's phone service. And that wasn't the only thing turned on; Kim was flirting more and more with her new neighbor. I told him he was an idiot for not fooling around with her, especially since Lauren was probably fooling around on him.

Just then Slow Eddie, that wise guy with all the answers, warned Eddie, "Kim's trouble. She has an agenda to ruin your relationship with Lauren because of their past." So Eddie listened to Slow Eddie and avoided going to happy hours and other places with Kim, telling her he had to catch up on his writing. That was another reason Eddie didn't like Kim; she never once asked him anything about his writing.

Eddie did catch up on his writing. And he wrote long letters to his parents and Sara. A few months earlier on the phone, Sara and his parents told him they enjoyed reading *Blue River*. It was his sister's opinion that meant the most to Eddie since she minored in English in college. Sara told him that she would love to edit his next book for him; and she even offered to be his agent. Eddie told Sara it all sounded good to him and that he'd send her his new manuscript when he finished writing it.

Lauren picked up Eddie at the San Francisco airport. Her new tenants, a young couple from Santa Rosa, would move into her house the next day. Lauren had everything packed and was ready to move south as soon as she and Eddie got back to her place to pick up his van. Besides having her car's backseat jammed to the roof with clothes, she had Eddie's van loaded with the rest of her things — making room for her futon bed in the cargo area.

They spent the night at a rest area off I-5, eighty miles north of Los Angeles. Lying down together in the crowded cargo area, he told Lauren that Kim flirted with him all the time, even parading around in her underwear when she knew he was coming over. "Oh, that's just Kim," Lauren dismissed with a laugh. "She's a flirt."

Lauren went on to tell Eddie about her partying days with Kim, including all the sexual flings. Eddie listened, but I got my two cents' worth in when I convinced him to tell her, "Look, maybe it's because I'm not from hip California, but I don't like hearing about your stupid past with that idiot."

After an awkward silence, Eddie told Lauren that he wasn't excited about living close to her best friend.

That Awful Beach

Eddie was grateful to have plenty of new territory in San Diego, yet each day when he was out selling I showed him awful images of the reunited party girls that drained his energy and left him stressed out by the end of the day.

Every single night when Eddie returned home from work, Lauren and Kim were either out doing something fun together or going out to do something fun together. It sure appeared to Eddie that Lauren had changed ever since she'd moved south.

Lauren loved their new apartment, the youthful quirkiness of Pacific Beach, and, of course, living so close to Kim. Pacific Beach had some used high-fashion clothing stores that Kim would take Lauren to and they'd shop for hours on end. They would leave the stores wearing new outfits that Eddie thought too revealing to wear in public, like sheer cotton beach bunny dresses of off-white, cream yellow, and baby blue. Even though Pacific Beach was similar to Marin County — a place by water with plenty of free-spirited people of all ages — Eddie was not going with the flow and enjoying the laid-back lifestyle of the surfers and carefree locals that were so much like Kim.

Meanwhile, Eddie kept plowing his new territory, managing to sustain the same numbers he'd had up north. But instead of the glorious freedom a writer needs to write the next book, and even though his list of readers was growing by twenty a day, Eddie was returning home to an empty apartment after I'd ruined his day with dark images of Lauren and Kim playing in paradise.

Yes, every day that Eddie worked like a dog, going from business to business, I was able to convince him that his girlfriend was up to no good with Kim, off somewhere in Kim's white VW convertible. These negative images were magnified during sales droughts of rejections that could come for hours on end; that's when I'd show him teeth-grinding visions of the girls drinking expensive wine at some La Jolla patio bar with a couple of rich California playboys all over them. I'd drive Eddie so mad with these periods of seething jealousy and resentment that one time when he was walking by a stop sign, he punched it so hard that it bloodied his knuckles.

Day after day this went on. Lauren would happily return to their apartment around six in the evening and often find her roommate curled up on their bed like a boy who'd been whipped hard all day. His eyes would be closed, but I kept him awake with lies about Lauren.

One evening after a particularly grueling sales day, I was able to really get him good. As usual, Lauren came home just after six.

"Kim and I went to Coronado. We had this fabulous lunch, then we walked on the beach for two hours and talked about everything. It was so fun. How was your day, sweetie?"

"Sold twenty."

That was all Eddie had to say, because that was all he was — a meaningless cipher, a number in the manswarm who joined a popular club comprised of a lonely group of men who lived for the numbers day to day until they were alone at night recovering from it all.

"You hungry?" Lauren asked softly, her lips close to his ear.

But Eddie didn't answer, wanting to punish her with silence. Then she came around to his side of the bed so that she could see his face. He saw she was wearing that see-through top he didn't like her wearing in public. He remained quiet. He knew that she knew that her clothing bothered him because more than once he'd mentioned to her that her breasts were exposed as if she "wanted men to gawk at them." Yet he shut his eyes and said nothing, listening while angry as she told him what he could have to eat while she went over to Kim's place to give her a permanent because "Kim met this really cute guy today." She kissed his cheek and soon he heard the clicking lock of their apartment door. Before long Eddie was asleep, which gave me a chance to show him a quick dream:

Lauren was naked and walking alone on that awful beach Kim had told him about. It was daytime, yet the sand and water were black as Eddie the dreamer saw an endless stream of naked men with their sinister eyes raking over Lauren's body. Eddie couldn't see Lauren's face as these men passed by her. He feared she'd be smiling, thrilled at the private show her flesh gave this manswarm of tanned vultures with their flat stomachs and golden hair, all of them with bulging eyes on the woman he loved.

Just then Dave came into Eddie's dream. Eddie's best friend was now one of those approaching men on the black beach — except Dave was fully clothed, wearing his favorite yellow shirt. But Dave was not smiling or gawking; it was as if he wanted the dreamer to see that Lauren was not some lust-inspiring object of form to be stared at. Then Dave smiled, but not at Lauren; he was smiling at Jenna, who was walking alongside Lauren. Jenna was wearing a long cotton dress and was barefoot.

Dave and Jenna embraced on the black sand as Lauren continued on, walking further and further away, until Eddie opened his slow-blinking eyes and wiped the drool from his mouth with the back of his hand.

I made Eddie get up and go over to Kim's place. Still in his dream-like stupor, I made him stand out of view in front of Kim's always-open front window. He could see Kim sitting on a chair while Lauren gave her a permanent. They were laughing, having fun; yet all Eddie could see was that awful quick dream that allowed me to tell him over and over, "She will betray you."

Splash of Rain

Weeks and months zipped by, along with case after case of *Blue River.* Eddie was certain his readers had vanished into the bottomless reading ether of southern California because he had zero feedback from them. The fact that there was no contact information inside his book didn't matter; a writer needs validation from his readers. All he knew was he was selling twenty books a day, and his list of readers was growing. He thought of calling some of them at the beginning of his list, then he decided against it because it would be too awkward and might destroy his desire to sell his book if he heard that most of them hadn't even read it yet.

Because of this absence of feedback, he was unable to come up with a title for his next novel in the works. So Eddie would just write; and he would move from word to word without letting me help him. Jenna inspired that. Yes, E. L. Dense was determined to write another book without using me — or rather, using me as little as possible.

But then one day came a "splash of rain," a term Eddie used when his story line changed for the better and seemed to take on a life of its own without any real effort on his part. The words poured onto his pages like some bulging bag of water that burst open at the seams and perfectly splashed magical words onto page after page until he was once again excited about writing another book.

About the time Eddie was getting used to Lauren spending lots of her free time with Kim, along came "est." Eddie discovered that "est" stood for Erhard Seminars Training, named after charismatic salesman and marketing guru Werner Erhard. est was a household word in California because of the millions of searching young minds who needed to "get" something. In this large group awareness training, groups of three hundred or more individuals would meet for a two-day intensive training seminar listening to lecturers until they could reach a state of enlightenment where they were freed of their sundry hang-ups and shortcomings and entered into a higher state of personal awareness. One by one, the seminar participants would "get" to this state of enlightenment and prove it by standing in front of the group and making a public declaration of their "getting it." In Eddie's opinion, each one was merely "getting" that they were willing to join the herd that needed this kind of training that, for all intents and purposes, was nothing more than a hot bath for the searching ego's desire to belong.

Kim had gotten Lauren to shell out big bucks to join her in one of the two-day est group sessions. Late at night, right after their first twelve-hour est session, Lauren returned home and told Eddie about the "incredible experience."

"Oh, Eddie! You have to take the training. It's so amazing! So many times I thought of you and how much this can help you."

"Help me? How?"

"Wake you up, Eddie. You can truly experience how very powerful you are. And I want to support you by paying for your training."

"Lauren, I don't want to sit in a chair all day and get brainwashed by some car-salesman-turned-guru. You go through it. That's fine for you. But I know it's only a temporary pop fad."

"Eddie, I know est can bring us closer together. I want you to take the training for us."

I'm in training every day I sell my book!" Eddie snapped, not wanting to be hounded about est any further.

By the next night, about the time Lauren was to have supposedly finished her training, there was no Lauren. She didn't return home until three in the morning. Eddie was asleep — or at least pretending to be — when she got under the covers, snuggled against his backside, and kissed his shoulder.

"Sorry I'm so late," she whispered and giggled playfully.

I'll admit it was my idea to play this kind of game with Lauren. I waited until I sensed she was waiting for Eddie to ask her where she'd been until three in the morning. So I made Eddie keep his mouth shut and wait her out. I'll bet that Slow Eddie didn't like that game.

"Kim and I went to an IHOP after the training. Then we walked all over downtown. We were so excited after the training."

Then Eddie turned to those green eyes that sparkled with aliveness. "Who went with you?"

When she blinked twice fast before answering, I knew she was thinking about lying to Eddie. But she didn't. "A couple of guys from the training. They bought our breakfast . . ."

"And walked with you?"

"Yeah. They were like our chaperones. Kim likes both of them. She's so funny. We laughed all night. I wished you were with us." Then Lauren kissed Eddie's neck and told him that during this last session she really "got" how much she loved him and that she didn't compare other men with him.

"Well, that's good," Eddie rolled his eyes.

"No. No, really, Eddie. That's a big breakthrough for me. Can you say the same thing?" She punched him playfully while he pondered his answer.

That morning Eddie went to work tired after he kissed Lauren goodbye while she slept. All day he reflected on whether he would take the est training, asking some of his new readers if they knew anything about est. A few of them had heard good things about est and some even knew people who had taken the training. "Did you notice any positive changes?" Eddie would ask them.

One woman said that her sister took the est training and that she seemed happier, more at peace.

During his lunch break at a deli while writing at a table, Slow Eddie told Eddie, "Take est. It will help you sell books."

Change Me

"It's always the last ones 'to share' and expose their power who have the most trapped energy." Those were the words Slow Eddie whispered to Eddie during the second day of his est training. I resisted and fought like hell to keep my power over Eddie while Eddie Dense sat on a chair sweating it out with three hundred peers.

Nearing the end of the training, only a handful hadn't "gotten it" and proclaimed it in front of the group. But to really "get it," those words had to be true. Eddie had watched them all; one by one they would join the herd of "gotten its." And he could see that many of them were like children — wanting to be a part of the group but not really reaching into their bellies for something buried deep within their fearful sense of becoming something better than they were.

Knowing Eddie like I do, it was the fact that Lauren paid a lot of money for him to "get it" that made him get off his chair and head for the front of the room to face them. On his way Slow Eddie told him, "You do not love Lauren because you are closed off to knowing what love is. Until you give up seeing the world as 'you' against 'it,' she can only be a part of your resistance to reaching your Blue River."

"Change me," Eddie whispered back to Slow Eddie as the seated group stared at his slow-blinking eyes and his lips that were twitching from the push of his buck teeth.

Eddie's sharing lasted thirty-five seconds. Reaching his freckled arms above his head, he dug deep into his belly and repeated the estian words exhorted by the trainer which burst forth from his throat in spitting terror while his eyes were open and on the blur of his captive audience. The words were not important. It was the awakening of aliveness in every cell of

Eddie's body at that very moment that made the group instinctively applaud as if one cohesive mass. It was the sound of their approval that filled every inch of Eddie's body with aliveness.

When he returned to his seat, I was stunned to silence and knew that Eddie Dense was now immersed in Dave's elusive Blue River. My suspicion was confirmed when at the very end of the training as all were exiting the room, a middle-aged man with blazing blue eyes reflected back to Eddie that Eddie was one of the few who truly reached a place intended upon completion of the training.

Outside that downtown San Diego auditorium, Eddie saw a luminous world for the first time. Everything he saw was alive with a glowing energy — moving traffic, buildings, traffic signal lights, and people. On the corner a homeless old lady was ranting beside her grimy shopping cart that was jammed with all her shabby belongings. Eddie stopped to listen to her angry self-diatribe about the evil monster in America — the media. "Oh, how it exploits human fears by exploiting stories of death and greed, fear and corruption."

There were other things she was saying that were inaudible, yet Eddie knew she was right. And he could see that she was only a reflection of the fearful pedestrians that ignored her — many of whom held the faces of those he had just been with for two days.

Just then it hit Eddie right between the ears: This old lady was the fearful mind we all have, except she was voicing her every single thought that the majority of humanity drowns out with myriad temporary distractions and vices.

Eddie returned home after walking downtown for hours just as Lauren had done with Kim after their training. And just as

Lauren had been, he was anxious to wake her and share his experience.

Standing in their bedroom doorway, he paused to watch her sleeping on his side of the bed. Lauren was smart; she knew that he would have to wake her because he could only sleep on "his side" of the bed. Clarity was there for him. He could grin knowing that she had "used" her mind to sleep until he returned home. By contrast, when she had finished her training, he had let his mind "run him" with all kinds of negative images and words that had only made that moment and the following day miserable.

"Yes, Eddie, she is smarter than you," Slow Eddie reminded him.

He sat on the edge of his side of the bed and gently rubbed her shoulder, hoping to wake her without speaking. When he answered her sleepy query, "How was the training?" he startled himself with a new voice when he said, "It was amazing." She noticed right away how deep and alive his voice sounded and told him so.

"I hope it holds," he smiled.

"It will," she kissed him.

They stayed up until dawn talking because it was Sunday, then they went out for breakfast where Eddie was tested. Lauren informed him that Kim wanted her to go down to Ensenada, Mexico, for a couple days before they began working for est as group training facilitators.

"Facilitators? What's that?" he inquired with his new voice that held no trace of the Eddie she knew.

"We would help market est to fill seats at seminars and then become trainers."

Lauren was surprised when Eddie told her that it might be a good opportunity for her and Kim, and that he would support her in any way he could.

Even Eddie was surprised by the way he reacted to Lauren's plans. All day his voice remained powerful, even when they went over to Kim's apartment and found her with an overnight guest — a man who took the training with her.

Jealousy or Trust

All day Wednesday I made Eddie think about Lauren and Kim in Mexico. The two attractive est graduates left in Kim's car Wednesday morning and were to return early Friday morning before border traffic got too heavy. I didn't really get to Eddie until one of his new readers told him that est held seminars in Ensenada because many affluent Americans lived there. That was all I needed to give Eddie a giant headache.

Thursday and Friday were nothing but long, anxious hours of selling with Eddie's old voice that had returned. Sales were good despite the negative images I gave Eddie of Lauren in Ensenada. He'd sell a book and record the reader's name and phone number in this notebook; but when leaving he'd see Lauren lying nude on a white Mexican beach with Kim and two male est graduates. Several times an hour he'd tell me to "stop it" because he trusted Lauren to be loyal to him. Eddie's jealousy was all my doing, and I loved it.

Friday during lunch Eddie wrote in his notebook:

> *It's a matter of jealousy or trust. My mind will not allow trust to run my day, though trust is by far a much better thing to have. This terrible feeling of being fooled by this wonderful woman I've come to care for and desperately want to trust haunts me all day, until my legs are mere toothpicks drenched in exhausted nerves that feel weakened whenever I move or stand, or even when I sit to rest.*
>
> *Today I hope she's not home when I get there. I want time to soak this tired body in a hot bath, to quiet my jealous mind before I explode in a thousand directions. When I search my*

memory, I cannot recall being lied to by my parents or deceived by anyone in my life in such a way that really hurt me. So where does this jealousy come from? Lauren is my first girlfriend; and though we are about the same age, she is the one who has a past love life. And she has been open about her life experiences to the point that it bothers me.

My ego will not let go of her past. That's a problem when an average guy like me has a beautiful girlfriend; other men want her whether I'm there or not. Now that she's away in Mexico with her friend Kim, I cannot help but think that bad things have happened. What bothers me most is I must know the truth.

My mind is a jealous mind. Even if she tells me she is loyal, my mind will not believe her. So either way I feel we are headed for a falling out. But not a falling out of love. If I really knew love and how to keep some interior doorway open to let love flow, then and only then do I believe we would have a good chance of staying together. To whomever I write these words, and to whatever it is that compels me to scribble these ghostly words — words that always mean nothing because they are always behind me — change me to trust her.

Friday evening at eight, Lauren's glowing, tanned body and sun-lightened hair returned home from Mexico. Their eyes met from ten feet away. Both knew right away that things had changed. Lauren was incredibly sensitive to anyone's mood or "energy," as she called it. They kissed. She left Eddie's lips too soon to suit me, so I made him interrogate her; but not in a suspicious, petty way that insecure boyfriends can do when they feel threatened. She knew his old voice was back when he asked her, "How was Mexico?"

"I loved it," she answered with overt haggardness from too much sun and partying.

"What'd ya do?" Eddie held his fake smile.

She answered while removing her clothes and on her way to bed to get some sleep, "Lots of sun, too many margaritas, not enough sleep, and too much good food."

He could see her shoulders and head slumped forward when she sat on her side of the bed. "I hope you don't mind if I sleep now," she sighed.

Just when I wanted to press her about who she was with in Mexico, Slow Eddie took over. "Sleep, sweetie. You're beat," Eddie whispered while covering her with a comforter.

Lauren slept while Eddie went for a long walk on the beach. He kept me quiet by telling me that jealousy is a venal thing that's big-time ugly when compared to trust. "I choose to trust, so shut up," he told me.

I knew Eddie wasn't serious about trusting Lauren for long.

The Lies Have It

Months passed in paradise. His old voice seemed to be back for good, yet Slow Eddie was right about the est training helping him sell books. His numbers were about the same; it was his ability to handle rejection that improved.

Eddie was driving to Orange County to find new territory. That was just one of many things I kept warning him about. I tried to tell him that he could run out of territory in San Diego with over two thousand copies of *Blue River* left to sell. No way could Eddie move out of San Diego with two thousand books in his van. Eddie's new worry was leaving Lauren in San Diego after breaking up with her.

Their life together had diminished to a point of no return ever since her trip to Mexico with Kim. The further away he drove to find new veins of prospects, the more he was certain he wanted to be free from Lauren. He'd sell for a week at a time in Los Angeles, then two weeks at a time. He'd stack enough cases in his van to sustain him, and he'd sleep in the van's cargo area to save money on motels. He'd shower and change clothes in public beach restrooms in Venice or Santa Monica.

Sales were good in Los Angeles. Surviving in such a polluted metro area gave him a real sense of what it would be like when he broke it off with Lauren. It also gave me time to come up with a way to make their breakup less painful for both of them: Lie to her.

Of course, Eddie didn't want to admit it at the time, but he was driving Lauren to another man by withholding his trust and love.

At that point Lauren was on her way to enlightenment, or at least that's what she believed. est was good for her; but Eddie — poor Eddie — I still had him where I wanted him, listening to me instead of Lauren. It is so true that it is easier to live with someone if you communicate your feelings right away. Lauren was surrounded by people at est who loved her and supported her emotionally. Somewhere between rest and handling rejection in the territory, Eddie was only supported by me and his growing list of readers. That's good for me and bad for any relationship. Yes, Lauren and Eddie were doomed — headed for a fall.

I gave Eddie his plan: When all his books could fit in his van with room for him to sleep, he would hit the road. It was getting close. He estimated that sixty-two cases would be about right, some 1,800 books. There were sixty-eight cases in storage.

Driving back to San Diego after another difficult two weeks in L.A., he concocted a story for Lauren, which he planned to tell her that evening after she got home from an est training seminar. But she had good news first. She'd been elevated to an est trainer which meant more money and responsibility. Even Kim saw that as something that would mean the end of Lauren and Eddie.

Right after Lauren told Eddie her "good news," he told Lauren that his Aunt Susan in Council Bluffs was terminally ill and that he wanted to see her before she died.

"You've never mentioned your Aunt Susan to me," Lauren stated bluntly, as if she knew a lie when she heard one.

"She's my mother's sister. I called my mom from L.A., and she said she needs help taking care of her. And I could help out by tending bar on weekends."

Eddie could tell that Lauren knew he was lying, that there was no Aunt Susan; but she let it go, resigning that their relationship was over. Kim often told her best friend that "Eddie was too much in his head" for her. Lauren knew that Kim was right, yet she loved Eddie. Kim was willing to move in with

Lauren to save both of them rent, but Lauren didn't tell Eddie that.

The last week Eddie was in Pacific Beach, he worked closer to San Diego in Ramona, Vista and Escondido. That final week in their apartment was filled with silence. Lauren was angry with Eddie because her suspicion of his lie was confirmed when Mary Dense called her son one night when he was out.

"How's your sister?" Lauren asked her.

"My sister? I don't have a sister."

"I thought you had a sister who is very ill."

"No . . . not that I know of," Mary chuckled.

Lauren didn't tell Eddie that his mother called that night. She never revealed to Eddie that she'd caught him in his lie. But that lie meant that Lauren didn't have to tell Eddie she'd been attracted to another man, an est trainer she'd met in Ensenada who had recently moved to San Diego to work for est in the training center.

Two lies made their final days together a drag. One lie was spoken, the other hidden, but both equally destructive.

After hugging goodbye outside Eddie's loaded van, Eddie said he'd call her. Lauren knew that call would never come, and yet she believed they would see each other again. No drama. Each had helped the other get what they wanted.

When Lauren went back into her apartment, she found a letter from Eddie he'd left on the kitchen counter.

Dear Lauren,

We have separated without me telling you how much you've meant to me. Why we didn't stay together is not as important as the incredible mystery it was for me to find you. Along my journey to California, I truly imagined finding someone who would help me get published. I found you.

Any independent writer can make mistakes with grammar and skirt most of those educated things that critical readers reject and dismiss. I've learned that none of those critics would write a novel — because they can't. You alone helped me and made my book better.

I've stood before thousands of those critical readers and watched up close as they rejected me after reading a few passages from my little book. They said no from a critical eye because my work invalidated what they've been taught to know is "good writing." Yet you alone knew I'd become a better writer by selling my book this way. You helped me by knowing this venture would force me to become better because of the investment it takes. Without your help, Lauren, I would be even more lost because I would not have some eight thousand readers behind me. I believe this endeavor will somehow lead me to a place that conquers time and opens a door that allows love into my heart.

I cannot live around your light, est, or any other person or thing until I'm out of this darkness. Thank you for getting me closer to my Blue River — to even seeing it after the training. You are one of the few in my selfish world who had the courage to show me that I have a jealous mind. I wish you the best.

Until next time,

Eddie

Free to Struggle

That May was hotter than usual in Arizona. At a time when Eddie thought Lauren's light was too bright — preferring his own darkness — the harsh Arizona sun was almost too much for Eddie. Sweat poured from him day and night as he attacked Phoenix. Since his van had no air conditioning, he would toss and turn on his sheets in the torrid cargo bed while wedged between stacks of *Blue River* that reached to the roof. Some nights he would have to go to a Glendale truck stop to shower in order to cool down his body enough to sleep.

Night after lonely night, day after scorching day, he'd think of Lauren lying beside him beneath their ocean-breezed window in Pacific Beach. I would scold him a thousand times a day: "You should go back to Lauren. Nobody cares about your little book. Nobody cares if you die selling the damn thing. Tell Lauren you 'got it' before we both drop dead from this friggin' heat."

Eddie refused to quit Phoenix, though it was literally getting hotter every day. The perfect strip malls Eddie needed for quick pitches were so abundant in Phoenix that at first Eddie believed he would sell out his book there. But then he had to leave, mostly because his fast-food diet trashed his bowels and made him crap his pants three afternoons in a row.

Before Eddie ran out of underwear, he slogged north in his loaded van to the cooler elevation of Flagstaff. He'd lost fourteen pounds in Phoenix in just eleven days. This was a period in Eddie's life I particularly enjoyed because I could constantly press him about his future.

It wasn't like Eddie was starving; he could always sell books. One obvious fact was that Eddie was out of California where his book had had a chance to be discovered. But not out here.

These friendly people living in the midst of so much space kept reminding Eddie that each book sold was another book lost in the maddening longshot of picking up a publisher who would validate his writing.

It was in Flagstaff that Eddie began keeping a journal to track his expenses. A journal was something a Phoenix CPA told him to keep after Eddie sold him a book. Flagstaff was also the first town where Eddie sold a book to a public library. He wrote in his journal:

> *From now on I will try to sell a book to the library in every town I work. That way I can be on the library's shelf with other books and in some way live forever, or until the book is weeded or falls apart. I can be like Johnny Appleseed, leaving my book in a thousand places and proving I was on this earth. This new prospect of having my book in libraries excites me. Now I can live that real, invisible American fantasy of being everywhere at once, with a real chance that my book will be read by dozens of people I could never reach. It's all so thrilling to have this real potential for a long reach to readers not even born yet. Life is good in Flagstaff, Arizona.*

Ass-Backwards

As he traveled east across I-40, Eddie got to thinking about how Lauren had rediscovered meditation at est and how proud she was after sitting quietly for a solid hour during her lunch break.

Working hot towns like Winslow and Gallup convinced Eddie to get a motel in Albuquerque. That's when things got bad for me. Inside his cool but cheap motel room, he told me to "shut up" because he was going to meditate in a cool bath for an hour. He began by counting his breaths. I came into his head constantly, mostly telling him to stop this meditation crap and pay attention to me. I fought like hell, showing him images of places he could go and sell his book out then live there. When he dismissed place after place, I fired off images of Lauren partying with est graduates and trainers.

That Eddie! I gotta give him credit for staying in that tub for an hour and doing his best to shut me up. His cool bath was nothing but a "hot bath" as far as keeping me quiet. I must admit that since I've been in charge of Eddie for a long time, that bath in Albuquerque did give me a scare. It was during one gap of silence for perhaps three minutes that he really scared the hell outta me. I caught another glimpse of Slow Eddie just like it was near the end of Eddie's est training. It seemed that Eddie was activated to a higher frequency and he stopped the broken record I could usually play between his ears. This time Eddie scared me because he relaxed me right out of his head and without any help from the herd, like at est. I think he might have kept me out longer, except for that old pattern of worrying about the future. That's when Eddie started to cry, releasing a ton of stress from San Diego and Phoenix.

He pounded Albuquerque on tired feet for four days, averaging eighteen books a day, which eliminated three cases from his crowded van. Heat again made him drive north to the tourist haven of Santa Fe, which reminded him of Scottsdale. Santa Fe's *Blue River* prospects were tight and resented Eddie walking past their "no soliciting" signs posted on or near the front door of nearly every business.

North again into the rugged beauty of New Mexico's Carson National Forest he plowed on — not finding new territory until reaching a much cooler Durango, Colorado. Downtown Durango started out good for Eddie with quick sales — even a couple of doubles and one triple. But just when he was feeling good about being on a roll, he met the man that threw him into a panic.

With only two books left inside his light briefcase, he handed one of them to a middle-aged man, the manager of a clothing store. Eddie's goal was to sell these two books and get a motel early so he could rest as long as he could. But trouble came when his prospect opened the *Blue River* cover and saw that the last page was at the front of the book and the pages were upside down. Eddie took back his book to examine it, explaining, "I guess the cover was put on backwards — ass-backwards. Haven't seen that before. Don't judge a book by its cover," Eddie fake-laughed, cracking his dry lips in new places as he removed his other book from his briefcase. Again the pages and cover were "ass-backwards." No problem. It was Fast Eddie to the rescue when I made him say, "Well, four bucks for one of these rare gems . . . even though it's a collector's item." More painful cracks as he held his smile until the prospect agreed to pay three bucks for the flawed book, which he signed and dated with the inscription: *James, thanks for covering me.*

He exited the store fast with the other ass-backwards copy of his book inside Lauren's gift. The van was parked six blocks away, not far from the library where he expected to meet with the librarian after he worked the downtown area.

I took over from there. Eddie cursed Lauren's father and the binder all the way into a drugstore where he bought lip balm.

Eddie was incredibly anxious on his way to the van, fearing the worst, and all the while oblivious that I was running him. So much noise was going on in Eddie's head, including a high-pitched ringing that continued as he opened case after case of *Blue River* and found the same ass-backwards covers on every single book. After screaming expletives, he pounded his fists into a case of books until his knuckles were bruised and bleeding and numb from his spent anger.

Exhausted, poor Eddie filled his briefcase with a dozen copies of his flawed book. When he walked by his driver's side window, he slammed his briefcase into his reflection, cracking the glass like a spider's web. He looked down at his wristwatch and saw that he still had time to sell. That's when Slow Eddie told him to go get a motel room and soak in a tub to quiet me.

Within fifteen minutes he was soaking in a deep tub filled with hot Colorado water. He was rubbing his temples with a hot washcloth while I kept asking him how in the world he was going to sell all those ass-backwards books. I also reminded him how tough it was to sell books without a flawed cover. About that time Eddie started to cry — more than I'd ever seen him cry since he lost Dave and Jenna. They were horrible convulsing sobs that made his belly thrash up and down like some fish fighting to stay in the water. Yeah, those sounds coming out of Eddie were just awful.

Sometime later there was calm. He had released enough tension to reach a quiet place where he breathed consciously and told me to "shut up" when I tried to talk to him. Slow Eddie was telling Eddie he was listening to me way too much, and that if he didn't learn to relax and quiet me he'd experience more pain.

I'll give the guy credit, he did shut me up for ten minutes during that hot bath. That's when Slow Eddie answered his query, "What do I do now?"

"Well, Eddie, I suggest you have some fun with it and pitch every prospect with a sense of humor. Tell them the truth, that your printer goofed by putting the cover on backwards. Tell them you just discovered this and you'd love to sign one of them for three or four bucks . . . so you can work your way back to your printer and clobber him. Have fun with it, Eddie. You have to sell them, right? If they balk at four bucks, drop your price to three and look as hopeful and pathetic as you can. Look on the bright side, Eddie; you don't have to pay for these flawed books. Now you can pay off your balance faster. Turn this around, Eddie, and profit from mistakes with a positive attitude. They're all golden lessons, Eddie."

Well, the next day Eddie sold books like gang-busters around Durango, entering and leaving each business with the heart of a hungry lion whether he sold a book or not. At no other time in his selling history could he recall having such fun with laughing prospects who thought his ass-backwards book were a novelty. They bought because he sold its value with a sense of humor. He even added a closing line when he showed them his thick notebook filled with buyers of his book: "When I call ya for my next book, mention you bought an ass-backwards copy and I'll give you free shipping on my next book."

That evening he soaked again in the same Durango motel after saturating the town with forty-four books sold in less than two days at four bucks a copy. The next day was Sunday, and he wanted to do something different before driving to new territory. Two words he asked Slow Eddie over and over as he gapped me out of his head in that Durango bathtub . . .

Now Where?

Mesa Verde National Park was about forty-five miles west of Durango on Highway 160. He saw the ancient cliff dwellings in a brochure in the motel registration area when he checked out and sold a copy of his book to the motel clerk.

His van had slowly climbed nearly six thousand feet to reach the parking lot where he could then hike to the cliff dwellings that were thousands of years old. Eddie was the sole tourist on the marked path that led to the canyon dwellings. Ten feet down into the rock via a ladder was a room about ten feet by ten feet. He climbed down and stood in one of the cool, dark rooms and could hear the wind howling against the red canyon walls high above him. He felt small and vulnerable when he realized he had no home of his own. "NOW WHERE?" he screamed from the room.

Back on the path to his van he decided on Austin, Texas, and traced the route on his atlas.

The new view during his drive fringing the western side of the Nacimento Mountains in New Mexico was incredible at sunset. Colors all around him were changing so fast, and he was free to take in the scenery since there was no other traffic in either direction. There were no service areas with businesses, so selling was not on his mind. This was the kind of scenery that Slow Eddie made Eddie focus on. It was as if Mesa Verde had awakened his visual sense.

His slow-blinking eyes went from thing to thing — the earth and the scudding clouds, every rock and tree, even the colors between all these living things he observed and saved in his memory as if he would write about them one day. These were all such vivid things that Slow Eddie told him to see at this very moment; yet I, Fast Eddie, was able to come in often and inflict him with a montage of broken-record warnings — ominous reminders of Eddie's need to survive in new territory and to operate without any kind of home base.

That stretch of I-25 south of Albuquerque to Socorro was decent selling territory for his ass-backwards product. He sold six copies to waitresses and truckers at a truck stop when he put six bucks worth of gas in his van. Just as Slow Eddie told him to, Eddie did have fun selling his book and laughing at each prospect's confused expression when riffling through the sorry pages. "Yeah, my printer goofed. But if ya turn it upside-down and start at the back, it reads straight through. At least all the pages are in order."

I gotta hand it to Eddie; he was selling those ass-backwards books at a pretty good clip.

From Socorro, New Mexico, he got on Highway 380 and headed east for Roswell, working sleepy little towns on the way like Bingham, Carrizozo, Capitan, and Picacho. These were mostly Latino prospects who were very friendly, yet his book was not funny to them. They were confused. He had to reduce his price to three dollars for most of them.

In Roswell he was ready for another hot bath. On a spooky billboard next to the motel Eddie checked into, the town of Roswell claimed to be "the UFO capital of the U.S." But what really spooked me was that Eddie meditated for twenty minutes without letting me in. Later on while he was watching the motel's television, I was able to bother Eddie about where he would live next.

For some reason that Slow Eddie was appearing more and more — especially in the morning. I guess he was trying to kick Eddie's day off to a good start. Slow Eddie said things like, "Lighten up; get happy, Eddie, and wipe that scowl off your face. Have some fun selling your ass-backwards book." Slow Eddie was even telling Eddie to try it his way all day and just see if it gave him more sales, versus Eddie's usual means to an end fueled by his grim determination. I sure didn't like that advice.

Off we all went, on foot, with twelve ass-backwards books stacked inside the snazzy gift Lauren had given Eddie. Slow Eddie took over, except for an occasional gripe here and there from me. Mostly I'd complain about poor timing, like when the prospect would be busy or the phone would ring and Eddie would wait and wait for nothing.

Again, Eddie did it Slow Eddie's way and had fun. His first Roswell prospects were in an auto parts store. The manager was free and so was a female employee standing nearby; that's when Eddie was able to pitch both of them at once. A chance for a double! Eddie let Slow Eddie talk. "I published my first novel, and my printer goofed by putting the cover on backwards. Do you do any pleasure reading?"

After positive nods, Eddie handed them each a copy and pointed out the summary on the back cover. As they read the cover, Eddie paid attention to his breathing while imagining each one paying him four bucks for his flawed book. After reading the back cover they flipped it over to the front cover. Eddie's timing had to be perfect when he said, "The pages are in sequence; ya just have to forget the cover," he smiled. "Anyway, I sell them for four bucks each. I'd love to sign one to each of you, or for a gift for someone."

Eddie left the store five books lighter and with twenty bucks in his pocket because he asked the manager if he had any other employees who might be interested. Roswell was easy and fun for Eddie because he had changed his attitude. His confidence made him feel lighter, "less dense."

After Roswell he drove south down 285, making quick sales in Artesia and Carlsbad before heading east on 180 to Hobbs, New Mexico. Around six in the evening he drove into Texas feeling terrific after selling thirty-six books for the day in New

Mexico. Eddie wouldn't let me talk to him above the radio; he just turned south on 87 and headed for San Angelo, where he would get a room and count his money.

The "$29.00 room special" at the Sandman Motel in San Angelo dropped to twenty-five dollars after the author sold a book to the motel clerk. Eddie was resting on the motel's bed with the TV on while counting his take for the day. One hundred forty-eight dollars minus thirty-nine for expenses was a great day, considering his book sales from now on were all profit. No way was he paying for his printer's mistake.

While soaking in a hot bath, I was able to anger Eddie about Lauren's father and the way he was going to tell him about his ass-backwards book when he made his last payment to him for the "good copies" already sold.

Suddenly, Eddie just dropped it. Eddie was changing. He noticed his feet weren't as sore of late and that he had more energy at the end of the day — all because of a new attitude. I would simply have to wait him out.

Texas Lessons

By late June Eddie was a walking zombie with a positive attitude. Austin was poor territory for sales, sometimes moving only ten books in a grueling day if he was lucky. He was sleeping in his van two out of every three nights. Eddie had to be dead tired in order to go to sleep fast when he slept in his van, which was still crammed with cases of *Blue River* to the roof in more than half of the cargo area.

Those times he'd sleep in his van, he'd shower in the morning at some truck stop for five bucks or trade a book for a shower. Then he'd have a lousy breakfast and write in the café while he was still strong and not spent from the day. Yes, Austin taught him about perseverance until he'd had enough of that city and drove south to Lockhart and then to Gonzales before going further south to Cuero.

Cuero is where he broke down sobbing. It was during the day inside his cargo area when he was restacking cases that had shifted and fallen during a turn before he parked. He began punching the boxes, admitting to himself that his book was a piece of crap. Not only because of the cover, but also because it was poorly written and now Eddie was ashamed to be selling it.

After his long crying session he felt better. Although he had about $450 on him, he didn't like spending money on motels. As he took a good long look at his reflection in the van's window, he admitted that this frugal attitude had taken a toll on his body. He needed a haircut; his fine red hair hung in shaggy, curling tufts above and behind his ears. His sensitive skin was red and dry from the constant exposure to a relentless Texas sun and wind that had given him patches of blotching and flakiness that made him look like an albino. Eddie could see that his body was really falling apart.

Prowling for only ten books a day was too hard on him. Gas and food were gobbling up half of his revenue every day, and his diet was appalling. He'd wolf down greasy café food with weak coffee, and all the while his hungry eyes with their dark circles would be scanning the room looking for a prospect. It might be a waitress, a cook, a clerk at the register, or a friendly trucker who looked approachable.

You'd better believe I was busy. The moment Eddie entered a café, I'd tell him the best place to sit in order to have a shot at multiple sales. Funny thing about Eddie; he was getting good at keeping me quiet between sales calls on a main street. It was another Texas lesson: Keep me quiet some of the day in order to finish the day strong.

His Texas atlas sent him seventy miles west to San Antonio. Once there he decided that a cheap motel with a bed and hot bath would be a much-needed oasis for his tired body. First he called Ike and Mary collect at their bar and let them know he was alive and well in the Alamo Motel just four blocks from the Alamo. He told his mother he was having the time of his life seeing America while searching for the next place he would call home.

Never could he tell his parents that there was no place in the country he wanted to live — that the "America" he envisioned and longed for seemed more and more elusive every day. To honestly let them know that he was struggling as at no other time ever before in his life would only cause them endless worry.

After his chat with his mother and father he took his hot bath, whereupon I hounded him about looking for some kind of work to do when his books were all gone. His next book was not coming along well, and he probably only had one book in him — an ass-backwards one that was killing him.

"Shut up," Eddie yelled at me in the tub.

It must have been about an hour later when Eddie was nodding off to sleep in the cooling water when Slow Eddie said softly, "Sara believes in your writing more than you do. She told you to keep writing about your life experiences while selling your book, and that she could edit it into the story line to enhance it considerably. You need a good editor, Eddie. It's hard to find a good editor who really cares about your book like you do. Eddie, listen to me. It's no coincidence you're in the Alamo Motel. This is your last stand. You must surrender to this struggle or be crushed by your remaining books."

"I can't," Eddie cried.

"Why not?" Slow Eddie asked softly.

"I don't know how to make it last! This is all I have!"

Over the next four days Eddie worked San Antonio and managed twenty books a day. He stayed at the Alamo Motel every night in order to recover from the Texas heat and wind that burned and blew relentlessly. Three loads of dirty laundry were done, which gave him more room in his van. A barber traded a haircut for a book; and Eddie bought Vaseline for his dry skin.

During his last night at the Alamo Motel he saw a weather report on TV that warned of a heat wave coming to Texas the following week; so he headed east on I-10 to Houston, working the little exit towns along the way.

Houston was too big for Eddie. A giant metro area like Houston could make him feel desperate and tired — like a panhandler. I promptly convinced him that if he were to ever have trouble with his van, he would be lost. I reminded him of the time he was in Los Angeles on the Santa Monica freeway when he blew out his spare tire. He spent hours cowering like a whipped dog from the bottomless pit of strangers slicing past his pleas for help. Yes, it was easy for me to convince Eddie that he was no match for the metropolis.

He worked the suburbs of Westfield and Tombull before turning north on I-45 toward Dallas. It became cooler the further north he drove. Many of the service exits on the way to Dallas were good spots for selling doubles, which convinced Eddie to give Dallas a try.

The weather in Dallas reminded Eddie of summers back home. Ducking in and out of businesses was enervating as he moved from hot to cool a hundred times over an eight-hour period. Remembering Sara's encouraging words had bolstered his will to write — and he did more than ever, taking four or five writing breaks a day. He wrote:

> *My hungry eyes would meet and greet every face within view when I entered a business. If I saw fear in their eyes when they saw my briefcase, I came to know they had no money. Yet I would pitch them anyway. This slow voice would come out of me when I asked to see the manager, even though my mind was always wanting to jump in and get things rolling. But my slow pace relaxed them. No matter how their day was going, it was refreshing to hear this stranger slow things down.*
>
> *"I'm a writer from the upper Midwest. I published my first novel. Do you or anyone close to you do any pleasure reading?"*
>
> *The answer was always "yes" because I was poised to click open my briefcase and show them my book. This is when my timing had to be perfect — when I handed them my book and told them my printer goofed and put my cover on backwards so that the pages were all upside down. I'd have to tell them fast that I'm selling these flawed copies for four bucks just before*

they started reading the back cover's review. When each prospect finished reading the review, it was painful for me to have them turn the book upside-down to follow the page sequence. That's when I'd tell them I'd love to sign a copy "to you or anyone close to you." If they balked, I would offer two copies for seven bucks, or, as a last resort, one copy for three bucks. Either way, I'd hit the sidewalk with a quiet mind.

Those gaps of silence between sales gave Eddie the location of his next best prospect. He was getting better at not counting his books sold or money taken in, and not letting me bother him about a dry spell. He had figured out the hard way that the more I talked, the less energy he had for selling.

Attractive women were one of the ways I could reach Eddie when he was working. I could tell him he needed new clothes in order to at least flirt with single women with some confidence. The numerous times that Eddie was too big of a coward to ask a girl out, I could really bother him — especially after work when he was headed for his van or some dive of a motel alone.

Regrets I fed him about things he didn't do or say had always kept Eddie's self-esteem low. He didn't "get it" that I was the voice that made him a big chicken and caused him to beat himself up for being a coward. It was insane, I know, but he let me do it; so I did it — until one night.

Thanks for Nothin'

The Benbrook Motel near Fort Worth had eleven occupied rooms; and Eddie's room, #6, was right in the middle of them. It had rained for ten days straight. Assembled in that place was a collection of misfits and dysfunctional knuckleheads, the likes of which he'd never before seen. On one side was an unemployed alcoholic truck driver who argued with his nagging wife every single night; welfare mothers with crying babies in stinky diapers were in rooms 5 and 4; and an elderly Middle Eastern couple sat outside their room on aluminum folding chairs chain-smoking while complaining incessantly about the world. The rest of the rooms were filled with specters coming and going at all hours. Worst of all, Eddie knew he was one of them.

Despite the rain, sales were good for those two weeks around Fort Worth. The week before, he had signed a book to a mechanic who'd bought a copy as a birthday gift for his sister. The mechanic wanted the author to sign his book to "Ellen" and write "Thanks for nothin'" above his autograph.

At the end of his second week at the Benbrook, Eddie lay in bed having trouble falling asleep. He was vacillating about whether he should check out of that dive the next morning or pay for another week in this good sales territory. That's when the neighbor babies started bawling, which intensified the itching all over Eddie's body caused by the cheap laundry detergent used to wash his bedding.

Eddie kicked himself free from the twisted sheets around his ankles, bounced off the foam mattress, and looked for something to punch. The desk drawer below the TV took the blow from his left knuckles. He grimaced in pain with his screaming little neighbors and thought he broke his hand.

He hustled his injured hand to the rust-stained bathroom sink and let cold water run onto his throbbing knuckles; they were bleeding in several places and already turning black and blue. It wasn't me that told him to turn on the light and look in the bathroom mirror, but that's what he did. Next he put his pathetic face right up to his reflection while keeping his hand under the falling cold water, and he said right into his slow-blinking eyes, "Thanks for nothin'."

Eddie was waiting for some kind of response, but nothing came. "Nothin'," he mumbled into his eyes and then across his forehead where nothing came from me or Slow Eddie.

This gap of silence was something new for Eddie because it held longer and longer . . . and longer until he whispered, "My mind is not going to run me anymore. All I have to do is look for nothing between all things and listen to the silence between sounds. Thanks for nothin'," Eddie smiled at his reflection before hurrying out of his room into the humid night with his hurting hand.

There was the Arab couple smoking in their chairs, watching the characters of the night go by. Eddie waved at them and they waved back, smiling as he went to the back of his van and unlocked the double doors. He hopped into his dark cargo area and rearranged the cases of books to make more sleeping room. Then he stepped outside and admired the increased space he had made.

Just then he saw his books as something good that sustained him, something that supported him and kept a roof over his head. He removed a copy of his book from an open case and opened his book to a random page, whereupon he focused on the white margins that surrounded the text, then the white space between the lines, then the space between words, then the whiteness between the letters. He whispered, "Thanks for nothin'." It was now so crystal clear to Eddie that without the emptiness of space there would be no words — only solid blackness from the ink. It was "nothing" that made everything possible.

He sat in the open back doorway of his cargo area looking up at the small number of stars that were visible in the night sky. A dawning of awareness came over him. He had allowed me, his mind, to fill his space with sounds, sounds with warnings about fearful things that were hiding his true self — Slow Eddie. Eddie listened for the next words. Slow Eddie's voice was there. "It will be difficult to keep your mind quiet, Eddie. It's been talking to you ever since you were a little boy. Like your parents, you've always avoided inner peace. That's why you printed your book. You thought *Blue River* would change your life. It can only change your life situation — which is always temporary, Eddie. Your mind has always been in charge of your life."

"Who are you? " Eddie asked the blackness between the stars.

"Slow Eddie."

"Can you stay with me?"

"That's up to you. When you reach your Blue River I'll be there. You can choose what you want. It's all up to you, Eddie."

As usual I started talking and, incredibly, it was a while before Eddie realized it. He started asking questions like: What now? How much money do I have? How many books do I have left?

Eddie noticed that he didn't recognize my voice in his head immediately because it was habitual and lightning fast. Again, Eddie's eyes shot upward to the vast space and silence, a place where Slow Eddie might live. Nothing came. That's what he wanted.

Back in his shabby little room he couldn't go to sleep. Lying there in darkness, his neighbors asleep, he paid more attention to me than he ever had — and I didn't like it. I wasn't allowed to broadcast to his heart the usual mordant doubts and fears that would never fail to make his feet sweat at night. But Eddie stopped me this time. Yes, Eddie was onto me and I didn't like it.

Without even consulting me he decided to check out of that dump and head north to Oklahoma. He packed up his things, and I had nothing to say about it. Things were changing.

Broken Record

Eddie didn't sleep at all that night, so by four in the morning he was rolling north on I-35. Three-and-a-half hours later he'd entered Oklahoma and was having breakfast in a small truck stop café in Ardmore. He sold three books to three waitresses before his breakfast arrived. That's when he paid attention to me, observing how I was rambling about prospects in the café instead of shutting up so Eddie could enjoy every bite of his meal.

Then Eddie pulled out his notebook from the inside pocket of his briefcase and with his still-swollen hand began writing:

> *I have this trenchant (if that's the right word) new way of observing my busy mind and how I've allowed it to use my energy. Oh, God, I do see how most people are in their head most of the time and only now realize how my country's people are run by this kind of mental chaos.*
>
> *Two political parties are organized and run by a bunch of lawyers and rich businessmen who are nothing more than agents representing their organized party — an interest-driven monster that knows most of its base supporters are fearful egos with an us-against-them mentality.*
>
> *And then there are those wealthy media messengers who feed our fear-dominated country the latest negative news and problems without a positive resolution. Their biggest advertisers are automakers with their big combustible engines that poison our air, but the poisoning is justified because of big profits for them.*

Yet the number-one insanity is how any country allows one man to start a war by using words — mere labels like "freedom and democracy" because young men won't die for corporations like Ford, GM, or Exxon.

Here I sit, one isolated American in this truck stop café in Ardmore, Oklahoma. I'm low on resources; yet because of that fact, I'm able to now see for the first time in my life that Blue River is a clean, flowing, natural self-energy that can never be exploited by the manswarm if I pay attention to it. This river of consciousness is not being polluted by those in a rush to get somewhere. Blue River is not something I will ever find in the imagined future or long for from the past. It is always present — seen wherever I am — as long as I stay relaxed and don't let my mind run me.

Before Eddie returned his notebook to his briefcase, he looked between the angry lines he had just written, at the whiteness of space that was so much more than nothingness implies. Eddie smiled and continued eating his cold breakfast, savoring every bite with all of his attention.

An hour later he left the café with eleven books sold at four dollars each. Truckers, waitresses, cooks and cashiers bought *Blue River* because he was not a desperate man. One of the waitresses gave him an idea and directions to the town's public library that was just opening for the day.

The library was open to having Eddie at a book signing, despite his cover. The library director said she needed a week to advertise his signing in the local paper to get the word out. "I've never heard of someone selling their book like you have. It's remarkable and must be very difficult. The fact that you are willing to give ten percent of your sales to the library at the signing is good for both of us," the director stated.

"That's what I was thinking. Plus it gives me a chance to sell a bunch of books at one place. Do you really think your patrons will buy it the way the cover looks?"

"I think if you explain the mistake your printer made and pass the book around so they can see it, some might. I can't say how many. If you had some kind of flyer I could post, it would help."

"What if you posted it upside down?"

The librarian laughed at the writer's suggestion, even though he was serious.

As he was exiting the library, I tried to warn him about pitching a group of strangers in a library with his shoddy-looking book. He answered me in prose, repeating his poem several times:

Oh, dark space
Between my ears
Keep things quiet
Especially my fears.

Eddie had an Ardmore printer make him a bold-type flyer and ran off a hundred copies.

Independent Writers Sells Novel Backwards
Self-published novelist E. L. Dense will be in the Ardmore Public Library on Thursday, August 16th at 8:00 p.m. He will talk about his novel *Blue River* and sign them for $4.00 per copy.

Eddie dropped off his flyer at the Ardmore library; the director copied it and posted it in three places inside her library.

That day was the end of my broken record I'd been playing in Eddie's head since he first published his book. My voice would go on and on about how he had to sell twenty books a day. I must have badgered him five hundred times a day about that. I know exactly what happened. That ass-backwards cover forced Eddie to either suffer or change his attitude — all because he gave Slow Eddie a chance to be heard when he relaxed in a bathtub. And Eddie liked what he heard.

When a man is blown down by different things and keeps getting back up on his feet, it is usually because he has family and friends who help inspire him to do so. However, when a solitary man like Eddie can be inspired by his own experiences, there is no storm on earth that can destroy him.

Eddie worked the small businesses in Ardmore like a tornado with legs, handing out flyers to surprised prospects who bought his slipshod-looking book at a record clip. I know he was breaking records because there was no more chatter coming from me about selling twenty books a day.

Eddie was excited about his new sales approach. Now he could imagine another signing in the next town, and then the next one. Before long, Eddie was even getting better looking.

Tiny towns like Dickson, Baum and Mannsville were worked quickly with flyers posted about his first book signing.

Breakthrough

Eddie was on a roll — a consistent hot streak selling books as never before. For five of the next six days, he worked towns in a forty-mile arc north, east and west of Ardmore, leaving over two hundred flyers posted with over 150 new readers. Then he worked towns south of Ardmore that bordered Texas by the Red River, places like Petersburg, Rebottom, Leon, Burneyville, Marietta, Lebanon, Willis, and Enos. In Durant, a town of 13,000, he sold quite a few books to people who had heard of him. He estimated that he had talked to five hundred people in five blistering days.

The night before the book signing he decided he would stay in the Ardmore Motel just three blocks from the library. In the motel's lobby he picked up a free copy of the local four-page newspaper and saw that his signing was front-page news. Slow Eddie told him to rest all the next day so that he would be fresh for his signing that night.

Although he had no clue what he would say at his first book signing, he refused to let me give him ideas or pester him about it. I was totally left out of his big day; although I was able to show him what it would be like if people showed up at his signing just to have a good laugh at the ass-backwards writer who had the nerve to have a book signing in their library.

The Ardmore library had put out twenty folding chairs for the unknown author's signing. Over sixty people of all ages crammed into the library's meeting room, lining all three walls around the seated twenty. Since most of them he had met in the field that week, I couldn't bother him much because he could see that his legwork had paid off.

E. L. Dense stood beside the friendly library director with copies of *Blue River* stacked tall in four rows on a table in front of him. I must admit that it reminded me of a scene drawn by Norman Rockwell. There he was, in slightly wrinkled gray corduroy shorts and Dave's favorite yellow shirt, with still no idea of what he was going to say to these people after the director introduced him to the quiet group.

"Thanks for coming," Eddie smiled. "This is sort of like writing fiction; I can remember your faces but none of your names. I want to thank those of you who bought my book, even though my printer goofed up the cover."

A little laughter.

"How many of you have read my book?" Eddie motioned for them to raise a hand.

Nobody raised a hand.

After an awkward pause Eddie continued. "That could be a good thing. I was in a town east of Ardmore — Milburn. I was near this big lake in this old gas station and bait shop tryin' my best to sell my book to the owner, this old man who was hard of hearing."

A few laughed in the audience indicating they knew who Eddie was talking about.

"He told me he's been there for forty-eight years and that I was the first writer who ever tried to sell him his book. Well, you can imagine how I felt when I showed him my ass-backwards cover."

The audience laughed because many of them seemed to know the codger Eddie was talking about and could well imagine his reaction to the book.

"Anyway, either the old man couldn't see what I was tryin' to show him or hear my explanation, so he bought a copy for four bucks and I hightailed it outta his place after signing it to him. When I was drivin' down the road, my imagination showed me that the old man went to show his first customer my book, and the customer brought the flawed cover to the old man's attention. Well, that's when I imagined the old man got mad because he thought he'd been ripped off by an ass-backwards writer. But worst of all, an outsider. That was the last straw for the old man. I pictured him ranting and raving about how rotten the country had become, telling everyone that America was not free because of crooks like me who can roam the countryside and rip him off! And those were the last words the old man ever uttered because he dropped dead right there in his bait shop with my book clutched in his lifeless fingers. All because somebody goofed at the bindery where my book was put together. The good part about this fiction is that everyone in three counties who heard about the old man who died with my book in his hands wanted to read my book, and so it sold like gang-busters."

The audience was tickled with Eddie's little story.

For an hour Eddie answered questions about his self-published book: the cost of printing, how he found a printer who would give him a break, and how difficult it would be if he had to raise all the money up front. "Your friends and relatives are your best source for backing your dreams because they know all the work you've put into your writing."

Seventy-one copies of *Blue River* were signed and sold by the end of Eddie's first book signing. It really made the author feel good when one young lady told him how he had inspired her to keep writing. She told Eddie she had not written in months until he had stopped into where she worked and sold her a copy of his book. She also told him while he was seated at the table signing books that she admired his courage to keep selling his book.

Leaving Ardmore that night after his signing, Eddie was in the magical embrace of a breakthrough with library book signings. He now knew he had a new way of marketing books. Yes, Eddie was getting further away from me.

Sooner or Later . . . Normal Insanity

Heading north on I-35 and closing in on Pauls Valley, Oklahoma, Eddie had a marketing decision to make: Should he stay away from bigger cities like Oklahoma City and Tulsa and work the little towns for book signings as he had in Ardmore, or should he work the bigger cities with more readers and cut down on his traveling?

I tried to get my two cents' worth in and tell Eddie to work both, but that calm voice I call Slow Eddie told Eddie to slow down (duh!) and stay in the country where people were more friendly and less jaded, and to get more signings in small-town libraries during the week.

So Eddie really slowed down and got more tactical, setting up separate signings in Pauls Valley and Ada — towns separated by thirty-two miles of Highway 19 with dozens of small towns splayed out in all directions. He sold books, put up new flyers, and did interviews with little weekly newspapers to promote his signings.

His next two signings went well like his first one had. Eddie was pleased and thought he was onto something.

Slow Eddie was running the Eddie Dense Show now. Even though I kept hammering Eddie to listen to me, Slow Eddie had convinced him that positive change is slow, yet well worth the wait if he was committed to living a better life. Of late, every time I would try to warn him about the usual things — like being low on gas or the number of books he had to sell — he'd calmly tell me, "Quiet."

It was now as if Eddie were floating on air in the rain along these tiny "Main Streets." These were rural places where cooling late-summer rains poured down and soaked the dusty earth for only minutes at a time most every day. Eddie was on a high.

It was the end of another selling day, and Eddie was sitting in his stocking feet in a shoe-repair shop while the elderly shop owner was in his back room replacing the worn-down heels of his working shoes. Eddie was taking in the masculine smells of leather and polish and oiled tools and machinery the man had used in his craft to extend the life of footwear for a thousand of his Sooner customers.

It was at this time I managed to have Eddie think about his past — until he caught me. Then came a wave of calmness inside Eddie that flooded me right out of his consciousness. Slow Eddie put a pristine image of a slow-moving blue river behind Eddie's closed eyes. At first this river was soundless, flowing between golden fields of prairie grass; then it made the relaxing sound of a smooth-trickling, gentle force of clean-flowing blue water that blocked out any other sounds and smells around him.

A tinkling bell above the shop's front door opened Eddie's eyes to a customer — her face down and obscured by her exaggerated effort to close her black umbrella before stepping clear of the door she held open with one elbow. Eddie never pitched customers of retail businesses; however, he wanted to say something to this attractive woman wearing burgundy corduroy slacks and spotless tan cowboy boots with pointed toes.

"Will it ever stop raining?" she drawled and laughed upon seeing the relaxed stranger with red hair. Before Eddie could say anything, the shop owner came out from his back room and took her claim check number that she handed him across his cluttered counter. When the old man ducked back into his room, it was Slow Eddie who asked her if she knew what a "Sooner" was.

She flipped back her lush red hair that was short and cut stylishly to match the shape of her face. "You're askin' the wrong person," she drawled and laughed before adding that she was from Arkansas.

"Where in Arkansas?" Eddie smiled.

"Eureka Springs," she smiled back.

"Really? I'm goin' there when I leave Oklahoma."

Eddie felt foolish when the old man brought out a pair of men's boots that must have been her husband's. She paid her bill and left with the boots.

That's when Eddie realized he was really lonely — so lonely that he was willing to tell a stranger he was going somewhere he wasn't.

Thanks to the shop owner's handiwork, he left the shop a bit taller. I told him he had well over a thousand books to sell and that his van was in need of tires and a tuneup. Right then he shut me out and again saw that blue river that was so calming in the shop.

As he neared his van, I made him think of Lauren and how good it would be to have her visit him here in another world for a lost weekend. I made him get a bunch of quarters and call her from a phone booth outside a motel — just after he'd checked in and sold a book to the clerk.

"Lauren, this is Eddie."

"Eddie! How are you?" she exclaimed as if she were really glad to hear from him.

"Oh, I'm fine."

"Where are you?"

"In Oklahoma. Sellin' books like gang-busters. I wasn't sure you were still there . . . or . . . who you might be with," he winced.

"I'm still here," she said coyly without answering the other half of his query.

"If you can, I wanted to see if you'd fly out here for a lost weekend."

"I'd love that! Next weekend would be perfect for me. I don't have to work."

"I'll get ya a round-trip ticket to Tulsa and call ya with the itinerary."

"I'd have to leave here Friday after three and return Sunday evening."

"Okay. I'll call ya this Sunday."

"Great! Thanks for calling, Eddie. I look forward to seeing you."

"Same here. Bye."

"Bye, Eddie."

When he put down the receiver he checked the coin box for change and immediately regretted calling Lauren. Back in his room, he sat on the mushy queen-size bed and removed his shoes. That's when I got him good. I went on and on about how he only wanted to sleep with Lauren and then at the end of her visit show her his ass-backwards books that her father was responsible for. That way she could tell her father that was why Eddie was not going to pay him for the balance of his books.

Eddie stopped me. Then that darned Slow Eddie came in and told Eddie he needed to complete his relationship with Lauren; and if he did just that and had some fun at the same time, then that was a good thing for both of them.

That night, in total darkness and flat on his back, he listened to the rain changing from pounding torrents of water to pattering sprinkles. He turned on his side, switched on the bedside lamp, and grabbed his writing notebook. He wrote:

The drought is over for me. I called my ex-flame, Lauren, today. I asked her to come visit me in

Oklahoma next weekend. She said yes. Now I regret calling her. Sooner or later this had to happen. I want our past healed so that we can move on without repeating the normal insanity. This reunion will resolve many issues for me . . . I hope.

I write this from a motel outside Tulsa. I must sell books like crazy this week so that I can get us a nice room and take her to nice places. Oh, God, wait'll she sees how much I've missed her since I left her that letter.

Next Time

Eddie's palms had been sweating on his van's steering wheel and in his pockets as he made his way to baggage claim inside the Tulsa airport. His stomach had been telling him since that morning that he was doing the very thing he'd resented when they were together: deception.

He had gotten a haircut and washed his best outfit — a pair of khaki pants with an ice-blue knit shirt he knew Lauren liked. The night before, he had polished his new-heeled selling shoes with mink oil and put in the new shoestrings he'd bought for them.

Outwardly, Eddie looked like he was doing well; even their room at the Holiday Inn a few miles from the airport was prepaid for two nights. The stage was set to impress his old flame; however, his plan was to tell Lauren all the things he'd written in his notebook during the week. And he would tell her these things just before her return flight to San Diego.

He told her he'd meet her at the luggage belt. Nervously, he looked at his wristwatch, even though its battery had stopped a month prior. He knew he was fifteen minutes early, yet she was already waiting beside her bag when he got there. There were only brief seconds to look at her before she spotted the shirt she had bought him in San Francisco.

Lauren looked better than he'd imagined. An off-white cotton skirt and lacy blouse draped perfectly over her shapely figure. She radiated health. Her smooth tropical Brazilian skin enhanced her brown sun-lightened hair which offset her sparkling green eyes. And no makeup, as usual; she had nothing to hide or highlight. Just like her mother, Lauren glowed with incredible energy that made everyone look at her.

The moment she saw Eddie approaching, I was made a silent observer. Slow Eddie took over. She had to have seen that he'd aged much more than the months since she'd last seen him.

As they embraced he looked at her. "It's good to see you," he smiled. Eddie savored the moment because he knew that from that point on words would follow words; and before long, certain words would bring back the past in images of her trip to Mexico with Kim.

First, she wanted to drop off her bag at their room. That took two hours. Breaking the ice after their long separation was the best way to begin their weekend together.

One of the many things Eddie liked about Lauren was that she was low maintenance as far as wanting to be wined and dined. As long as Eddie was giving her an enhanced level of attention, nothing else interested her. So it was her idea to "just stay in the room and talk."

Lying on the bed and facing each other with a foot of real estate between them, their conversation was open and free-flowing. Slow Eddie was giving Eddie the words to say. "When we were together, I knew you were with other men." Her eyes widened as he continued, "It doesn't matter who they were or how I knew. I just had to tell you I knew."

Explaining herself was unnecessary, especially after he told her that he understood everything. He knew she would never have strayed if he had been giving her the love and attention she deserved. And it didn't take a mental giant to know that the tears in her eyes proved he was right. I could see that if Eddie was more like Slow Eddie back then, she never would have betrayed him.

They had a late dinner in the Holiday Inn's restaurant and went for a long walk in a quiet industrial park that was well lit. It was then that he told her about his ass-backwards books that her father's binder goofed up and that he would show them to her later. She was appalled by the error and surprised Eddie by telling him she'd call her father and let him know that Eddie was not paying for any of those books.

"He's probably concerned by now since I haven't sent him a check. I was afraid to call him and tell him I was paid in full since he did help me get published."

"Eddie, you don't have to pay for those. I'll handle my father. He'll write it off. I'm sorry that happened, Eddie, but I don't see how you can still sell your book that way."

"It's hard. I have to really stay positive." Then he told her how lonely it had been for him. "I hope all this pathetic stuff about me and my book doesn't spoil our time together because I am really happy to see you, Lauren."

"I've been wanting to see you too, Eddie. We said goodbye in such a bad way. I'm just glad to be here . . . and to be your friend."

The weekend with Lauren went well. As she prepared to board her flight, they agreed to keep in touch this time. And if she wasn't in a relationship when he sold-out his book, she'd fly to wherever he was and they'd celebrate.

On his way back to the motel, I was able to hound Eddie about the money he'd spent over the weekend and that he'd probably gotten Lauren pregnant. But Slow Eddie stepped in and told him not to listen to me.

Three Strikes, You're In

Eddie ditched Tulsa the next morning like a trailing slug, keeping the slime of his past one micro-thought behind him. Eddie made me listen to his derisions of the past by saying out loud, "I can't go forward if I keep looking back. My past is like looking in a rearview mirror, to be glanced at briefly here and there when needed, but always returning to the present very quickly. I know that my past was only a chance I took and not to be made into some pathetic habit that I let ruin me."

Purposely, the author-salesman skirted the Muskogee turnpike at Broken Arrow to save a couple of bucks. He sold books in Coweta, Porter, and Tullahassee on his rural route to Muskogee, where he parked downtown and hit the bricks hard before businesses closed. The following day he would work the capital of the Cherokee Nation in Tahlequah and had hopes of replenishing his depleted savings by then.

Fall came fast — especially when he was back to sleeping in his van. No longer were those unforgiving Texas prairie winds blowing dry heat and dust into his nostrils. Trees were alive after cool nights, no longer drooping and parched from the unrelenting heat. Better weather had even improved the spirits of his prospects; they seemed to be more alive and fluid after a long summer that had drained all grace and ease of movement from every living thing.

Blue River was not one of those books that was good enough to be passed on from reader to reader. When running into readers here and there, Eddie found out by probing them that the book's story line was just interesting enough to stay with it until the last page but nothing to rave about. Of course, that fact really bothered Eddie since he wanted to believe he had over nine thousand readers who would be anxious to read his next book.

On the bright side, there was a leading character in *Blue River* who was fed up with America's criminals committing repeatedly the same crimes when released from prison. This character had a plan to end criminal recidivism, and Eddie's readers loved it. This character wanted the government to build a massive penitentiary in northern Alaska to house these repeat offenders from all fifty states (which would pay for the project collectively). "This would deter the media's message of fear to the people and give society real freedom," his character proclaimed. "Our vicious criminal justice system supports fear and destroys any sense of freedom for the jaded majority by releasing these cowardly incorrigibles before they are truly ready. They will know that 'three strikes, you're in' means isolation in northern Alaska. Professional mind rehabilitation will be given to inmates who are ready to stop poisoning the earth with their toxic minds and contribute in positive ways."

There were other things his readers enjoyed about his character's manifesto. "The goal has to be that this jaded majority (America's middle class) will finally take action necessary to reach its Blue River, a place where this positive current of human energy will slow down America's frenetic pace and bring about a conscious flow of all things. This will be a slow process, one mind at a time; yet the key is to reach every single mind willing to reduce the level of fear inside a country that has *not* lost its mind but, rather, lives in a mind dominated by fear and addicted to its ever-growing consumerism that will eventually destroy itself. But maybe that's the way it's supposed to go down, so that some kind of united race can bring about a higher state of consciousness."

Blue River had many such solipsistic ideas that Eddie's readers found interesting yet too fantastic to implement. Sara planned to tell her brother, "I think you have something in *Blue River* that can reach and even move many readers, though I believe that it's written in a fractious form that invalidates educated minds who will resist it, dismiss it, and make it insignificant." Sara had read *Blue River* four times, each time finding more clues that would help her edit his first novel or his next book. At Creighton University, Sara Dense had a reputation for perfection with peers and faculty. Though this may have been an era for loose relationships and partying in the Midwest, Sara remained aloof to it all. She earned her degree in business marketing with an English minor in only two-and-a-half years.

In Muskogee, Eddie was in the shop of a middle-aged locksmith who was riffling through *Blue River* when he stopped at passages related to the penitentiary in Alaska. Eddie could see the man's sinister tattoos of black and red skulls and green snakes coiled under the man's hairy forearms. Then Eddie could literally hear the hardened man clenching his teeth as he read, which Eddie knew meant trouble.

I watched in slow motion as the locksmith put the book down onto his counter and then reached down for something while asking the author in an ominous tone, "Three strikes . . . you're in?"

I answered for Eddie rather cynically, "Yeah, for three-time losers."

Well, all hell broke loose when that guy brought up a black baseball bat and let the business end of it rest on his muscular shoulder while he walked around his counter. Eddie closed his briefcase and backed out of the door with it as the ex-con kept coming; he even started swinging his weapon at Eddie's head as Eddie left the strip mall at a dead run.

Slow Eddie came into Eddie's head about the time his heart rate normalized. "You know, Eddie, you could've learned a lot from that guy if you would've asked him things. You don't know what it's like to be in prison, or even what it's like to be a victim. You're recounting what you hear and see on TV and read in the newspapers. Learn from people, Eddie. That's how you become real and write from experience."

Eddie went on to his next call knowing that what Slow Eddie told him was what his readers would have more or less voiced — that *Blue River* lacked the substantive punch to really move them to pass the story on to others. The story had failed to move them to that positive degree that really matters to every novelist. This is what Sara knew but was reluctant to convey to her brother while he was in the throes of selling his book.

Yes, Eddie had great ideas like anybody. And working them out is the hell he avoided — just like the herd he'd always despised. I tried to tell him this while he was writing *Blue River,* but he didn't want me around his pages at all. I can recall telling him, "Sure, you can tell 'em about the way things should be, but you don't really experience people like a *real* writer does. Fiction — that's what you are, Eddie."

Hitting Bottom

Muskogee readers put $110 in Eddie's pocket by the end of the day. Autumn weather was perfect for selling books throughout southeastern and eastern Oklahoma. He was able to sleep comfortably in his van to save money. Sales were over thirty books a day without even setting up a library book signing. After three weeks of working hundreds of little Oklahoma towns, he counted his inventory and was elated to know he had just over nine hundred books left. That really energized Eddie. "Sell 'em out" was his mantra as he believed he was closing in on his Blue River. For so long he'd believed that wherever he was when his books were all gone, he would be shown his peaceful place that Jenna had talked so much about.

Yet something terrified Eddie that he had managed to deny ever since his reunion with Lauren. Deep down Eddie believed he had gotten Lauren pregnant in that Tulsa Holiday Inn. He was afraid to call her and hear the news from her, so he faced the problem like a man — he didn't call her.

Cold rain poured down hard sixty miles north of Tahlequah that early October morning when he was parked beside the Grand Lake O' The Cherokees — one massive body of water not far from the Missouri and Arkansas borders. A worn sign on a nearby post advertised that eight bucks would put his van on a small ferry and save him over an hour of driving on meandering poor roads east of the lake as shown on his road atlas. This shortcut would save him time to I-44 that would lead him northeast to new territory in Joplin, Missouri.

An old man — a fair-skinned, full-blooded Cherokee with a leather face — operated his four-vehicle ferry that was docked and dead in the water as if unused all day. Eddie thought the old guy might be sipping whiskey from his black thermos while seated on a deck chair under a beige umbrella at the very end of the careworn dock. Off to the ferry captain's side, Eddie could see a faded red fishing pole with a silver reel, its line cast into the quiet lake as heavy raindrops pelted the surface like plunking marbles.

The captain appeared as if he couldn't care less whether or not he caught any fish; however, he was visibly happy to see someone he could ferry and possibly converse with over the twenty-two-minute ride across the monstrous lake.

After Eddie paid for his ferry, the old man went into action by extending his loading ramp to the shore so his customer could drive his van onto it just as rain really started pouring down.

A few days previous in Tahlequah, one of Eddie's Cherokee readers told the writer that there were three Cherokee dialects and seven clans in the Cherokee Nation. Eddie was interested in finding out more about this now, because the ferry captain had to be at least eighty years old and most likely knew many interesting things about the Cherokee people if he was an area native.

About the time the ferry left the shore the wind really started to pick up, making it difficult to hold a conversation. The sky looked ominous and ripe for a storm or even a tornado.

There was no talking from the half-popped ferry captain who was at the helm straining to maintain his course as Eddie got behind the wheel of his van to escape the rain. It wasn't long before the rocking motion of the ferry made Eddie nauseous, and he closed his eyes. I got right between Eddie's ears before that Slow Eddie could open his big mouth. I made Eddie feel the weight of his books behind him, showing him images over his past twenty months of selling throughout the Southwest as the remaining books in the cargo area creaked and bobbed and shifted with the rising waves.

The pitching ferry's roller-coaster-like dipping and rising with the waves made the lone passenger feel like hurling, so he opened his door and dry-heaved toward the moving slick deck. The smell of burning oil and gas from the ferry's engine made Eddie even more nauseous as every breath he took was stifling and making him dizzy. I was back in charge of Eddie now.

Eddie's swirling memory of what his recent Cherokee readers told him about this magical lake was taking hold. They had told him about their travel-worn ancestors and how their Trail of Tears ended near here at a place called Blue Springs, where the gushing waters were blue like the bluebird. It was a sign to them that the worst of the journey was behind them — that they could rest now and be at peace because to them the blue water was a promise that from then on things would improve and there would be no end to the lasting peace.

Yes, it was Eddie's readers who led him here because it reminded him of his own Blue River; but death was in this blurry haze of swirling lake water that was gray and brown and furiously rocking the ferry.

The captain had his hands full. He knew plenty of storms like this one, and he knew they were rare at this time of year; yet they were halfway across the lake and it made no sense to turn back now. Oblivious to his passenger, the old man had no control of his ferry which was spinning around and around in the swirling vortex of screaming chaos with howling winds and rain that hit the skin like needles fired from a machine gun.

One giant dip into a swell forced Eddie to topple out of his van and slide under it, holding onto anything he could get his hands on. The superstitious Cherokee people had seen a blue promise that life would be better from now on. But not for the ferry captain. Eddie looked for his hunched back at the helm, but the captain was nowhere to be seen. Had the old man been thrown into the lake and lost in the maelstrom of cold black water? Eddie shifted his position under his rocking van, unsure whether he was at the front or the back of it.

Just then two wheels on one side of the van were raised entirely off the deck and dropped back onto it with such force that the frame of the van punched and bruised Eddie's chest, causing him to slide out from under the van — out of air — and crawl back in behind the wheel. Some thirty cases of *Blue River* were banging against the shell of the cargo area behind him. Every case was tossed at once, hitting each side of the cargo bed with such pounding fury that Eddie could now see his death coming. It was on the other side of his windshield in vivid splashings of lake water and rain that formed ghostlike tracings of Dave and Jenna.

Slow Eddie stepped in to make sure Eddie did not die from these terrorizing things I could show him. But suddenly the van rolled over on its side onto the bobbing deck of the ferry-go-round gone mad. Eddie climbed back to the cargo area where all his product had tumbled to a jagged pile of hard-pointed, thirty-pound cardboard missiles that tumbled into his shins, slamming and gouging its pointed weight in a dozen places on his body at once. Both of his temples were hit, punching him into a semi-lucid state of numbness. Yes, Eddie's book was literally attacking him with every rocking swell that finally shoveled his van off the ferry and upside-down into the roiling lake.

Blue River stopped beating him up, though many cases covered him while he lay face-down on his roof as water streamed in and splashed cold on his face. Loose copies of his book began floating around him.

I'll admit that before Slow Eddie showed up, I had really bothered Eddie about the loss of all his product. He resisted losing all his income until Slow Eddie showed up in the middle of that lake and told Eddie, "Let it go. They're all gone, Eddie. You did it. You're here!"

It was incredible. Eddie relaxed with the van as it went down slowly into the now-calm lake water that had by this time filled about half the cubic space of his graduation gift — a space that was now darker than the bottom of a tar pit. Slow Eddie kept Eddie calm under the circumstances as the van continued to fill with water to within a few inches of the top, which was actually the floor of the cargo bed. Methodically, he balanced his toes on cases of books, moving here and there while feeling for his foam mattress. He felt the van's roof hit the bottom of the lake and settle some seventy feet below the surface. After taking in as much air as his lungs could hold from the last remaining pocket of air space, he dove down and found pinned under cases of his books the bed he was told by Slow Eddie to find. He freed the mattress and kick-swam to his front seat where he had to feel down low for his window. Bracing his back against the engine's covering, he let the bed float above him while holding onto it with one hand so he could get a good kick into his window. It was here that I reminded Eddie about the two gifts from Lauren: his briefcase and inside it the list that was all of his nine thousand readers. But Slow Eddie came in fast and told him, "Let 'em go, Eddie."

Eddie did, yet the terrible loss of all his hard work made him mad. But his anger fueled his legs to kick hard at his cracked driver's side window. He was nearly out of air when he gave it his all — one powerful kick with both legs that smashed away most of the glass. The last thing Eddie did was the most incredible part of his ordeal. When he was nearly unconscious while floating to the surface, he dug his fingers clean through the mattress and forced through his hands and arms up to his elbows while extending his chin into Sara's gift.

Just before reaching the surface and losing consciousness Slow Eddie told him, "Jenna told you that Chi is just like a river

— a flowing of energy to be traced back to its Source. That's where you will find stillness, Eddie — your Blue River."

That night the Grand Lake O' The Cherokees was calm. The storm was over and Eddie was still. His unconscious body floated all night until dawn when a local fisherman spotted a floating white object from his Mercury-powered boat. The old man wasn't strong enough to bring Eddie into his boat, so he secured the foam raft to the side of his craft and towed his catch to shore. On the shoreline the old man got a pulse from Eddie's throat and left Eddie attached to his mattress while he hurried off to a phone.

By the time the fisherman returned with the ambulance some thirty minutes later, they were shocked to see that Eddie was again floating some thirty yards offshore with his head resting on Sara's gift. They finally got Eddie inside the ambulance and sirened him off to the nearest trauma center, which was about ninety miles away in Tulsa. They tried to revive him with oxygen, but he remained unconscious with a weak pulse and shallow breathing. Both of the paramedics had seen near-drowning victims like this, and they had the feeling Eddie was doomed to be a brain-dead vegetable with little hope of ever regaining normalcy.

When they searched his wet clothes, they found no billfold or identification. The local police had no missing person report that matched the description of the young man fished out of the big lake. They took his fingerprints while Eddie was on life support in intensive care; however, nothing came up because Eddie didn't have a criminal record.

After three weeks passed, the Tulsa hospital became concerned when no clues had surfaced on the identity of the redheaded man on life support at a cost of $5,600 per week.

Tulsa media would broadcast on the "unknown man in a coma" about once a week; however, for the most part, the story never really got out of Oklahoma, except for here and there in tiny blurbs buried in newspapers.

Late Thanksgiving Day, the gathered Dense family in FIKSHEN became acutely concerned when Eddie hadn't called home. Sara and her parents knew that something had to be wrong. "On Thanksgiving Eddie would at least call us collect to wish us a Happy Thanksgiving," Mary assured the agreeing Sara and Ike.

It was during that holiday-missing of Eddie that Mary decided to call Lauren in San Diego to see if she'd heard from her son. Sara and her father listened intently as Eddie's ex-girlfriend told Mary that she last saw Eddie in Tulsa when they got together for a weekend, and that she hadn't heard from him since.

"Tulsa?" Mary repeated so her family could hear. When she got off the phone with Lauren, she told Sara and Ike that something must be wrong.

Ike said bluntly, "Well, just call the Tulsa Police and tell 'em your son was last seen in Tulsa."

"Do it, Mom. You're not going to wait until Christmas and go through this again, are ya?" Sara declared.

When Mary called the Tulsa Police, the officer at the desk told her he'd have a detective call her tomorrow because he was off duty now. Ike stayed over and slept on the sofa so he could be with Mary when the detective called.

First thing the next morning, Ike called the car dealership where he had bought Eddie's van and got the make, year, and vehicle identification number so his wife could give the information to the authorities. Mary was ready with Eddie's social security number and insurance information the next morning. Sara and her parents waited by the phone all morning until Sara convinced her mother to go ahead and call the detective in Tulsa.

Lieutenant Brown was on the phone with Mary for twenty minutes getting all the information he could, including Eddie's physical description. The veteran detective assured the worried mother that he knew of no unidentified accident victims who fit her son's description. He told her he'd call her at home or at the bar if any leads surfaced, and he promised to get back to her within seventy-two hours to apprise her of his results after an extensive search. "Frankly," he told the concerned parent, "I don't believe you have to worry because most of these searches turn out to be resolved in a positive light."

But they all worried anyway, mostly because it was so unlike Eddie to not call on any big holiday. Three days later Detective Brown called Mary and told her that nothing showed up on her son or his van statewide. The Dense family could only pray and wait.

Meanwhile, the redheaded vegetable on life support the nurses called "Dreamer" was fed intravenously. Oddly enough, he showed some brain activity, indicating he was probably dreaming — hence the nickname. Soon "Dreamer" was able to be taken off life support and breathe on his own while in his rare dream state, which reduced considerably the cost of his care.

A renowned Oklahoma City brain surgeon ran extensive tests on Eddie and reported his findings to the cost-conscious hospital board members who would prefer that the comatose patient be transferred to a state facility in Oklahoma City.

It was in early December when Detective Brown read a newspaper article about "Dreamer" and drove over to the Tulsa hospital to see the unidentified man who was found floating on a foam mattress in the Grand Lake O' The Cherokees. Of course, the detective was amazed that the redheaded comatose young man fit Mary Dense's description of her son. Now he had to call her and let her know.

Sara and her parents flew to Tulsa the next morning where Detective Brown met them and drove them over to the hospital. All hoped it wasn't Eddie; however, when Mary entered the intensive care ward and saw her vegetative son, she fainted into the arms of Ike.

The trio cried at Eddie's bedside for a good hour after Eddie's doctor gave them the sad news in his office that it was unlikely Eddie would ever wake up from his coma.

The Tulsa media were there to interview the distraught family and report to their viewers and readers that the mystery man in the coma finally had a name: Edward Lesley Dense. It was Sara who informed reporters that her brother was self-published author E. L. Dense, and he'd been selling his first novel, *Blue River,* in Oklahoma when he was pulled out of that lake. S. O. Dense, the business marketing "A" student, was livid on camera — demanding an investigation into the bizarre finding of her brother on a lake on the very foam mattress she had given him for a graduation gift.

"How did he get there? And where is his van?" she queried the press outside the hospital's front door as Ike and Mary stood quietly nearby. The parents had been stunned with the news that Eddie's hospital bill was nearly $97,000; and since Eddie had no insurance, the hospital was holding them responsible for payment.

Over the next few days, Ike and Mary made arrangements to fly Eddie home on a private charter and were informed of the medical supplies and special needs for his home care. Detective Brown was assigned to Eddie's case and went to the big lake to look for answers, and Sara decided to rent a car and go to the big lake herself to do some investigating.

While Ike sat in an alcohol-deprived stupor in Eddie's private room going over in his busy mind how they'd have to sell the bar to pay for Eddie's future care and all the bills piling up in the hospital, Mary was a doting caretaker. She watched the doctors and nurses carefully and performed every detail for Eddie — the changing of his excrement bag, his bathing and shaving needs, his feeding — every facet of his care. She'd talk to Eddie as if he were conscious, and several times a day she'd lift her son's lazy eyelids and say loving things to those vacant blue eyes that made poor Ike drop his head into his hands and sob like a middle-aged baby. "We're going home, Eddie, so Mommy can take care of you," Mary Ellen would baby-talk while patting her boy's forehead that was freckled and darkened from the late summer sun.

I. M. Dense didn't mind hearing his wife baby-talk to their comatose son. Ike was beside himself because Mary told him if he had so much as one beer, she'd file for divorce and turn over her half of the bar to Sara. Ike was afraid of Sara. His serious daughter would surely drive off his regular customers and "convert the bar to a smoke-free establishment," she'd told her father, if she had her way.

One time Sara was waiting outside her parents' smoky bar to pick up some cash while a city fire inspector stepped outside with Ike to have a cigarette after passing their annual inspection. Embarrassed was not an adequate word to describe how Ike felt when the fireman offered his hand to Sara when the just-passed bar owner introduced his daughter. Sara refused his handshake, adding, "There's nothing more cynical than a fireman smoking in public."

It was Sara's gift that saved her brother from drowning and gave Eddie "the longest dream" — words that Eddie's doctor told his family when Sara asked if her brother could feel anything. The same doctor told the family that Eddie's brain waves indicated he was in a dream state and to not be concerned if he flinched or tossed about. "It is a nervous system reaction," the doctor informed the sullen family.

During Sara's drive to the big lake — to the very spot marked on a map by Detective Brown where Eddie was found — radio personality Paul Harvey's familiar voice boomed out of the car radio. "The mystery man in a coma in Tulsa, nicknamed 'Dreamer' by his nurses, after several weeks has now been identified by his family from Council Bluffs, Iowa. Edward Lesley Dense is a self-published novelist who was peddling his first book, *Blue River,* in Oklahoma when he was found floating in the Grand Lake O' The Cherokees. The police have no clues about what happened to the young writer E. L. Dense. And his doctors do not know if he'll ever wake up from 'the longest dream.' Now there's a story that we hope someday Mr. Dense will get a chance to write about."

Itchy Fingers

Sara turned off the radio and tightened her grip on the steering wheel. Her creative mind for marketing was causing wave after tingling wave to move across the top of her skull. The notoriety of Paul Harvey and the vastness of his listening audience gave her a settling assurance that her family could recover from the financial hardships of this terrible ordeal, and she resolved to tell her mother that worrying about Eddie was a waste of energy.

When Sara arrived at the spot where her kid brother was found floating on the bed she had given him, her flinty green eyes scanned the lake. She knew that Eddie would never use his bed for leisure floating because he was too cautious about water after the drowning of Charles and the loss of Dave and Jenna right next to the Missouri River. She was positive that Eddie had not been carelessly playing on the water.

The lake was far too big to walk around since the total shoreline was over two hundred miles. From her map she could tell that her brother probably approached the lake from the south, on the other side, since the last time they'd heard from Eddie he was in Texas and southern Oklahoma.

Sara's short red hair was banded back to a sheaf the size of a shaving brush. She had started wearing glasses soon after Eddie left home to write his first novel. She wore gold-colored metal frames with round lenses that made her smart eyes look even smarter. Because Sara took good care of herself and had no vices, her green eyes were always clear. And since Sara was in control of herself and her life, she didn't need a man to take care of her. No serious dating in high school or college proved she wanted more out of her life — just like Eddie did.

It took her forty minutes of driving on rural roads to get to the south side of the lake. On these roads her map was useless to her, so she kept her bearing by keeping the lake within sight for most of the trek.

There were four things Sara needed to find: Eddie's journal, his list of customers, the pages of his second novel he'd said he wanted her to edit, and his remaining copies of *Blue River.* But it was the mission to keep her family from going under financially that served as her primary motivation. She was determined to not let that happen.

It wasn't until her sixth attempt to stop somewhere on the south side of the massive lake that she saw the same worn ferry crossing sign that Eddie had seen. That's when her adrenaline really started to pump from the notion that Eddie's van, holding perhaps a thousand copies of *Blue River,* took a ferry ride and was now at the bottom of that giant lake. She alone believed his books were like bricks of gold — sunken treasure to be raised to the surface at any cost. Because S. O. Dense was no dummy, she was certain she could turn Eddie's second book and journal into something the pleasure-reading public would buy.

All of these things about her brother's work were itching at the tips of her fingers, which perpetuated her habit of nervously rubbing the tips of her thumbs rapidly back and forth across her fingertips — just as she had when she was about to take her finals in college or when she first heard that her baby brother might be in an irreversible coma.

There wasn't a business within fourteen miles in any direction from the spot where she found the ferry sign and its landing area by the rickety, gray barn-wood dock that might have launched her brother into his longest dream. Redolent fumes of oil and gasoline were all about the dock area with no ferry in sight.

At the nearest gas station, the station owner informed Sara that A. J. Blundell operated a ferry part time — maybe two days a week or whenever he was sober.

"Who owns the ferry?"

"Blundell does. He works when he wants to," the man drawled slowly.

"Is it a licensed ferry? Somebody must regulate its safety for public use," Sara stated with such certitude that the man became reticent. "Do you know where Mr. Blundell lives?"

"In a camper. He's all over the lake."

"It's such a big lake . . . How do I find him?"

The man shrugged his slouching shoulders, adding, "You'd need a helicopter to find A. J. Hard tellin' where he is."

"Does he have family around here?"

"Nope. No kids. And he's too stubborn to have any friends," he chuckled, revealing the brownest horse teeth she'd ever seen.

Before exiting the station, Sara asked the man if Blundell's ferry could sink in the lake.

"Yeah . . . I wouldn't be surprised." Then the station owner removed his soiled green ball cap, scratched his balding head with his black nails, and told the redheaded Columbo he hadn't seen the old man since that big storm awhile back.

On Sara's drive back to Tulsa, she made her plans to get to the bottom of that lake. But that meant she'd have to stay in Tulsa and get her mother's credit card to cover her expenses until she could use the media to raise enough money to find her brother's van at the bottom of that awful, big lake.

Again, she nervously rubbed her thumbs across her fingertips as she gripped the wheel while pondering what she would say at her next news conference in Tulsa.

Sara Takes Over

Sara arranged for all three Tulsa network-affiliated television stations and the city's biggest newspaper to be at the airport when her brother was wheeled onto a private jet that would fly him home.

Ike was having hand tremors from his recent sobriety and his decision to sell his house and move into FIKSHEN in order to help pay for the care of his only son. It was Sara who told her father he'd have to sell his house in order to shore up coming expenses. Mary told Ike he would sleep in Eddie's old room and that she wanted Eddie in the living room so he was close to her room. "I want him in the room with the most space and light. I want him to be around television, all our meals . . . as if he were awake," Mary sobbed.

Poor Ike. His life as a married bachelor was over. Unbeknownst to him, the only hope he had of keeping his bar afloat was in Sara's plan to market her brother's doleful condition to the media and sell his writing to an altruistic public. Oh, how he craved a cold beer or two!

What Sara and her parents didn't know at the time was that the publicity generated about E. L. Dense's condition had stirred a cyclonic demand to read the over five hundred ass-backwards copies of *Blue River* the author had sold in Oklahoma. The Dense family was unaware of the ass-backwards books because Eddie never wanted to tell them about it until he was sold out. But boy-oh-boy! Those fortunate five hundred Okies who took a chance and paid their four bucks were loaning, hoarding, and selling their signed and dated copies for as much as three hundred dollars a copy to local collectors who knew a good deal when they saw one. Every single buyer of *Blue River* in the state was widely known in his or her respective community and considered a celebrity, of sorts. Many of those five hundred buyers put their books in their safe deposit boxes and refused to sell them. The copies that were passed around were getting ten to twenty reads per month. Amazing!

That's what Eddie hated about human nature. Now that he was in a coma and the public knew about it because of the media's propensity to report tragic news, they wanted to read his book. No way would the same reporters give a good crap about Eddie's hard work when he was working his tail off and getting nowhere. But drop dead or vegetate in a coma and they all want ya. That's the cynical part of America that Eddie hated.

And that's exactly what Sara saw, and she was going to make her brother prosper from his tragic circumstances. When Sara summoned the now-familiar camera crews and reporters to the Tulsa airport as she sent Eddie and her parents home on the private jet — paid for out of the blue by a wealthy Tulsa benefactress — she allowed close shots of her brother being wheeled onto the silver jet. Yet that was part of her plan, and she had arranged in advance to be given personal copies of each and every photograph and video-taped segment of her brother.

Millions of Oklahoma six and ten o'clock news viewers watched as the poor young writer boarded that jet with his parents after his sister gave him a tearful kiss goodbye. That shot then appeared on the front page of the Tulsa newspaper the next morning.

As the silver jet taxied onto the runway, Sara spoke with passion into several handheld microphones, pleading for anyone who could help her find her brother's van at the bottom of that big lake. She was direct and looked like a million other Okies with her red hair, fair skin, and plain, straightforward goodness. "My brother told me he kept a daily journal. I want to retrieve it and the pages of the next book he was writing. That's the only means our family has to provide long-term home care for my brother. His van has to be at the bottom of that lake, and I hope and pray someone out there can help me find it. I want to thank all of you who have called the hospital and those of you who have sent cards and money to my brother. Oh, and Paul Harvey, thank you for your support. Your compassionate words have validated my brother as a true American artist, and I know he would be proud of that. Thank you."

Everywhere in Tulsa Sara was gawked at and identified as "Sister Sara," a name the media attached to her.

Coincidentally, Sara was staying at the same Holiday Inn where Eddie and Lauren stayed during their reunion. Sara discovered that when she called Lauren in San Diego from her room, as her mother had asked her to do. On Thanksgiving, Lauren had begged Mary to keep her posted on Eddie's whereabouts. Sara hated having to call her because she knew that Lauren cared about her brother and this news would be hard on her.

Kim answered the phone in the two-bedroom apartment they shared in Pacific Beach. Lauren came to the phone fast when her roommate said it was Sara. They talked for an hour. Mostly it was Sara talking and Lauren listening to every numbing word about her ex-boyfriend. As Lauren cried, Sara thought it strange that she herself hadn't cried that much since arriving in Tulsa. It didn't mean that Sara didn't have feelings for her only sibling, it simply meant that she had trained her mind not to go to those places — to stay away from those thoughts and images that could bring emotions to a sensitive heart that chose this way of guarding itself against a cruel world filled with hurtful things.

Late in their phone conversation, Lauren revealed that she was pregnant with Eddie's child. S. O. Dense had a first impulse to not trust Lauren, rather than feeling the joy of being "Aunt Sara" to Eddie's offspring. That's how she found out about their weekend at the Holiday Inn in Tulsa. Sara asked, "Are you sure Eddie's the father?"

Lauren explained how she and Eddie had gotten together in Tulsa for a reunion and how well Eddie appeared to be doing since he had gotten them a nice room at the Holiday Inn near the airport. Sara only blinked, not even mentioning to Lauren that she was calling her from the very same place.

When the call was over, Sara was unsure whether to tell her parents about Lauren's pregnancy — especially her mother, since she had her plate full with caring for Eddie. *Maybe later,* Sara declared inwardly and gave it no more thought as she reached for the Tulsa phonebook at her bedside. She found two diving companies and called them.

Within three hours of landing in Omaha, the Dense family was in the FIKSHEN living room. Mom and Dad had carried their now 127-pound son in from the car's backseat and put him on the same sofa that had been furnished with the mobile home. Mary had already made arrangements in Tulsa for a special medical bed to be delivered within the hour by the store's owner, along with everything on the list from Eddie's doctor in Tulsa that the comatose patient needed for his home care.

Now Ike and Mary stood looking down at their son who lay motionless on the couch. The window curtains were open to let in the winter light that would dim and rise from the torn, gray clouds racing above FIKSHEN, enhancing the horrid, palpable gloominess permeating the Midwest during the cold winter months. They were both exhausted from the ordeal that they knew could go on for the rest of their lives.

Mary called her daughter at the Holiday Inn when Eddie was tucked into his new bed facing the west windows that looked out to the frosty green trailer, which his mother knew meant so much to her son. “He’s tucked into his new bed safe and sound,” Mary baby-talked, then pooched her mouth out to listen to Sara.

Sara told her mother she’d called Lauren and delivered the grave news. There was no mentioning the fact that Mary would be a grandma by late spring. Sara also told her mother she would keep Lauren informed about Eddie. Then she went on to say how she was getting estimates from divers who could bring up Eddie’s things inside the van, including all the remaining copies of *Blue River.*

“But you have to find the van first, Sara,” Mary whined as she flipped on a light near Eddie’s bed.

“I know, Mother. I’ll find it.”

Mother and daughter chatted briefly. S. O. Dense never liked explaining herself, and her mother knew better than to ask Sara about how she was doing regarding her plan to help with Eddie’s care or how much money she thought she’d spend.

Sara was preoccupied with the ass-backwards books. Lauren told her about Eddie’s predicament with the books when Sara asked her if the books were paid for. *How could he sell those books that way?* she wondered. *And how can I sell them?* she added.

When Sara went to bed, it really hit her that it was her gift to her brother that saved his life in the lake. She thought of those boys drowning in the river and the tragic deaths of Dave and Jenna. Now Eddie was in a coma that he may never come out of. The images braced her for the incredible amount of work ahead of her. Yes, it was truly Sara’s time — a chance to save her family from the poorhouse. But she didn’t cry herself to sleep; it just wasn’t her style.

Two separate professional divers interviewed with Sara at the same time in her room. Each man was surprised to see the other until Sara assured them she was not doing a bait-and switch in order to get the best rate. "I want you working together on this venture."

Tim was a middle-aged man with over twenty years of diving experience. Mike was considerably younger than Tim and had only five years of diving experience, but he was extremely competent and taught diving classes during the summers for several youth organizations. Each man had dived to the depths of the Grand Lake and knew it to be over seventy feet deep in places. They agreed they would need the support of water craft equipped with a pulley basket to bring up Eddie's books and personal effects. They could provide all the equipment they'd need for the job but agreed again that it could take hundreds of hours of diving time at one hundred dollars an hour before finding the van.

"Is that one hundred dollars an hour per man?" she blinked.

Tim nodded yes first, and then Mike joined in.

"So it's two hundred dollars an hour?"

Again they nodded.

"And does that include the cost of all equipment?"

"No, ma'am. Equipment costs would be on top of the hourly rate," the older diver drawled, and the other man nodded in agreement.

The men looked at each other while seated at the little round table by the window as the five-foot-six, thin redhead paced around the room. They were flabbergasted when she finally asked them, "How much would each of you charge me to teach me how to dive . . . to do the job myself?"

Each man was hers from then on. Feminine guile had won. She knew that they had been concealing the fact that they wanted this project in a bad way. She exploited that. The older diver told her it was too big a job for a woman. Her stern green eyes glowered behind her lenses until the man corrected himself. "I mean . . . uh . . . for one amateur diver."

"How much?" she pressed with brusque impatience.

The men knew she was serious and told her they'd work with her and give her a better rate. Finally, she got them down to one hundred dollars an hour total for both of them, and they agreed to defer payment until after she had recovered her brother's property.

"You do know that each of you will be exposed to the media during your search?"

Both nodded with satisfaction. Again, Sister Sara had the upper hand, using her mind to stroke their egos.

She showed them the spot on the map of the lake where the ferry was docked, and she iterated how imperative it was to get started right away while the public's eye was still on this. They would start the next morning, and she would type up a contract for all three of them to sign. She shook each man's hand upon agreeing that they would pick her up at five the next morning.

Within thirty minutes of the divers leaving her room, Sara had updated her four media sources at the newspaper and three television stations. They would all be at the lake at the ferry's dock to report on her expedition to the bottom of that huge lake. After another thirty minutes, her contract with the divers was typed and copied by the hotel manager.

She returned to her room to rest, pleased with the fact that she no longer had to plead or beg for money to find the van. For the first time since her arrival in Tulsa, everything seemed possible and expeditious, the way Sara liked things to be. Only one thing could halt their diving — the weather. And there was no use in worrying about that. That's how Sara was different than Eddie; she didn't bother her mind with things out of her control.

Sister Sara's Sunken Treasure

The media were there to capture this needle-in-a-haystack endeavor as the divers, equipped with underwater lighting, slipped into the cold water from the ferry dock. On the dock Sara told the press that the divers warned her that if the weather cooled another five degrees, they would most likely have to wait until March to continue their search.

On the first day the divers began their underwater search from the dock and headed in the direction where Eddie was found. They would mark their stopping point with a weighted buoy and resume their search from that point the next day. Each diver would swim slowly near the bottom with lights on, cutting a swath no more than fifty yards wide — so small that they may never find what the press called "Sister Sara's Sunken Treasure."

Right when the last of the media reports and crews had returned to their vehicles for warmth, Sister Sara stood alone on the oil-stained dock that smelled of fuel and fish and the cold air of a coming winter that threatened to postpone the hunt. Sara was acutely aware that time could diminish the public's interest in Eddie's writing. Her flinty Dense eyes scanned the lake to the horizon in three directions, seeing only gray water that chopped and flapped its undulating weight against the hoary wood beneath her spotless white sneakers.

The goggled divers in wetsuits and thirty-minute oxygen tanks began raking the bottom, familiar with the things they brought to light thirty, forty, and then fifty feet below the surface. Thousands of beer bottles, cans, and flickering fishing lures littered the lake's floor among patches of green and gold flora that sheltered catfish and bullheads and menacing carp. Compasses in hand, the divers moved slowly in the direction of the north side of the lake. Four hundred yards from shore, the divers saw an eight-foot rowboat, both of its oars flat and embedded in mud with a tackle box. Twelve minutes out had covered a thousand yards of the lake bottom. Tim signaled Mike to move east fifty yards, as planned, to work their way back to the shore before their tanks ran out of air.

Their redheaded boss was waiting on the dock when her divers surfaced to the east of her, their black flippers shiny wet. "Any luck?" she shouted.

"Nothin' yet!" Tim barked.

Sara left with the divers after reporting "nothing yet" to the reporters who proposed to return the next day — weather permitting.

In her room the light on her telephone was flashing, indicating that she had a waiting message. The hotel manager informed Sara that an anonymous Tulsa benefactress had called him and insisted on paying all charges for Sara's room for as long as she stayed. This news made Sara cry tears of joy and call her parents to relieve their minds of the sixty-two-dollar-a-day bill they would not incur. When she asked how Eddie was, her mother answered from the kitchen phone at an increased voice level for Eddie's ears that she refused to believe could not hear her, "Oh, he's just doin' fine!" Then she told her daughter how she put honey on Eddie's throat to help heal the wound from where the doctors first inserted an endotracheal tube with oxygen. "Tomorrow we're decorating the tree while we listen to Christmas carols. You know how Eddie always liked Burl Ives singing 'Holly Jolly Christmas,'" she sang into the receiver.

Sara winced when she heard that familiar smacking of her mother's lips when she sang the lyrics of the title in baby talk as if Eddie were two years old. It broke Sara's heart, and she got off the phone quickly after that.

The second day of diving from the eighteen-foot craft, with Sara on board, turned up the same results as the first day had — except half of the reporters didn't show. With the next day's forecast for high winds, the divers had announced their intentions to call off the third day of diving.

Sara was thankful that the guys were able to use four tanks apiece on the second day, doubling their search compared to the first day. Since the lake was over four miles across, it was a daunting task, indeed.

On their drive back to Tulsa with the salvage boat in tow, Sara sat between her divers in the truck, their bodies smelling of freshwater and sweat from two hours of searching. Ahead of them was the same brooding gray winter sky that hid the calming blue and the powerful sun from all things on earth. She thought of her brother's elusive Blue River and how he so wanted to reach it. She knew it would be in his journal and all over his next book, this metaphor for inner peace and immortality that was truly a sunken treasure she alone could value at millions of dollars.

By the time they dropped Sara off, she had convinced them to change their minds about diving on the following day. The divers agreed that perhaps they could dive for a day or two more the way the weather looked; yet they told her that even if they found the van, they might have to put off recovery of the cargo till spring. At least the men thought so.

Once inside her room there were no messages. She opened her address book and called the reporters that didn't show at the lake. Her nature was to blast them with castigations and to withhold future updates because of their waning interest. But she needed them all. And she hated that. Nevertheless, she informed them of another fruitless day, yet ended on a sanguine note telling them, "It's another day closer."

The next morning Tim and Mike were not looking forward to telling their feisty client that they would probably be doing their last dive until the weather warmed again in the spring. When they parked on the street in front of the registration area with the boat in tow, the diving tandem saw Sara and a host of reporters coming toward them. Younger Mike drawled to Tim while finger-combing his matted hair, "I wish I'd've showered and brushed my teeth this mornin'."

Before Tim could stop laughing, Sara was giving orders to them. "Mornin' Mike and Tim! We're gonna do a little training now in the pool here. I'll wear Mike's suit and gear and, Tim, you're gonna teach me the basics of diving for the newspaper and TV reporters."

"But, Sara, there's only a day or two at the most . . ."

"I know what you said. But I'm gonna dive even if the lake freezes. I called a diving company in Denver, and they've dived at the North Pole. They said they'd dive all winter. They're giving me a quote tomorrow."

She had them again. They would either dive all winter or be paid off now and be out of the picture. No Denver diving company existed — or at least the one she said she'd called. S. O. Dense was not going to let these two Okies delay her from finding her brother's things. No way was she returning to FIKSHEN for three agonizing winter months of watching Eddie atrophy into a breathing skeleton while her mother baby-talked herself into an insane asylum. Since her mother's side of the family was prone to fits of hysteria and downright madness, Sara was desperate to do whatever she could to avoid seeing her mother succumb to the same fate.

S. O. Dense was no dummy; she had called a man referred to her by Detective Brown who used to dive for the police. The retired Navy Seal told her that the lake could be dived all winter in wetsuits as long as there was a hole in the ice for entering and exiting.

The media covered Sara's diving lesson in the hotel's indoor pool.

On the way to the lake later that morning while seated between her divers, Sara got to the bottom of their "weather permitting" concerns. Each of the men had winter plans they were used to and had set up their lives to never dive off season. Tim was a successful house painter and had numerous interior painting jobs lined up for Tulsa property management companies. Mike liked to go to Santa Monica and surf for a month this time of year before spending the winter working in his father's machine shop as a pipe fitter.

So Sister Sara told them to give her a few days' notice if either of them wanted to quit diving for her. Both agreed, and once again under a slate-gray sky they hit the water in Tim's salvage boat and headed out for their anchored yellow buoy that marked the spot where they last searched for "Sister Sara's Sunken Treasure."

She Danced on the Water

It was colder on the boat than it was for the divers seventy feet below her. They were on their eighth day of searching the Grand Lake's bottom and still had a few dives to go before even reaching the halfway point to where Eddie was found. On the second dive of the day Tim surfaced early, calling out to the boss to bring the boat over to him. Sara's heart skipped and fluttered, for she thought something bad had happened to Mike.

When Sara cut the engine and steered to within ten yards of the senior diver, he raised out of the water Eddie's brown leather briefcase by its handle and held it up like a trophy while whooping and screaming at Sara's gaping jaws. He handed her the sales case as he held onto one of the ladder's rungs and enthusiastically shouted, "We found it!"

She reached down and squeezed his hand. "You really found it!"

"We found the ferry first a couple hundred yards before the van. We could see a body pinned under it. He must've stayed with it all the way to the bottom! Boy, I gotta tell ya, Sara, your brother must've had a helluva ride! The van's flat on its roof! He swam out of the driver's window after he broke the glass! Don't know how he did it. It's awful dark down there."

"Did you see the books?"

"Yeah, they're there. We'll have to break the windshield to get the cases out of there with our tanks and diving gear. Hand me that hammer," he pointed.

When she gave him the hammer, she pointed to another yellow buoy that had just popped to the surface.

"That's the spot, Sara! Anchor the boat close to it. Drop the basket and set the depth to seventy-three feet. You know how to work the pulley?"

"Yeah!"

"We've got about half our air left. We'll send up a case at a time. We'll go as long as we can!"

As he inserted his mouthpiece and prepared to go under again, Sara quickly added, "Tim, if you see a notebook or any loose pages in the van . . ."

"I gotchya! There's a bunch of clothes . . ."

"No! Leave 'em!"

He gave a thumbs up and sank below the surface.

Sara positioned the boat near the marker, dropped the cargo basket, and lowered it by pushing the pulley generator button that would drop the steel basket exactly seventy-three feet via a nylon rope that stopped automatically. As the basket lowered to the divers below, she opened the unlocked briefcase. Inside the air-tight case were four copies of the ass-backwards *Blue River* Lauren had told her about. When she riffled through the dry pages, she was more confused than Eddie's prospects because he had been able to explain to them its flawed appearance. Sara had no clue how her brother could sell such a pathetic-looking product to the public. Next she saw the thick notebook that held his list of customers. And there in the accordion holder at the lid of the case she saw the two hundred pages of his next book, along with four yellow notebook pads filled with his journal entries since he left home.

She danced on the water around the briefcase and raised her thin arms to the gray sky in celebration just as the pulley beeped, indicating it had stopped at the bottom of the lake seventy-three feet below her. Everything she needed to begin working on her family's behalf was now here. Finally, she could use her degree in marketing to rescue her family from certain bankruptcy.

Flashing lights on the generator told her that the first case of books was on its way to the surface. She watched the red descending numbers get closer to zero until a soggy, dripping case appeared ready to be removed from the basket. She quickly emptied the basket of its contents and sent it back down to her divers.

The cardboard peeled off with ease like the crumbling shell of a hard-boiled egg. Carefully she handled a book, it's water-soaked pages clumped together. She was hopeful they could be dried out and sold to collectors. This was a treasure whose fate and value she alone would control — just as she alone controlled herself growing up in her dysfunctional Dense household by staying in her room reading and studying and preparing for this sort of thing without complaining. Yes, S. O. Dense had reached the very point that Eddie made in his book: that women would pursue logical things until they had control because men could be manipulated with praise and could do the work necessary to keep them content.

Meanwhile, seventy-three feet below her, Mike was inside Eddie's van handing Tim a case at a time that he would place in the recovery basket. They were able to bring up nine cases before their air ran low. They surfaced briefly to change their tanks, then returned to the salvage site to bring up the remaining twenty cases.

After her diving session at the hotel, no reporters ever showed at the lake again. As case after dripping case lined the length of the salvage boat, Sara was thinking how she had to contact her media people, and then she had to find an expert who would know the best way to preserve the books for optimum quality retention. But first she had to call Detective Brown and inform him of the drowned man under his ferry and its location.

The divers agreed to help her unload the books into a storage locker close to her hotel room; but first they would all wait with the loaded boat in tow until the media showed up to document the found treasure. Tim and Mike became statewide celebrities and relished the newfound fame that Sister Sara had promised them. Yes, these men got the praise they lived for.

Every reporter showed up to interview Sara and her crew and to capture the treasure of E. L. Dense. She told the cameras, "Now I have a chance to tell my brother's story and maybe sell enough of his books to provide the home care he needs. I want to thank Tim and Mike for finding my brother's van. First, they discovered the drowned man who ferried my brother the day of that big storm. Apparently, the man has no living relatives or friends that could report him missing. Then they found Eddie's van near the ferry. The van was upside down on the bottom of the lake. They found his journal and the handwritten pages of his next book. About nine hundred copies of *Blue River* were recovered. Most importantly, I want to thank all of you for your interest and support during this horrific ordeal my family has endured."

When the reporters had gone, Sara had a bottle of champagne delivered to her room for the salvage trio to celebrate their completed mission. As the divers sipped from their glasses and chatted about the day, Sara called two marketing companies from the Tulsa phonebook. One of them was known to be the best and the most expensive agency of its kind in Oklahoma. Del Wagner of Tulsa Marketing told Sara to look no further and to deliver the books to his three-story building in downtown Tulsa where he would store them "safer than any storage facility." Sara agreed to meet with Mr. Wagner at six that evening if he would supply help unloading the books.

The books were carefully unloaded into the impressive building under its crenelated roof of ornamental brickwork. It's terra cotta parapet and art-deco-style awnings represented prosperity to Sara.

Wagner told his new client he'd give her a ride back to her hotel so that the divers could go on their way. Sara hugged Tim and Mike and told them to come by her room at noon the next day, and she would pay her $4,200 diving bill. "Bring me an invoice," she told Tim.

"Yes, ma'am," he returned with a smile.

When Eddie Wakes Up . . .

Ike was more than willing to work longer hours at the bar so that Mary could stay home with her son. That way he could drink at will during his long shift and fall into bed in Eddie's room after closing when his wife was asleep.

There was no peace for Ike's busy mind. His financial woes were intensified when he got the $3,800 bill for Eddie's new bed in the same stack of bills that revealed Sara's $4,200 cash advance on his credit card to pay for "those damn divers."

All day and night at the bar he'd complain and gripe about how his son's tragedy was going to run him "into the poorhouse without a pot to pee in." Rheumy-eyed regulars would sit stoop-shouldered on their barstools waiting for their bartender to refill their glasses as the endless diatribes of doom and despair went on and on.

Over and over Burl Ives filled FIKSHEN's walls with "Have a Holly Jolly Christmas," Eddie's favorite holiday music. And Mary would remind her husband of just that whenever he asked her to lower the volume "so I can hear myself think, for Christ's sake."

"Oh, be quiet and drink your coffee, you old goat! It's Eddie's favorite. When Eddie wakes up, I want him to know that everything is just the same as before!"

"For God's sake, M. E. Dense," Ike grumbled loudly as his double chin creased and his jowls flapped above his coffee mug, "you keep playin' that damn song over and over and he might just wake up and run the hell outta here and never look back!"

Such was a sampling of the verbal bouts in the Dense family that outsiders found hilarious, partly because never once did the Dense couple crack a smile at whatever each one spewed at the other. Skinny Mary's scatter-brained countenance and fine red hair were a comedic contrast to Ike's shining bald head with bushy red sideburns and Buddha belly made by Budweiser.

"When Eddie wakes up, I'm going to tell him all about his Sister Sara and how she found his van at the bottom of that lake, and how she's gonna finish his book for him," she'd baby-talk and purse out those bird lips until Ike's belly screamed for his first beer of the day.

Yes, Ike's wife was unwavering in her faith that her only son would return to them one day. It would drive Ike nuts when Mary would brush her son's teeth after each IV feeding of his protein, vitamin and mineral formula and talk to her boy in her Elmer Fudd voice, "No, sireee! When Eddie wakes up, he's gonna have no cavities whatsoever."

Two days before Christmas a registered nurse came by the Dense home to see how mother and patient were doing. The nurse agreed with Eddie's doctors that his condition was a gross impairment of both cerebral hemispheres; he was not brain dead, but he was in a persistent vegetative state that could go on for years.

The nurse observed Mary taking her son's blood pressure, which she'd been doing twice daily since Tulsa. Right away the veteran nurse could see that the patient's urinary catheterization and IV tube feeding were being handled correctly by the doting mother.

When Christmas Day came, it was Ike, Mary and Eddie in the FIKSHEN living room listening to Burl Ives. Ike hadn't had a drink since the day before. Seeing his son in this condition was wearing on his heart. Mostly his heart ached because he was now seeing the total annihilation of his family — forever gone in a ghostly flash of maternal regression. Every day he sadly reiterated to himself that Mary was "losing her mind." Each morning at 9:30 before he gladly drove to the bar to open it by ten, Mary would call to him in that pathetic voice of Mrs. Elmer Fudd, "Daddy's goin' to work now, sweetie. He's comin over to say goodbye to you 'cuz he wuvs his boy Eddie so, so much!"

Ike would sigh and his thudding footsteps that made the walls of FIKSHEN shudder would approach his bedridden son, who was now rolled around to face the morning sun coming through the open curtains on the east windows. The top portion of his electric bed was elevated just enough so his thick, closed eyelids could catch the first orange glow of every morning. As those giant horse teeth emitted haunting whistles of air, his father would be standing there looking down on the only chance he had to have Dense grandchildren. He would lean down with a brooding grunt from his aching back and kiss his son's freckled forehead that smelled of sweet baby soap. Mary would smile and expect her husband to say something every morning. "Daddy's off to work, Eddie."

"Bye-bye!" Mary's happy voice would chirp until Ike's steps were lost to the slammed back door.

That's when Ike's best part of the day began — when leaving for a sixteen-hour day behind the bar. Yet fearful thoughts of his bossy daughter returning home one day would come and go throughout his day: like the money she'd insist on for this, that or the other thing for Eddie; like the newspaper and TV hounds she'd surely have poking their noses into FIKSHEN; and like, worst of all, the thoughts about having two Dense women running his life at home.

"When Eddie wakes up . . ." Ike would snort with disgust after each gulp of his beer. "That's a joke," he'd quip at the end of his swallow that would twist his lips to appear more spiteful and more hopeless as the day wore on.

Sara was pleased with the way Del Wagner got things rolling. He contacted Paul Harvey's office to make sure the radio host was aware that Sister Sara had found her comatose brother's sunken treasure. His marketing approach was more than a level above hers when it came to selling those water-soaked copies of *Blue River,* and the bonafide Tulsa celebrity took over handling the media.

Red-faced Irishman Delbert Wagner, a former Tulsa weatherman who had a voice as familiar there as Paul Harvey's, had a simple plan and rate for his new client. "I get half of what we sell. If I sell nothing, I get nothing. My list of Tulsa people with money is all we'll need to sell your brother's nine hundred books — no problem whatsoever, Sara. I know that a Tulsa fundraiser dinner to raise money for your brother's care is the way to go. I'm quite sure we can get Paul Harvey to speak — his schedule permitting, of course. Whatever the number of books in that van is the same magic number at the fundraiser. Now, I know for a fact that the good people of Tulsa will pay five hundred dollars a plate if we act while this story is hot. Expenses should be around eighty thousand, roughly. We should split around three hundred sixty thousand. Now, these are rough figures, Sara. Could be a little more or less. That's my plan to get rid of those books, Sara. Yes, no doubt about it, that's the best way," he drawled with a big grin.

Sara was impressed with Del's keen squirrel-like eyes that were a butterscotch color and that flickered and paused with clarity and animation. After a slight pause in their conversation, Sara proposed having Del's firm manage Eddie's writing. That's when she told him, "My brother's book, *Blue River,* has a tremendous potential in Oklahoma after these nine hundred copies are sold. I can edit the book, put a new cover on it, and end the story with Eddie's near-drowning. His journal could be another book for readers in this state, and I want you to go after them."

Del huffed out a big sigh and sat back in his rocking office chair with his hands locked behind his big skull. He pursed his lips, twisting them from side to side as if intrigued. Then he said, "Ya know, that's all real good stuff ya got goin' there, Sister Sara, but I was just thinkin' how easy it would be to find investors to publish and market the books in Oklahoma. I read recently that today writing is ninety percent marketing. I hope you agree," he smiled.

"Yes, that is true. I believe that my brother's second book would do well in Oklahoma if it was marketed by direct mail to readers who buy via mail order. A well-done letter about Eddie mailed to every rural mailbox in the state . . . That's where the big numbers are, Mr. Wagner. No doubt about it."

Again Del rocked back to chew on it as Sara kept quiet. Sara was happy with the man across from her who had completed the perfect agglomeration for the end result she desired: Dense prosperity. She decided that when she got back to her room she would pore over Eddie's journal and begin reading the second novel he was working on. Inside his journal she hoped to find his comments on his flawed cover. And she wanted to avoid Lauren for her mother's sake. But now she let Del do some thinking. She had confidence in him because he had done a great job finding experts to dry out Eddie's books. Yes, Sara was happy.

The Fundraiser

It took Del Wagner only seven weeks to manifest the "Sister Sara Benefit for Eddie" in the ballroom of the Tulsa Hilton. Nine hundred twenty-two wealthy Tulsans paid five hundred dollars a plate for a dried-out, waffled, ass-backwards version of *Blue River* set next to their plate; a fabulous dinner; twenty minutes of Paul Harvey's witty remarks; and Sister Sara's twenty-two minutes of closing remarks explaining *Blue River's* condition, the ferry disaster, and her brother's life before and after the tragedy. She also talked about how this ordeal changed her life before she quoted some of Eddie's words from his journal.

Wearing a black satin strapless gown with an orange silk scarf wrapped about her throat and one shoulder, she opened Eddie's journal notebook and revealed his words into the microphone. These were a few lines he'd written on the road when he left home:

> *While driving further and further from the only home I've ever known, I was forced to use my mind to diminish the awful images of failing on my own. Often this made me feel better. I would imagine the friendly faces of people I'd never see, and I'd see the positive things they'd bring out of me and onto my pages — things that would make me a better writer. Where would I be without them? I could never write a good book without them. I know they will help me when I need help.*

Sara looked up from her brother's journal and scanned the audience through her hawkish lenses. She faltered a bit when she thanked them, saying with real tenderness, "Yes, my brother found those people. All of you out there are people who never knew my brother or even had read his writing. Yet you gave him five hundred dollars to help with his home care. All because you'd heard his story and wanted in some way to be a part of it. On behalf of myself, my parents, and especially Eddie, thank you for making all of this possible."

The applause was deafening. Sara bowed her head with humility and rare tears streaming down her face as she left the podium. Del Wagner met his client backstage and told her how great she looked and how fabulous she was out there. And he told her to stop by his office the next morning to pick up her half of the fundraiser proceeds minus expenses, which he would go over with her in detail.

On the way to her rental car, she knew that her family's share would be close to two hundred thousand, thanks to the discount Del was able to negotiate for the Hilton ballroom — including tables, chairs, and the elaborate table settings usually reserved for retired astronauts, politicians, and evangelists.

Her red Dense eyelashes, still wet from the magical evening, blinked lazily at the vanilla rind of a moon that was straight ahead and low over the ink-black sky. She felt like Eddie had felt after his est training — something she was anxious to take from his journal and put in his next book.

She couldn't get to the phone in her room fast enough, anxious to relieve her parents of their mounting financial worries. First she called her tipsy father at the bar to let him know she was sending him a big certified check the next day. Ike could hardly hear his daughter for the phone being close to the jukebox, and Hank Williams Jr. was touting his "Family Tradition" loud enough to be heard all the way to Louisiana. When he finally made out what she was saying, he couldn't believe his ears! "That's great news, sweetie! Call your mother!"

Sara laughed after hanging up the phone. Somehow hearing her father's unctious, half-drunk voice was a loving thing to her now. She was tickled by his predictable weaknesses.

Mary was beside herself upon hearing the good news, repeating every word to Eddie in her strident baby-talk she used all the time now. Mrs. Fudd sang out, "Now we don't have to sweep in the stweet, Eddie!"

Then her mother put the phone to her brother's ear so Sara could tell him she loved him. But her mother kept the phone to Eddie's ear, whereupon Sara could hear his haunting breathing that would even creep out Hitchcock. That awful noise made by a breathing dead man made her sad because it was her brother, a young man cut down in the prime of his exultant youth.

Upon poring over Eddie's journal she wrote in her own journal:

> *My poor brother was closing in on his own Blue River. I know that more than ever now. To him "NOW" means that he lies breathing in darkness in the very place he wanted to leave. Now he gets shaved and bathed by our mother in an obdurate contemptuous finality of silence that scares to death all of us who love him — because all of us who love him secretly wish he were dead. With every breath taken by his healthy lungs and a pounding heart that refuses to quit, we all know he is changing us — changing who we are and what we must do to keep caring for him without falling to pieces. The world is ass-backwards. That's what his book was telling me over and over again. Because most of us, when we are troubled or burdened to our limit, will say, "I'm losing my mind." Eddie tells us that is*

all ass-backwards when he wrote in his journal at a rest area in Utah:

All of us must know we are not losing our minds. The fact is our minds are losing us and running away with the very peace we all must truly want instead of this mind-dominated insanity that pours this noxious cloud of me-against-the-world onto every living thing and chokes it until all life is gone.

The fundraiser had really empowered Sister Sara and gave her the freedom to finish editing *Blue River.* She'd been editing it almost every day and night since the van was found. Now she could put her degree into action. She had only been at half-speed because of her mind's business and all the details it kept pouring between her ears leading up to the fundraiser. Now she had the glorious freedom to run at her speed — full throttle. She attacked her typewriter at the round table by her room's window with a fierceness her brother never had. She was tearing apart Eddie's *Blue River* and making it the world's.

Time To See Eddie

By late February, when Tulsa was really blooming and booming, that same generous person who had paid for Sister Sara's room rented her a fabulous two-bedroom apartment in a downtown Tulsa building she owned for only two hundred dollars a month, for as long as she stayed in Tulsa.

Elsie Krumbaugh was that generous benefactress. The seventy-eight-year-old widow and heiress to her husband's worldwide fuel additive manufacturing enterprise had paid for a table at the fundraiser and had bought thirty-six other plates in the room for friends and business associates. Elsie never read Eddie's book, yet she informed Sara that she was willing to invest or help in any way to see that the new edition of *Blue River* was published. Sara told Del not to look for any investors — to focus his attention on marketing statewide the third printing of her brother's book.

Elsie confided to Sara that her only son had tried to kill himself with a pistol when he was a young man. The bullet lodged in his brain and he too remained comatose for six months until he died at home. That's why Eddie's story appealed to the altruistic woman.

Sara found a quality printer who did his own binding and guaranteed his work upon seeing Eddie's botched cover. It was Sara's idea to have the new book printed in blue ink since it wouldn't cost any more than black ink. Since Sara was a perfectionist and a control freak, she insisted on no typos in the new edition. There were none. She also designed the hard cover's jacket.

Over the previous four weeks, Del's firm had four-color brochures printed and mailed to sixty thousand potential direct-mail buyers in Oklahoma who had bought novels via mail order.

A newspaper clipping collage of Eddie's ordeal and a personal letter from Sister Sara offered each prospect the new limited-edition hardcover *Blue River* that had been edited by S. O. Dense for thirty dollars and no postage. In the first three weeks of the massive mailing, twenty percent of the prospects sent in their checks totaling three hundred sixty thousand dollars. "That's an incredible start!" Del cried out to his elated client. "I do believe we have something here!"

Del was trying to sell his client on the idea of a book-signing tour statewide with a video of Eddie at home. He said it would generate a bunch of sales. But Sara said "no way" without explaining why. She hated explaining herself. In her journal she wrote that she was not going to show her brother in this condition and parade him around just for book sales.

"No more speaking engagements for me, Del. I want you to market my brother's books, distribute them, and don't bother me with anything except our fifty percent of the net." She'd either hang up the phone or get up and leave Del's office. Sara was cool. Del inwardly called her "smart and final."

During the two weeks it would take until the book was ready, Sara decided to go home to visit her family. Elsie had told her many thing she'd done and wished she'd done for her son that Sara was taking back to FIKSHEN. For the two weeks she'd be at home, Sara had told her mom, "I know we can do some good things for Eddie that could really help him."

The day before she boarded her plane, she had a black tote bag filled with the things Elsie had given Sara for Eddie's home care. She knew that the money she was sending home would really remove the stress from her parents, and now she could be free to decide where she wanted to live during her winter visit back home. Sara was tired of the attention in Tulsa; all the staring and finger-pointing was taken modestly only to justify the fact that Oklahoma was a hotbed for Eddie's book-launching.

Ike was waiting for his daughter at the passenger off-loading ramp in Omaha's Eppley Airport. She smiled upon seeing her father's red bulbous nose crimson and shining in the fluorescent lighting of the terminal that was peopled by the hearty souls of the Midwest she'd always regarded as the friendliest people in the whole country.

Riding across the Missouri River, she could tell he'd had his car washed and detailed for her because of the fresh scent of the evergreen tree hanging from his rearview mirror. "How's business at the bar, Dad?"

"Oh, it's been slow, but we'll have a busy weekend," he sighed.

"Can you believe that fundraiser, Dad?"

"Oh, sweetie, that money was a godsend to us. I was beside myself with all the bills piling up." Again, it was the familiar way he had of lisping his Ss that tickled her.

She was struck by the familiar starkness of winter compared to the blooming Tulsa. She could see the forked branches of the bare trees and dirty snow plowed to banks three feet high in front of the solid, ugly two-story homes of brick and wood so common in Council Bluffs and throughout the upper Midwest. The lane to FIKSHEN would be ice-packed with a blue tint that sparkled and gave the illusion of riding on a glacier made of sapphires.

Ike parked on the tire trail close to FIKSHEN's back door and carried in his daughter's suitcase. Her mother was standing at the head of Eddie's bed announcing Sara's approaching footsteps for snoring Eddie. "Here comes someone you know!" she sang.

Sara smiled at her mother and her eyes went to Eddie's face. Those brooding eyelids were closed, his upper lip vibrating with each exhalation. She handed her mother a cranial pillow she was concealing behind her back, something Elsie had given her for Eddie. "It will keep his head tilted back and lift his chin to prevent aspiration," she told her mother as she gingerly replaced Eddie's pillow with the gift.

"How 'bout that, Eddie? A new pillow!" Mary beamed.

The Christmas decorations were still up and the tree was withered and decorated with blinking lights and red tinsel in front of one of the west windows. After hugging her mother and kissing Eddie's warm cheek, Sara pointed to the tree and said, "It's February, Mother."

"You have to open your Cwismas pwesents from us, Sawa!"

Sara saw the wrapped presents under the tree and smiled tenderly, which assuaged her statement. It was now apparent to Sara that her mother was turning into Daffy Duck, just like the cartoon character she loved to watch every Saturday morning with little Sara and Eddie.

"Look at this, Sara!" Mary gently raised one of Eddie's eyelids so Sara could see that Eddie's once-blue eyes were a yellow-gold color. "It's from the anti-infection medication. But they sure are a pwetty color," she baby-talked.

"Let's sit down and talk, Mother," Sara coaxed her mother as she sat down on the sofa. Sitting together, Sara told her mother about one of the incredible things for Eddie's home care she'd brought from Tulsa. It was a portable cassette player with positive subliminal affirmation tapes with audible ocean waves. Another gift from Elsie. "Under the sound of the waves are hundreds of thousands of healing messages for Eddie's brain, Mother. They're promoted by a Tulsa doctor who has proven that the subconscious mind will receive these messages and heal the brain."

"Isn't that incwedible what your sister bwought you for a Cwismas pwesent, Eddie?"

Sara got up and went to her room at the front of the mobile home to get Eddie's gift in her bag. On her way to her room she saw her father sitting on his bed in Eddie's old room. He was changing his socks when he called out, "Sara, I'm going to the bar. We'll have lunch tomorrow, okay?"

"Sure, Dad. With Mom too?"

"Oh, no. She'd never leave Eddie alone." Ike donned his parka quickly and scuttled out the back door before his wife could stop him and make him kiss his son goodbye.

Sara could tell that the money had stopped the worry about losing the bar, yet there was a palpable heaviness coming from her father — an unspoken grief that was a constant reminder of his son's hopeless condition that pounded away at his lifelong denial of his own mortality. Sara summed it up well in her journal when she wrote:

> *My father has lost his only chance to bond with his only son. I've read in many books, like* Iron John *that the boy must leave his mother and go off in the wild with his father to initiate him into manhood. Now my father is alone and it's too late. He can only watch his wife regress back to the days when Eddie was a baby. Now she gets to praise and adore her boy all over again in this endless cycle of maddening baby-talk and pathetic attention that all boys and men resist and resent deep down. Because the male knows he is addicted to her praise, he will spend his life either breaking free of it or living in its stunting grip until shamed to dust.*

Sara peered out from her bedroom curtains to see her father get into his car and drive away leaving a cold, foggy trail. There were so many times she had overheard him say to her mother that this or that customer had died or was paralyzed by a stroke and was now reduced to shitting his diapers and being spoon-fed in some nursing home where the "air was filled with a million drossy putrefactions that would make even a vulture vomit from the stench." Oh, how it all seemed so unreal to Sara that her father too could die from such a stroke now that his heart was stricken with grief about Eddie and Mary.

Sara turned from the window and headed for her brother with her bag of natural healing goodies, knowing deep down that Eddie was nothing more than a breathing wooden Indian with a pulse.

Within five minutes Sara had the cassette player set up and the tape inserted, ready to play from Eddie's bedside table. She asked her mother if she preferred to have Eddie use the earplug or to play it without so she could hear the waves with him. "It automatically rewinds and keeps playing," Sara added.

"Oh, I'd wuv to hear the ocean waves with Ed-dee!" she sang.

On and on, over and over, the waves played with the volume not too high, yet the subliminal healing messages were undetectable by the human ear; only the endless running in of the ocean washing over sand could be heard — sometimes more pronounced than others.

Sara spent her first night home watching Eddie breathe. She opened her presents on the vinyl floor in front of the Dense Christmas tree with Mother Dense narrating every move with cartoon-like animation and genuine joy. "Sawa's opening her pwesent from you, Eddie. The one with the bwue wibbon. Your favowite color!"

Sara joined in with Mrs. Fudd upon opening Eddie's gift to her. "Oh, Eddie! A blue candle! I love it! I can light it when I take my hot bath tonight! Thank you very much!" She kissed her brother on his white, freckled forehead and whispered into his ear, "Merry Christmas, Eddie. I love you."

The next morning Sara was up when her mother was feeding Eddie his intravenous protein formula with vitamin and mineral supplements. Mary had already shaved his red beard stubble that grew heavy around his throat after three days.

Sara dressed warmly in one of her winter coats that she'd worn her last three winters in FIKSHEN. Eddie's shortcut to the river appealed to her. She wanted to see the place where Dave and Jenna died so young, thus casting her brother far away from home.

Snow had stopped falling under the brooding sky, it's familiar gray-soaked clouds mocking the earth by obstructing the sun's warmth. This was the winter earth these clouds had turned so cold, hard and chilling to every nostril's breath that dared test it.

Her mind was on the existing social, political and economical systems that Eddie said were held in place by our educational system and the media — systems that had challenged S. O. Dense until now when she could see so clearly that if not for her brother's "brain death," the American system would not give a hoot about Eddie. And certainly a self-published writer would get no attention or validation from the academic world that caters to American corporations and their all-important bottom line. So if any corporation wanted to publish and distribute Eddie's books, it would cost 'em.

Del was right about writing being ninety percent marketing. *So why bother with flowery exposition and narratives in* Blue River*?* she asked herself as she reached the narrow snow-packed beaten path to the river. *Why not just write what Eddie wrote and mix in his journal writings up until his near-drowning?* she ruminated. She reminded herself that she would show her mother the literature Elsie gave her on Rolfing — a deep-tissue muscle therapy — and how Eddie could get ten Rolfing sessions that would straighten his fascia muscles from head to toe so he could at least sustain the exterior muscle integrity of a dormant body. Sara knew to ease these things for Eddie onto their mother, otherwise they might overload her and she'd dismiss them just because it was too much at once.

Upon reaching the east bank of the Missouri River, she looked to the south, toward the spot in his book where his friends died. But she couldn't move toward it. A sudden dawning about her brother made her legs unmovable as the cold north wind blew hard, causing her to adjust her collar closer to her ears. Then she removed one of her gloves to zip her coat higher and saw the blue river of veins that ran up and under her sleeve. Could she ever find that source of her Being where God the Creator shows our connection to every living thing? That's what Eddie was after — that Spirit place that he hungered to find ever since losing Dave and Jenna here . . . beside this river . . . a different kind of river . . . a river that can take and kill . . . and forever change your life.

Do We Stay or Do We Go?

Sara drove her dad to lunch in her car the next day. Ike had stored Sara's Gremlin in a friend's garage when he'd returned from Tulsa. During lunch she told Ike with animation how at the river she realized that Eddie was now at his Blue River — a place where there is stillness within. As usual, Ike uttered his phlegmy response without thinking. "For Christ's sake, Sara," his triple-lisp while chewing made her smirk, "are you sayin' it's a good thing he's a friggin carrot layin' there twenty-four hours a day?"

"Of course not, Dad. I know it's a terrible situation for Eddie and for all of us. I'm just in touch with how his mind is at peace now. I just want you and Mom to know he's not suffering now."

"Well, sweetie," Ike spit, "that's all well and good that Eddie's not suffering. But he doesn't have to see and listen to his mother acting like Daffy Duck day in and day out."

"I know, Dad," his daughter mollified with genuine compassion by placing her hand on his. "It's gotta be really hard on you and Mom. And I know I can't live here and see him like this."

"Where will you live?"

"I don't know. I'll go somewhere . . . other than Tulsa."

"Sara, you've got such a good deal with your rent in Tulsa. Maybe you should stay there awhile," he lisped softly.

"No, Dad. It's not where I choose to live."

"I can't blame ya for not wantin' to live 'round here."

"Dad, I don't see how Mom can stay with Eddie all the time. Doesn't she ever get a break?"

"She won't do nothin'. Maybe once a week if I'm there she'll go to the store or run an errand or two. She won't leave

Eddie for long. She's afraid I'll forget his feeding or forget to empty the waste bag."

"Why don't you and Mom move to Arizona with Eddie like you said you would if you sold the bar?"

"She'd be the same way down there," Ike sighed.

"But at least you wouldn't have these long winters."

"Yeah, I s'pose," he double-lisped.

Sara hesitated before she spoke, for she could see the pain caused by Eddie's condition in her father's eyes, so she broached the subject without manipulation. "Dad, if I moved to Arizona . . . would you guys move there?"

"I know your mother would. She's talked about retiring there when we both draw Social Security."

"But that's not for ten more years, Dad. You used to play golf. You could play year-round there."

"We'd have to have income. The money we get from sellin' the bar might last us seven or eight years at the most, but who knows what Eddie'll need?"

"Dad, I've set it up so you and Mom are getting a third of our fifty percent from Eddie's books. Eddie and I each get a third too. You and Mom should be able to live well on book sales, Dad. Believe me, I'm going to devote my life to editing and overseeing the marketing of his books. This is what I want to do with my life."

For a change, Ike was pondering what to say. He wasn't aware of the split he and Mary would be getting from his son's book sales.

"You know my friend Elsie who rents me the apartment?"

"Yeah."

"She gave me these forms from her attorney that we have to take to your lawyer so we can have Eddie placed in your custodial care and finalize the disbursement process for our half of Eddie's book sales. I already have a top-notch marketing firm for this edited third printing of ten thousand copies of *Blue River.* They get fifty percent of the net like we do. Elsie paid for the third printing. She gets her investment back first, which is about $56,000, roughly $5.60 a copy. The marketing firm provides the prospect lists, but we pay for the literature and postage costs for mailings. So far returns are excellent, Dad — about twenty percent. This printing could be sold out soon, so we'll print another ten thousand. It's doing about five times better than direct mail usually does."

"Is that right?" Ike was surprised to hear all this good news for a change.

"Dad, Eddie's a good writer. I made him a better writer. I don't want his work bought because he's some pathetic charity case, yet his personal story is hot right now with the public. And I must exploit that in order to get his work read."

"Uh-huh," Ike nodded, feeling a bit ashamed because he hadn't even attempted to read his son's book.

"Dad, talk seriously with Mom about moving to Arizona. It'll be better for all of us — especially November through March. Okay?" she smiled.

"I'll talk to her," Ike shrugged his shoulders with body language that said, "It's a waste of time."

That Saturday morning Sara awoke bleary-eyed to hear her parents laughing at the cartoons on TV. Ike and Mary sat on the sofa. Eddie's earplug was out of his ear and on his shoulder as if his parents wanted him to enjoy the cartoons with them. This Dense laughter was like a cool oasis in the middle of a hot, barren desert. Sara even joined them on the sofa, soon laughing along with her parents just like she and Eddie used to do every Saturday morning. Their morning laugh session was good for all of them.

On Sunday Ike said he'd watch Eddie when Sara talked her mother into going shopping and then catching a movie matinee at the Council Bluffs Mall.

At a health food store, Sara bought Eddie some jojoba cream for his sensitive skin he'd damaged the previous summer. Mary was excited to be out and about and now wanted to know all about any "special things" for Eddie that Sara thought were good for his home care. Sara saw the need for her brother's muscles to be used because of how thin he was now. "When we get home, we can move his arms and legs for him and see if that can help his muscle mass." Mary thought that was a great idea.

It was after the movie that Mary confided to Sara that she needed to get a life and do things for herself. That's when Sara told her mother she would move to Arizona if they did.

"Arizona . . . that might be nice," Mary said with abstracted aloofness.

Yes, Sara could see that her mother was breaking down and becoming a human cartoon who might soon need home care herself.

That night Sara was listening to her brother's breathing, his air rushing through those giant horse teeth she knew embarrassed him. She thought about getting him braces but dismissed the notion, even though she knew this would be the perfect time to get them since he couldn't feel them or be embarrassed about wearing them.

Later, she and her mother exercised Eddie's limbs by bending them at his knees and elbows about twenty times each. They promised Eddie they'd do this every morning and every night. The girls had a big laugh when Sara mentioned Eddie's Charles Atlas routine. Mary talked to both of her children when proclaiming, "Yes, Eddie! You were a wegular Charles Atwas muscleman, weren't you?"

“Yes, Eddie,” Sara chimed in, “remember when you sent Charles Atlas your before and after photos, and he just returned them to you?”

The girls laughed so hard they cried.

The next morning Sara told her mother she’d stay with Eddie while her mother went to the store. During that time Sara wrote in her journal everything about Eddie she could sense. While Eddie was plugged into those subliminal healing waves of “Stillness Within,” she wrote up a storm knowing that these moments with Eddie in FIKSHEN had to be the last chapter of the next revised *Blue River*. She was anxious to begin Eddie’s second book to prove that her brother could write — and so could S. O. Dense.

Eddie’s breathing had put her in a blank-stare stupor after an hour of intense writing. The idea to keep her brother “alive” in his books appealed to her. Perhaps even now, as far as anyone knew, Eddie’s brain was living a normal life except for the things his body couldn’t do. But she couldn’t end the next book with the author trapped in his dead body. Inwardly she told her heart she could live for her brother and delay her own life.

At the end of her two-week visit — her clothes packed in her car and all the legal business handled — she felt good that her parents were legal custodial guardians and she was the agent and manager of her brother’s estate. She was certain her parents would sell the bar and move south.

“Stillness Within” was playing in Eddie’s ear when she kissed him goodbye and whispered to him that she loved him very much. Her mother would be alone again.

Eddie Moves

Del met his favorite client at her apartment and handed her a check for sixty thousand dollars — her family's half of the Oklahoma mail-order sales. "Sister Sara, *Blue River* is hot. I think we should triple our mailings in Oklahoma to descending income households and see what happens," he drawled and smiled at Sara's nod of agreement.

Sara's drive back to Tulsa had given her a much-needed break from family and writing. Now in Tulsa, sales were good and she could live anywhere she wanted. *Why Arizona?* she asked herself. She saw images of her father enjoying the sun on the golf course and smiled.

Just two days before Sara was to drive to Tucson and make her new home, fate stepped in and dealt the Dense women a blow that sent Sara back to Council Bluffs on a bereavement flight. Ike had literally dropped dead at his bar from a massive heart attack. Customers said he was gone before he hit the floor. Mary got the news at one in the morning from a good customer.

"Mary Ellen, this is Rex at the bar. I got some bad news, Mary. Ike dropped dead about twenty minutes ago. Paramedics just took him away and they said he went right away . . . was prob'ly dead before he hit the floor. I saw him. He just froze, grabbed his chest, and sailor-dived into the floor."

"Now, Rex, I know you're a practical joker. And this isn't funny if you're jokin' with me, Rex."

"I ain't jokin', Mary Ellen. Ike's dead."

Mary was flabbergasted — literally beside herself, unable to repeat to Eddie what she'd just heard. But ever the doting mother, she wouldn't leave Eddie to go to Ike. She called Sara. After breaking the shocking news to her, she told her daughter that she'd never felt so alone in her life. She added, "What would become of Eddie if anything happened to me?"

"What about me? I'd take care of Eddie," Sara cried.

Sara took a cab from the Omaha airport. By the time the cab parked behind her parents' cars, her father's ashes were already inside a cobalt jar on top of the color TV in FIKSHEN.

Mother and daughter had several sob sessions over the next few days; but then Sara tackled the family business with celerity. Within six days she had the bar and FIKSHEN sold. Meanwhile, the grieving widow fed, exercised, and lotioned Eddie with jojoba.

Sister Sara wanted to move her family the best possible way with Eddie's special needs paramount. She'd convinced her mother to pitch most of the Dense furniture except for her bedroom set, Eddie's bed, the TV and, of course, Ike. And Rex paid Blue Book value for Mary's car.

Sara hitched a rental trailer to her father's spacious Buick and drove them to Tulsa where they'd stay with her for the time being. Eddie slept on the backseat with Mother Dense monitoring him from the front passenger seat.

During the whole trip Mary didn't feel like eating; she lost her appetite when she lost Ike. Their driver didn't want to haul Eddie into a motel room, but she became too sleepy from Eddie's ocean waves near Wichita and had to get a room. They placed him on one of the double beds, turned on the waves of "Stillness Within," and the girls joined Eddie in deep slumber within fifteen minutes.

The next morning all of Kansas was blanketed with snow blown down from Nebraska. From Wichita to Tulsa Mary kept up a constant monologue with Eddie above his ocean waves. This was the time she chose to tell her son that his father died. "Dat's why we're movin' away with Sawa. Maybe to

Aywazona, the Gwand Canyon State! Would you like to stop and see the Gwand Canyon?"

"Come on, Mom. We can't carry Eddie from the car over to the rim of the Grand Canyon."

"Maybe a postcard then," Mary laughed while checking his feeding tube.

Del had two of his employees help carry Eddie and their stuff into Sara's apartment. They put Eddie on the sofa while they moved Sara's furniture to the smaller bedroom and put Eddie's and Mary's things in the master bedroom along with Ike's ashes. Sara insisted on keeping her father's urn out of the living room.

Not long after they put Eddie on his bed in his new room, Elsie came down from her sixth-floor penthouse suite to meet Mary and Eddie, who had his earplug inserted. Short little Elsie leaned in close to peer at Eddie while holding onto the bed rail. Seeing Eddie really touched the widow emotionally — to see him there as she had watched her son so many years ago. Mary introduced the sweet old lady to her snoring son. "This is Elsie, Eddie. She lives in the same building with us now."

"Hi, Eddie," Elsie smiled, her eyes wet from memories. "I see you are listening to 'Stillness Within,'" she smiled down at the writer.

Elsie told Mary that she had other subliminal tapes that she'd bring for Eddie to listen to. "I listen to them every day," Elsie confessed with a giggle. "How are the exercises going?" she asked the girls.

"Oh, fine. Twice a day we move his wittle arms and wegs," Mary baby-talked.

"That's good," Elsie nodded.

Elsie invited them to dinner the following evening, but Mary declined because of Eddie. "Nonsense! I'll have our meal catered right here — if that's agreeable," Elsie drawled with an insistence that both Sara and her mother appreciated because they hadn't had a good meal in ten days.

A few weeks after their move to Tulsa, the Dense women had improved their lives considerably, thanks to the generous widow. Elsie would patiently sit with Eddie while his mother and sister went out for the evening to a live theater performance or to the Tulsa Opera House courtesy of their landlord, who was known to be one of the biggest patrons of the arts.

Elsie would bring a stack of tapes to play for Eddie while she read poetry she had written for her son when he was in Eddie's condition.

Boy of mine, so rare you are.
I never fail to think of you,
No matter where I am.
As when the seasons change,
The color of every leaf,
I'm the one that remains the same,
No matter where I go.

Then Elsie's wet eyes would stare intensely at Eddie's steady breathing, reminiscent of her son's teeth whistling with each breath. Yes, she was missing her son when she whispered to Eddie, "I miss my boy. That never goes away. There's this hole in my heart ever since he was hurt . . . by his own hand. I found an open Bible beside his body. The passage I knew he was reading was telling him to not be afraid to turn to the Lord in heaven, to be with Him in eternity. My silence within is what I must have to go on without my son. My son's name was Chad. I tell you this because I know you can hear me now, just as my son could. I'll tell you how I know this to be true. It was the morning I awoke to find that Chad had gone to heaven. I was sad . . . and somewhat relieved when he was no longer here with me. My husband was out of town, and I was afraid to call him with the news. In fact, I didn't tell him until three days later when he returned home and Chad's service was to be the next day. After they had taken Chad's body away, I looked under his pillow for the golden oak leaf I kept there. I had wrapped it in a little cellophane bag, and I always told Chad it would go to heaven with him when God wanted him there with Him. Well, the leaf was gone. And I wanted to believe what I told him was true . . . but I suspected it was taken or lost somehow when the men from the funeral home came and took him. I couldn't sleep, eat, or do much of anything but cry on the sofa in our family room where we'd spent so many wonderful times together. The day my husband was to return home, I thought I should finally make our bed; I hadn't made it since Chad passed. When I picked up my pillow, there was that sealed golden oak leaf. I sat down on our bed and stared in stupefaction at that leaf! I was tingling all over thinking that Chad had put it there before he left me," Elsie cried.

She wiped her eyes and removed the same leaf from her purse. "I want you to have this. I'll put it under your pillow, and I'll tell Sister Sara and your mother all about it. So if you decide to go off into the light, you can bring it to your mother and let her know that it was your time to leave her."

She placed the leaf under Eddie's pillow — the one her son had used — then stroked his red hair.

The Moxie Moron and the Next Move

Three summers passed. Eddie had been Rolfed by Elsie's Rolfer six times — about every five months. It had been two years since Sara had Del send a direct mailer on the new *Blue River,* including the collage of newspaper articles on Eddie, to nearly eight thousand buyers of *Blue River* that were on his list in his briefcase. About 4,600 of them mailed Del thirty dollars for the new edition, which Del thought was incredible. Again, Sara had validated her brother's hard work — by profiting on what he'd done.

The Dense trio still lived in Elsie's apartment building, even though the widow had passed away a year earlier. The dear woman surprised Sara and Mary when her attorney told them his client stipulated in her will that any or all three of them could live in her building rent free for as long as they desired.

The new *Blue River* had been literally rewritten by S. O. Dense, yet she only claimed editing credit. The new version was not told by Fast Eddie; rather it was omniscient past tense. Sara felt it would be easier for readers to follow the story. In the new version Eddie was the leading character, and at the end of the story he was alive and out of his coma. In the last printing, Sara added to the ending footnote: "The golden oak leaf was placed under Eddie's pillow. Elsie had told my mother and me that Eddie was just sleeping — that he was clearing his mind in order to write his next book."

On Elsie's deathbed she looked at Sara with her steady, gray, light-filled eyes and said, "Eddie will wake up when his next book is ready . . . and not until then. So let him sleep. Do not try to wake him. He'll be back when he's ready."

Early in her third fall in Tulsa, Sara met a man. His name was Junior Blend. Handsome Junior was a Tulsa bartender in one of the more upscale downtown bars. Since *Blue River* had sold well over a hundred thousand copies in Oklahoma, Sister Sara was a big celebrity in Tulsa and Junior recognized her the minute she walked into his bar. Junior went right after Sister Sara, buying her a drink when she sat down alone at a table near the bar.

"I'm Junior," he smiled with his perfect teeth and warm handshake when he delivered the glass of wine she'd ordered from the waitress.

Sara could spot a slick lady's man like a fly can spot spit; however, she was lonely. Pretty much no dating since college — no serious dating ever — had left her weak and vulnerable. That's why she gave Junior her phone number; to learn about carnal ways with men, those things that women her age already knew.

To her mother, Sara often called Junior her "moxie moron." In some ways Junior may have made a woman out of Sara, yet he could never be the man of her life. He had way too much ego. She had better things to do than try to change a boy into a man. She told her mother, "I don't waste energy on things I can't control. Men are right-brained. And that means stupidity until middle-age when their testosterone levels start to drop. If a guy doesn't have anything better to do than to try to seduce me, then I'll get bored real quick."

Mary laughed hard and then hurried into her bedroom to tell Eddie what Sara had just told her.

Life in the Dense household was going well. Mary lobbied for Eddie to be parked in the living room so he could be around them in the evening. Sara was quick and final when she nixed that idea. "No way! I have to have my space, and he has his. This isn't FIKSHEN."

After nearly four years in Tulsa, Sara was ready for a change. She'd been in Tulsa long enough to even pick up an Oklahoma accent. One day she saw a magazine's retirement ad for Sun City, Arizona. And before winter set in, she'd convinced her mother to move Eddie to Arizona.

"Won't you live with us?" she asked her daughter.

"No, Mother. I want to live by myself. I'm twenty-seven years old, and I've never really been on my own. I just need to have my own space."

Mary finally accepted her daughter's decision and knew better than to press her headstrong daughter to explain herself further.

Their move to Arizona was considerably different than their move to Tulsa. Sara hired a moving company to move all their things, including Mary's car. The Sun City retirement village property manager made arrangements to set up their new one-story duplex that Sara had purchased for two hundred thousand dollars. After Sara again drove her mother and brother in the Buick to their new home, she helped them get settled in Sun City before heading south to her new place in Tucson.

"Why not live in Phoenix closer to us?" Mary asked plaintively.

"Mom, I can't live that close to you two. I know I'd get pestered about every little thing and I'd never get anything done."

"What are you going to do that's so important?"

"I want to be free to travel . . . to write my own novel . . . and to not have to explain my life to anyone."

"We won't bother you."

"Mother, you and Eddie are in Sun City because you have registered nurses in the complex and all kinds of people to handle your needs. Even if you want to go out you can. I'm not going to live my life around Eddie's situation. I love my brother and I've seen to it that you and he are taken care of for the rest of your lives. Isn't that enough, Mother?" Sara asked Mary in her new sun-bright kitchen.

Yes, and Sara didn't want to live around her brother Eddie's endless whistling coming from his horse teeth. Now their mother had him parked in the front room as she'd had him in FIKSHEN. It was hard for Sara to say nothing about the huge sunglasses her mother bought for herself and for Eddie. His maternal caretaker explained that she would put the shades on her comatose son because of the intense light coming in from the two skylights — one in the kitchen and one above Eddie.

Under the surface, Sara's biggest reason for living away from her family was the cold fact that she had seen her mother age ten years in the four years since Eddie's tragedy. Sara's big fear was that she would be next in line to be Eddie's caretaker. If and when that happened, she knew she faced two options: Either she would abandon her freedom and devote her life to Eddie's care, or she would end up sending Eddie to a long-term care facility. Tough decisions were coming.

Sara believed Eddie would outlive both of them, lying there breathing through his teeth. And Sara could imagine when she was infirm and about to croak, he'd wake up from his coma and live his life oblivious to the fact that his mother and sister had spent the rest of their lives cleaning, grooming, and feeding him. *And for what?* Sara would ask herself, seething with anger because fate had dealt her this obligation to pick up the torch when her mother could no longer carry it.

All of them wore sunglasses when she kissed her mother and brother goodbye before driving off in the direction of Tucson with her rental trailer. Less than a hundred miles would separate them, but it would seem like ten thousand miles after living under the same roof for four years. Sara hadn't realized how trapped she'd been. She'd learned from *Blue River* that inner peace would come only if she could be free of her mind. Brother Eddie's writing had sparked the same dream in her — to find the true source of Being where immortality and inner peace dwell, where form dies, and where every moment we ever have is NOW.

Tucson

The Catalina Mountains were close to Sara's three-bedroom condo located just off the north bank of the ever-dry Rillito River. This was the wealthiest part of the desert city with well-spaced, million-dollar homes dotting the Catalina foothills behind and all around Sara's condo.

Rillito Park Racetrack, a horse track open for only a couple months in the winter, was next door to the west of Sara. The old track's massive graveled parking lot assured the new condo owner that there would be no construction to inhibit her privacy.

The River Walk was the feature that sold her on the location of her new home. On the north side of the Rillito, "The Walk" was a paved, two-lane trail. It was mostly level and stretched for five miles, and it was used year-round by thousands of local bikers, joggers and walkers. The River Walk on the other side of the dry riverbed was unpaved. It was obvious to anyone that Sara's side of the river was where the money was. The north and south sides of the river were accessible to one another via a wide pedestrian bridge that spanned the Rillito for 150 yards from bank to bank.

On the south side of the river were mostly well-spaced mobile homes — double-wides with carports that shaded chained dogs. Their once-bright pastel colors had been faded by the intense Tucson sun. They were skirted and adorned with Southwest landscaping, including sturdy palm trees and an assortment of pottery and desert foliage.

Behind the trailers was a massive organic farm that raised chickens and produce for health food stores. Roosters crowed mornings and early evenings, which beckoned to packs of coyotes hunting the river's dry bottom at night looking for a rabbit, a stray dog, or anything else they could find.

Sara found this area of Tucson incredibly fascinating, especially the other side of the river where real life's sights and sounds reminded her of her life in FIKSHEN — a life she no longer had to live, but something she could still observe and write about.

Tucson was certainly a creative respite for S. O. Dense. *Blue River* had sold 320,000 copies since Sister Sara took over editing and managing her brother's work. Del's continued marketing was proving more and more successful now that he was direct-mailing to Texas, Kansas and Nebraska prospects. The Dense family was secure financially, and major publishers were interested in *Blue River*. Del thought another publisher meant he would lose his revenue from the book, but Sara told him she was not ready for a conventional publisher because she was still holding onto her belief that big corporations were destroying America and dismissing new writers wholesale without compassion. These were Eddie's beliefs too that were all over his book. Yet secretly Sara was anxious to end Del's marketing literature that hammered away at her brother's condition so much that Sara felt as if she were only promoting a media-made charity case. She at least was not a celebrity in Tucson and thus was free to go anywhere unrecognized.

With each passing month, Sara was getting more and more used to the passive intensity of Tucson's weather and falling into an easy way of life that was far removed from Tulsa and Council Bluffs. The University of Arizona gave her the opportunity to become a better writer by taking classes that were taught by well-known professors lauded throughout the country. This university atmosphere appealed to her more and more as her writing improved. With every "A" in every class, she validated herself as a good writer within the Tucson academia — even though she had never told one person since moving to Tucson that she was the editor and co-author of *Blue River.*

In the mainline reissue of *Blue River,* which included Eddie's near-drowning and the life he led while selling his first two printings, Sara was proud of the fact that she never took Eddie's "voice" out of the original version. That feat was something that had required tremendous skill as a writer and was a major accomplishment she'd never been recognized for. Just like her brother, she was a cipher to the world.

Every morning Sara would hit the River Walk in her expensive walking shoes and head toward the rising sun. Hidden among the sporadic trees on her walk was a wondrous network of burrowed holes made by desert squirrels, diggers of thousands of angled holes that were entrances and exits for a vast underground labyrinth of tunnels that surely scorpions and snakes found inviting. On her right was the dry Rillito, alive with thirty-foot cottonwoods and dense brush as tall as a horse with prickly burrs and barbs that formed a web of entanglement protecting the nervous rabbits that had survived another night. Everything that grew from the earth was sharp and dangerous to the slightest touch. Even the flowers on close examination had spikes like needles that would draw blood if even brushed against. It hardly rained here, yet things grew and turned green, and the birds flourished here.

The sights and sounds of nature were captivating year-round and seemed close enough to touch. One day Sara saw an eagle perched in a tree near her parking space, and one night a large desert wolf pranced through the parking lot as if on a desert stroll. In the summertime snakes came out in the morning. She hated and feared snakes. One summer day on the River Walk she was looking out for snakes when a hungry coyote crossed her path. The animal was so tired that it walked right by her haggardly and waited patiently in the heat for traffic to subside so it could cross the busy River Road.

The dry Rillito brought life and death. At night packs of coyotes prowled the riverbed twenty feet below the River Walk. They were invisible to humans until a distant emergency vehicle's siren would make them howl in chorus. At times there were thirty or more.

Sara loved to watch horses with riders stroll the river floor on vast stretches of baked sand that was clear of vegetation for miles in places. The horses and their riders would enter from the graveled south side and descend one of the concrete ramps, which were always covered with horse dung.

After her first year of residing in Tucson, Sara knew she would make her home there for a very long time. Twice a month Sara would make the two-hour drive to Sun City to visit her mother and Eddie. Mary also liked her new home. Friendly neighbors, mostly widows like herself, visited Mary daily and taught her how to play bridge. Morning walks around the retirement village were possible for her since one of the Sun City walkers would sit with Eddie until Mary got in her laps that amounted to three miles.

"Are you dating yet?" Mary would ask her visiting daughter.

Usually Sara would snap back with a clenched jaw and pent-up anger, "No, not yet, Mother. I haven't met anyone that interests me enough to make me wanna take my clothes off."

One night when Sara was visiting, she was happy to see a few of her mother's widow friends stop over with a video. Sara turned up the volume above Eddie's whistling breathing and they all enjoyed the movie.

The next morning Sara went to a medical supply store and bought her brother a quality air purifier that would blow fresh oxygen throughout their living space. She wanted her brother's lungs at least breathing fresh air at all times, since the air in Phoenix was getting worse and all their windows were closed half the year because of the execrable heat.

She was always happy to return to Tucson — to return to her life of reading, writing, walking, and taking classes that interested her. She had already planned on taking courses in French and German within the next year because she wanted to explore Europe for a couple weeks.

Live theater began to interest her; she often attended plays on campus and at popular Tucson playhouses. Yes, solitary Sara was getting healthy and loving her life in Tucson. Writing in her journal, she likened living in FIKSHEN to "being wedged into a sardine can filled with turds from a shared septic tank."

And Sara was becoming jaded of men. Not just because they were men, but rather because they never approached her or flirted with her. Sure, she had that brooding Dense brow and those sullen, flat lips that looked like she'd just beaten to death a man or two. But she had a great shape, a brilliant mind, and a need to be desired. "Why won't those primates approach me?" she asked her reflection upon returning home after not being approached once at a local bar. Even though her face was scowling and ever so serious, she could not see that about herself. She was a Dense.

S. O. Dense was getting modestly rich from the new printings of Eddie's book. This made her decide that no man was worth changing for. Money gave her the freedom to be oblivious to a social life. Now she could be the way she'd always been and not beat herself up for what she didn't have. Compromise and sweet surrender were specious words that would soon ruin any relationship for the long haul. She could never tolerate a man who would lie to her. But Sara Dense was no dummy; she knew what was coming and why she made the choices she did. She wrote:

> *I will be my brother's caretaker and replace my mother one day, for I doubt she will live another ten years. What man would want that kind of life*

at home? I must spend this time learning to live alone well without companionship — because that's what's headed my way.

Sleeping Giant

Within a year of Sara's move to Tucson, she decided she could capably handle the marketing of Eddie's book by herself and terminated her relationship with Del Wagner. It was fitting that Eddie's new publisher and distributer was Atlas Publishing, a small press in Madison, Wisconsin. Books on audio were popular, and Sara was open to seeing how *Blue River* did on tape. Often the author would read the book on tape; but, of course, that was impossible for Eddie, and Sara was aware that her voice was out of the question. Atlas sent her numerous voice samples so she could select just the right one for *Blue River*. Most of the voices were of people she'd never heard of before, but she was able to find what she believed was the perfect voice for Fast Eddie, the narrator of the story. Yes, Sara had gone back to Fast Eddie, the voice in the original story.

Eric Rhodes was a professor at the University of Wisconsin. He taught creative writing and was an ardent fan of *Blue River*. Eric's voice sounded young even though he was forty-two. He had a slow Midwest cadence and pronounced certain words with an upper Midwest dialect just like Eddie had. Since *Blue River* sales were highest in the Midwest, Sara went with Eric to be the voice of Fast Eddie on the audio.

Six months later, jaded from no social life, Sara began taking an interest in the healing arts — positive things like nutrition, chiropractic care, massage therapy, aromatherapy, and Rolfing. Since Eddie had been Rolfed again in Sun City, Sara decided to experience this muscle-manipulating technique that straightened out the misalignment of the body caused by gravity and life's stresses. It was painful; yet after a day or two her muscle soreness subsided, and after each session she felt like her body was more balanced. She was getting to do many positive things for herself that Eddie couldn't afford to do when he was selling his book.

One morning before one of her visits to Sun City, her publisher called her and told her the audio version of *Blue River* was selling well in libraries, and Midwest retail outlets reported brisk sales after the first quarter. This was the good news Sara had been waiting for. Now she could go to Germany and find a German publisher to market the book and tape. Audio was bigger in Europe, and this was her chance to go there, mixing business with pleasure. It was a Dense kind of thing.

When Sara arrived in Sun City, her mother was exercising Eddie's arms and legs. Both of them wore their "Dirty Harry" shades while Eddie breathed like a bulldog. Mary had just finished trimming her son's fingernails and toenails, which Sara could see piled on a napkin on Eddie's night stand.

As was her custom, Sara began her visit in Sun City by telling her mother and brother about their book-selling business, explaining every facet from the latest sales figures to her plans to go to Europe.

But destiny stepped in and made sure Sara gave careful consideration to her trip before she packed her bags. Sunday morning, the last day of her visit, a neighbor lady knocked so hard on Mary's front door that Mary feared she might wake Eddie. It was Irene Flanders, a Dense neighbor from Iowa and one of her walking buddies. Irene, still clad in her pajamas and slippers, came right in through the front door and turned on the Dense TV set without saying a word. Soon they were all staring at a news story about Jason Whiteburg, an international publisher who was awaiting trial for embezzlement of the employees' pension fund from Zushikyten, Inc., a German-based media giant with subsidiaries around the world. He had been killed in a car accident near Palm Springs the previous night.

Just when Mary started to ask Irene something, Irene shushed her as a highway patrolman came on the screen and told viewers that Whiteburg had apparently fallen asleep at the wheel while listening to a book on tape. The Dense women were stunned to hear the officer reveal to the viewing audience that the tape was *Blue River.*

Mary was beside herself with the thought that someone had died while listening to her boy's book on tape. Sara's mind was in an acquisitive trap showing her images and words this event would have on her family's book sales. In a spinning fog of confusion, she called her publisher and left a message on his answering machine to call her at her mother's home.

"What does this mean? Will they blame Eddie for this?" Mary asked plaintively.

"Mother, remember what Elsie told us about keeping negativity away from Eddie?"

Mary comically covered her mouth, remanding herself while following Sara into the kitchen to talk.

"Mother, don't you see? This could be the greatest word-of-mouth advertising for Eddie's book. Think of the demand that dead crook will give us!" Sara whispered with animation.

"But won't people think the book is boring if someone fell asleep listening to it?"

"Mother, you're missing the point," Sara said as she rolled her eyes.

"Don't roll your eyes at me! Your father used to do that all the time," she scolded her smirking daughter.

"Okay, I'm sorry. That was rude. I hated it when Dad did that," she patted her mother's folded arms. "Mother, Eddie wrote about the media exploiting things like this . . ."

"Like what?"

"The media will not want to validate a book related to this creep. When they know their coverage helps sell books of a small-press writer, you'll see them back off. The media just gave us a goldmine, Mom. That's why I should get a publicist to exploit what the media gave us."

"What about Del in Tulsa?"

"No, he takes fifty percent, and that's too much."

"Why don't you go on Oprah?"

"No, I don't want to be gawked at like . . ." She stopped herself. She was going to say "like Eddie" because of the way her mother brought friends into their home to look at him, and then those people would bring people over to stare at him like he was a freak in a circus. But Sara didn't want to go there, so she asked her mother if she had any ideas.

Within the next thirty days, *Blue River* was a household word thanks to the media. One newspaper wrote: "E. L. Dense is a sleeping giant. This American novelist — though literally unconscious, in a vegetative state from an accident — has managed to do what the justice system could not do: bring a swift and powerful final verdict upon a dirt bag with legs who stole millions in pension funds from thousands of employees worldwide. Whiteburg fell asleep listening to the audio book *Blue River* while driving his Mercedes and died in a ditch. Thank you, E. L. Dense, for being part of a universal law called karmic destiny."

Sara hounded her publisher to find more distributors for the popular *Blue River*. Her publicist in Phoenix suggested she tour the country hawking the famous title on TV and radio, but Sara declined; she did not want to exploit Eddie's condition. After several days of soul-searching and fasting, she came to her final conclusion and told her publicist, "There's nothing more beautiful than a good mystery."

E. L. Dense slept in his shades, breathing purified air while covered with jojoba cream. His pale and lifeless body was exercised by his mother, and he grew richer with every sonorous breath as "Stillness Within" flooded his brain with waves of peace and contentment.

Six weeks later Sara flew to Munich, Germany, and signed the biggest book contract ever for an American novel in Europe: eighty million dollars plus five percent of every book or tape of *Blue River* sold by the publisher-distributor Zushikyten, Inc. — the very same company from which Whiteburg had embezzled the pension fund. A percentage of the proceeds from the sale of *Blue River* was to be deposited into the pilfered pension fund which would be monitored by employees, not some greedy corporate mind. This altruistic gesture by the Dense family was so well received by the public that orders for the book were coming in like gang-busters.

When Sara was about to sign the contract in Munich, Mary held the phone to Eddie's ear as his sister read the entire contract to her snoring brother. "I'm signing it now, Eddie. This makes it official! I'll be home in a couple weeks. I'm going to Paris, London, and Dubwin," she baby-talked into the phone before breaking down into violent sobbing.

All Alone

Amazingly, Eddie had been sleeping for twelve years and had become one of the world's richest men despite never having moved a muscle. *Blue River* was an international household word, and the swindled Zushikyten employees had recovered their pension fund after only eight months.

Now over seventy, Mary Ellen was so arthritic she had to use a walker. Sara hired a full-time registered nurse, Vicky, to care for Eddie and their mother. Sister Sara even bought the adjoining duplex in Sun City and gave it to Vicky rent-free for as long as she worked for the Dense family. Thirty-four-year-old Vicky, a Latino mother raising her son, Luis, alone, loved the arrangement. No longer did the competent nurse from Nogales have to drive in the awful Phoenix traffic or worry about Luis being home alone in the sprawling desert city.

Sara maintained a low profile, never telling a soul in Tucson she was connected to the popular novel that had sold half a billion copies worldwide.

Within a year after hiring Vicky to care for her family in Sun City, Sara bought the entire thirty-unit condo complex in Tucson where she lived. She made sure that her property management company kept the units on either side of her condo vacant for privacy. Sara was making plans to have Eddie and their mother move to Tucson and live next door to her with Vicky and Luis living in the other condo. But fate stepped in again: Vicky called Sara and told her that Mary had died in her sleep. "I went in to wake Mrs. Dense when she was not up for breakfast. I checked her pulse and she was gone. I'm so sorry, Miss Sara."

Sara was not surprised; her maternal grandmother had died in her sleep at about the same age. It pained Sara when she thought about Eddie and how, if he were to wake up, his parents would be gone. "And now, I'm alone," Sara sighed. "But I still have my brother. He's still alive," she cried on her bed.

That night, while strolling the River Walk and grieving the loss of her mother, she was anxious for Eddie to move in next door to her. And Vicky and Luis would live there too, with Vicky continuing to handle every detail of her brother's care. In the meantime, Sara would fulfill her mother's wish to join Ike in the same urn.

Over and over she kept telling her busy mind that she was still going to travel and live her life without Eddie's condition imposing on her lifestyle in the slightest. *In fact,* she mused to herself, *why couldn't Eddie live in the other vacant condo? That way Vicky and I could live away from that wretched sound of his breathing, and we wouldn't have to look at him every waking moment. I could have a camera installed and Vicky could monitor him from her place.*

It was too dark for Sara to continue walking along the River Walk; there was far too much rustling and slithering on the earth around her from God-knows-what. Her back was to the vanilla-orange full moon that hung low in the sky above the Rillito. The purplish-black Catalinas were looming off to her right — and she was all alone.

It was for good reason she felt empty. Knowing deep in her heart she would never marry — *I'm too rich for any man,* she sniggered — she let her mind tell her she was the sole survivor of her family and, for all intents and purposes, she'd die alone like Elsie if she outlived her brother.

She quickened her pace from being frightened and alone, and she thought of Lauren's child in San Diego. If it weren't too late, it was time to bring the only member of the new Dense generation into her life. Maybe Lauren and her kid could live with Eddie in his condo. No, she scoffed at the notion, Lauren could be happily married by now.

Les is Les

The next ninety days were rife with changes for Sara. She had been hit hard by the grieving process after losing her mother. Now she was focused on making Eddie, Vicky, and seven-year-old Luis as comfortable as possible in their new homes. Sister Sara paid all of Vicky's moving expenses; and she had Eddie flown down to Tucson, along with the urn that now held both Ike's and Mary's remains.

Sara recalled an uncomfortable incident from her childhood as she carried her parents' urn onto the private jet. When she was eight years old, she overheard a couple of her parents' hippie friends boisterously recalling a bizarre episode from their old house in Council Bluffs. They laughed about how Ike had pinched out some ashes from his father's remains and smoked them in his pipe. She never forgot overhearing that chilling story. One day she even asked her father if it were true. Ike only laughed.

Now the urn would be in Eddie's 1,800-square-foot condo, kept on his mother's antique cherry wood corner table on the other side of the living room from where he slept on his bed facing the river. This time Eddie would have his own space, and there were going to be some big changes now that their mother was gone.

Vicky and Luis really liked their condo on the other side of Sara. Nurse Vicky was more than an attentive caretaker; she literally had Eddie in her view twenty-four-seven because of the video camera constantly on her patient. And now Eddie had his own stereo, so there was no more need for earplugs.

Sara was free to focus on handling the Dense fortune, which was a full-time job. Writing another book seemed pointless to her after the incredible success of *Blue River.*

Sara found Lauren still living in San Diego after contacting Lauren's father's printing company in San Francisco. That's when Sara found out that Les, Lauren's father, had passed away a few years before. Lauren was thrilled to hear from Sara and was happy to drive to Tucson with her son, Les, the following weekend in order for the twelve-year-old to see his comatose father he'd heard about all his life.

Sara worked at getting Eddie's condo ready for his visitors. She had both bedrooms and baths furnished so Lauren and her son could spend Saturday night there. With the air purifier and the waves from "Stillness Within," it was certain that their host wouldn't disturb his guests. And Sara had a professional hair stylist come over to Eddie's place and give him a great haircut. His fine, red hair was cut shorter and spiked evenly, with the sides gelled back behind his freckled ears.

After his haircut, Sara raised her brother's eyelids and told him that Lauren and her son Les were coming to visit him. "Lauren says he's your son, Eddie. And Les is Les, not Lesley like your middle name. Les was Lauren's father's name, as you know. She named him Les Edward after you. I don't know his last name, but now we finally have someone Les Dense in the family! Isn't that great?" she laughed. "It's the perfect name for your son, don't you think? Anyway, Lauren said don't call Les 'Lesley.' Les is Les," Sara laughed again. "They'll be here Saturday morning. I offered to pay for their flights, but Lauren says she loves the drive from San Diego to Arizona. Lauren sounds like . . . an Earth Mother. I mean that in a good way.

"I'm really anxious to meet your old girlfriend. From your journal I feel like I already know her," she patted Eddie's frail shoulder that was clad in dark-blue silk pajamas. "When I wrote about Lauren, I wrote about your reunion in Tulsa. Even in the story line I wrote about how you conceived a child there. I'm glad Mom never read the new version of your book because I never told her that Lauren told me she was pregnant with Les. I knew she'd freak out, Eddie," Sara cried. "Now that she's gone I wish I'd told her. But you know Mom. She was really a Dense. Yeah, I felt guilty for not telling her, but I really wasn't sure you got her pregnant after reading your journal about the guys from est she was probably seeing. And I was greedy. I thought she'd try to get part of our estate. Now I know I was being a bitch, and I'm going to make it up to them, Eddie. And now that they're coming I feel like it might spark me into writing my own novel like I always wanted to. This one's just for me — unless you wake up and help me write it," she whispered. Sara kissed his forehead and turned on the ocean waves as she looked around Eddie's place and admired the Southwestern art adorning his walls.

And Eddie was getting a tan, but not from the Tucson sun. Sara bought him a tanning bulb from a health food store that would not damage his sensitive skin. Every other day Vicky would attach the light to his bed rail and move it down his body in ten-minute increments so that the entire length of his body would be exposed to the light.

There was another big change for Eddie: a Tucson orthodontist came and outfitted him for braces. Yes, Eddie was finally getting his teeth fixed. Not only would braces diminish the sound of his breathing, but also Sara really believed Eddie would wake up one day and be happy with his sister's decision about his appearance. Sara continued to maintain her faith that Eddie would wake up one day — a faith even greater than their mother's strong belief. That was the hardest thing about losing their mother, for now she would not be around to see her boy wake up. Mary had told Sara the previous Christmas that if she died before Eddie woke up, at least she will have died before seeing any of her children passing away before her. "That," she said, "would be a gift from God."

By Friday afternoon, the day before Lauren and Les's visit, Eddie had braces on his teeth. They were the latest kind that required no rubber bands. Instead of quieting Eddie's breathing, though, the interweaving of metal with his teeth gave each breath a metallic kind of whistle that Sara found humorous.

Twelve-year-old Les Edward was about to enter Eddie's condo behind his mother and Aunt Sara. Lauren looked radiant; she had ripened into a beautiful Earth Mother whom Sara admired right from the start. Sara had audibly gasped at the boy's resemblance to her brother. He had Eddie's fine, red hair, his mother's green eyes, and the same pimples Eddie had when he was young. When she first saw her nephew, she hugged him and looked at those lazy eyelids that blinked so slowly.

"You're twelve, right?" Sara asked.

He only nodded. Sara wanted to hear his voice but found out that Les was self-conscious about hiding his braces that covered his Dense horse teeth.

Aunt Sara ushered them up to Eddie's bed. Lauren went up to the side rail and touched Eddie's hair that she'd never seen spiked like this.

Les stood next to his mother, his green eyes blinking slowly while taking in this man who was his father. This was the man his mother had referred to eight years ago when she told him, "Your daddy is asleep. His name is Eddie . . . like your middle name." And two years ago she'd told Les, "Your father is a writer. Your Grandpa Les printed his first book. I last saw Eddie in Tulsa nine months before you were born. Now you know why you like to write poetry."

"You said he was in a coma since before I was born?" Les had asked.

Lauren nodded yes and explained, "Eddie nearly drowned . . . and he's been asleep since before you were born."

Now Sara was still beside herself from the boy's uncanny resemblance to her brother as Lauren pinched Eddie's cheeks and gauged the fat under his pendulous chin.

"He needs his facial skin toned," Lauren remarked. "I have this terrific muscle toner for the face muscles. I'll send it to you with instructions if you'd like."

"Thanks," Sara smiled.

They watched Sara lift Eddie's eyelids and listened to her explain the yellow-gold color. "His eyes are blue, but his medication changed the color."

Young Les smiled, revealing his own braces, after Sara raised Eddie's lips to reveal his new braces. "Eddie has braces too."

"Like father, like son," Lauren laughed.

"What do you think of your father wearing braces?" Sara asked the shy boy.

"It's cool. I wish I could sleep and wake up with my braces off," the boy said slowly, just as Sara had heard her brother speak.

Sara noticed Les had a handful of his favorite music recordings. "You can play your music here," she told him. "Eddie loves music."

Lauren fumbled in her purse. "Oh, would you play 'Crystal Blue Persuasion' once? It was Eddie's favorite song." Lauren handed Sara a well-worn cassette tape. "Les, tell Aunt Sara about the silicon solar cell and how it could replace fossil fuels."

But Les walked away, pretending to be interested in the art framed on the walls.

The women paid close attention to Eddie as "Crystal Blue Persuasion" played from the speakers Les wished he had in his room back home. Sara could see a flood of emotions sweeping over Lauren. When the song was over Lauren said, "Eddie said it gave him hope for the world."

Sara replayed the Tommy James and the Shondels hit song, and the women stared at Eddie. When the song was over Lauren said, "I'm sure Eddie would be thrilled with what you did with *Blue River,* Sara. I bought a copy of the new version. Les read it too. We both really enjoyed it."

Les played his rock music louder than his mother allowed at home; but Sara told Lauren, "If it wakes Eddie up, so be it."

When Sara showed her guests to their rooms, the most amazing thing happened: Eddie's left index finger twitched — but nobody saw it.

Flinch of Hope

Later that night when Sara and Lauren were chatting on Sara's patio and Les was listening to his music in Eddie's place, Les thought he saw Eddie's finger twitch. It wasn't until sometime later that Les casually mentioned what he thought he'd seen to Sara.

Sara bolted over to Eddie's bedside, turned on all the lights, and stared at his pale fingers. Since Vicky had the weekend off and had gone to Nogales to visit family, Sara wasn't able to confirm with her if she'd seen anything. Lauren and Les joined Sara on the other side of his bed. Sara had Les show her which finger moved.

"Do you remember what song you were playing when his finger moved?" Sara asked the slow-blinking boy.

Since Les couldn't recall the song, Sara had him play all his music. For two hours Sara and Lauren stood staring at Eddie's fingers while Les paced in and out of the condo, changing the music selections periodically. But not one finger twitched.

Sunday morning Sara and her guests went for a walk on the River Walk. The women chatted while Les trailed them. On Sara's side of the dry Rillito inside the Rillito Racetrack, a big carnival was setting up for the week. A huge silver-colored ferris wheel had been erected, along with several twirling rides around it.

"Can I go to the carnival, Mom?"

"We'll see."

"We'll see" turned out to be three hours later when the carnival opened for business. Since Sara wanted to stay with Eddie in case he twitched again, Lauren took her son to the carnival by herself. "We'll only be gone for a couple hours," she told her host.

About an hour later when Sara played "Crystal Blue Persuasion," she could have sworn she saw her brother's frail shoulders flinch slightly. But she waited . . . and waited . . . and waited, playing the song over and over until . . . there it was — a flinch from his shoulders. Then a big flinch excited Sara so much that she turned the volume up and screamed at Eddie, "Wake up, Eddie! Wake up! I miss you! It's okay to wake up now!"

Sara ran over to Vicky's condo as soon as she and her son returned home from a movie. "Eddie flinched!" she screamed at Vicky. "Like this!" Sara shrugged her shoulders to demonstrate. "He did it twice! Come on!"

Vicky and Luis stood by Eddie's bed as Sara blared "Crystal Blue Persuasion." Sara was singing along while crying, "A new day is dawning! People are changin'! Ain't it beautiful! Crystal Blue Persuasion!"

Eddie didn't flinch for his onlookers. And he didn't flinch later when Sara played the song and feverishly told Lauren and Les about Eddie flinching earlier.

"Does that mean he's wakin' up?" the boy asked the women.

"Yes!" Sara beamed and hugged her nephew joyously, whereupon she easily convinced her guests to stay over for another night.

The next morning Sara called Eddie's Tucson doctor to tell her that he had flinched. The doctor was reserved about it, informing Sara that comatose patients are known to twitch and flinch now and then, and it doesn't mean they are coming out of their coma. Sara fired back at the doctor, "Doctor, level with me. Could this possibly be the beginning of my brother waking up?"

"Yes, it could be. But I've also seen enough of these cases to know that it's all too random . . ."

"Then I can have hope?"

"Yes," the doctor answered reservedly.

After a late breakfast, Lauren and Les said goodbye to Eddie and headed back for San Diego, leaving Lauren's tape of "Crystal Blue Persuasion" for Eddie. Lauren was as hopeful as Sara that Eddie was coming out of his coma, and she was elated when Sara told Lauren that Eddie's estate would pay for Les's college if he didn't get a scholarship. That news was a huge relief to Lauren because she had no funds set aside for her son's college education. Lauren's father had left his daughter fifty thousand dollars in annuities, which she cashed in soon after his death to put down on a house she financed in Pacific Beach.

As they sat watching Eddie for hours on end, Sara and Lauren got a chance to really bond. Lauren told Sara how she had gotten out of est a few months into her pregnancy. She said she'd dated an instructor in the seminar training and had "freed myself from him a few weeks before I met Eddie in Tulsa."

They talked in front of Eddie as if he were listening. He was. Not consciously, but rather like a rock or a tree listens; it's just there, like an invisible energy that knows wind and rain and all seasons.

Over breakfast Sara had been quite agreeable to Les's desire to be adopted by Eddie. It was Les's idea. Lauren told Sara that Les thought the name Les Dense was a "cool name." The boy had wanted to be adopted in name ever since he'd read *Blue River* a couple years before. Les had written in his notebook at school:

> *Mom, after reading* Blue River *I know that Eddie is my dad. I would like to be Les Dense if it's possible.*

Upon hearing from Lauren what Les wrote, it hit Sara on an emotional level — and she was business-liking it too, knowing she could write off any funds given to Eddie's dependent as long as Eddie was comatose.

Weeks passed. Eddie was flinching and twitching more and more. Muscles around his face, fingers and toes would spasm and jerk as if he were having a bad dream. Vicky monitored her patient when Sara scheduled another Rolfing session for Eddie. That's when Vicky told Sara she thought Eddie would wake up soon.

"Soon" was at Christmastime, after Lauren and Les had visited for four days. Sara was sitting alone with Eddie. For some reason she decided to lift Eddie's eyelids. His eyes were blue again! Eddie's doctor said that would be a clear sign he was waking up. So Sara rode with her brother in an ambulance to the Tucson Medical Center where he could be monitored closely by doctors and staff.

After two days and nights of Sara waiting and sleeping on a bedside hospital lounger, Eddie and I woke up. But nobody knew it. When he opened his eyes he could tell someone was asleep close to his bed in his dark private room. *Where am I?* he wondered to himself.

Eddie and I had been asleep for thirteen years — and he felt tired. He couldn't speak or move. And I couldn't bother him with anything.

Yes, E. L. Dense was finally awake and had the most popular book on the planet — except he was the only one who didn't know it. Like a newborn babe, Eddie was innocent and empty of thought. I had been erased from Eddie's memory, yet I was ready to soak up life because Eddie had chosen to come back.

Yes, Eddie made a choice: to either succumb to death or come back to the world in his old form as Eddie Dense.

He's Awake!

Registered nurse Jessica Boyle was the first person to see Eddie's blazing blue eyes blinking lazily under his nightlight. They scared her at first because they were so awake and truly seeing her — seeing things about her she was self-conscious of, like the way she was unable to feel joy for a man who had been asleep for thirteen years and was now awake — and she could feel that he saw behind the mask that was layered with mascara, rouge, lipstick, eyeshadow, and a bronze skin-coloring cream that attested to her denial of middle age. She let him just look at her. He had seen more of her in these few moments than anyone at that hospital had in her fifteen years of being a fixture there.

The nurse woke Sara. "He's awake," she smiled at Sara's bleary eyes and told her she was calling her brother's doctor. When Sara looked at Eddie, she stood up in shock and stepped into his line of vision. Those lazy blue eyes were ablaze with a firestorm of raw purity like an innocent child. He was truly "still within" as his sister leaned her face over his chest and could see that he did indeed recognize her.

"Hi, Eddie. You're back," she whispered with tearing eyes.

She could see that he was not trying to speak and that he was not alarmed about his condition. She stroked his brow and told him softly, "Everything is fine. You're in a hospital in Tucson, Arizona. And we'll be going home soon."

There was no expression on his face or in his eyes.

"Eddie, can you blink twice" — she demonstrated — "if you can understand me?" She waited without blinking until he blinked twice.

Sara went out into the hospital hallway while his doctor was examining him. This time she would not alert the media. She didn't need them. The last thing she wanted for Eddie was hounding by the media. As she walked along the sparsely lit hallway, she had to hold her hand to her mouth to conceal her crying, for she was thinking how her parents would have loved to have been there at that moment.

The image of Les flashed through her mind and made her go to a phone booth and call Lauren. Lauren was so thrilled she said she would be driving to Tucson the following morning and bringing Les.

Back in Eddie's room, Eddie's doctor had been joined by another doctor and the head floor nurse. They invited Sara to join their robust conversation about her brother at the other end of the room. The two doctors were split: one wanted to remove the patient's feeding tube and catheter; the other wanted to wait at least forty-eight hours. Sara intervened, "What are the negatives for now versus forty-eight hours from now?"

Eddie's doctor told Sara that Eddie's bodily functions, including his ability to eat on his own, may be delayed for an indefinite time. The other doctor said it would be best to restore Eddie's body back to self-maintenance — that his body would respond rather quickly. Sara told them she wanted the tubes removed right away.

While extensive testing of Eddie's reflexes and sensory perception was being conducted, Sara stood in her brother's line of vision at the foot of his bed. Her gaze shifted from those blue eyes that emanated shards of light to the area of his atrophied body that was being tested.

"Can you hear me, Eddie?" his doctor asked. "If you can hear me, Eddie, blink like this," the doctor demonstrated by blinking twice slowly. Eddie would blink like a trusting child and Sister Sara's eyes would cry more and more with each good sign.

Later when the doctors and nurse had left Eddie's room, Sara stood at his bedside holding his hand. She'd given his dry lips a trickle of water. Then when his cracked lips rubbed against his braces Sara whispered, "I put braces on your teeth. You never liked your front teeth, so I did it. They're due to come off soon. Or I can have them removed now if you want. If they hurt now . . . I'm sorry," she cried.

Eddie blinked his lazy eyelids as if to say it was okay and squeezed her hand slightly to confirm it.

As Eddie rested contentedly, Sara slipped down to the cafeteria and called Lauren again. "He's still awake," she blurted.

Again, Lauren turned down Sara's offer to fly them out and confirmed they'd be leaving soon for Tucson. Les got on the phone and was just as excited as his mother was about Eddie. "Can he talk?" Les asked.

"Not yet, but he blinks his answers. He squeezed my hand. Speech will take time."

By the time Lauren and Les arrived early the next evening, Eddie was able to sip water and his protein drink from a straw. When Eddie's visitors from San Diego came into his room, Lauren leaned over close to Eddie's face. "Hi, Eddie. You remember me?"

Eddie blinked at her as Les moved into Eddie's view. Lauren told Eddie she wanted him to meet someone.

"Hi," Les smiled.

"This is Les. He's your son, Eddie," Lauren smiled. Both girls lost complete control of their emotions and had to regroup in the hallway where Lauren confided she had her doubts about telling Eddie about Les now. But Aunt Sara was loving and told her that the doctors said her brother needs stimulation right now.

That night Vicky stayed with Eddie in his hospital room throughout the night so Sara and her guests could get some sleep. Luis stayed in Sara's guest room. Lauren and Les, who again stayed in Eddie's condo, hadn't slept much since Sara had called them.

Resolving that life would begin anew for Eddie and herself from that moment on, Sara was numb and happy and exhausted when she took her parents' urn to the middle of the pedestrian bridge. She opened the urn and let the ashes fly out into the darkness above the Rillito. After tossing the urn into the dumpster, she had her nephew help her push Eddie's medical bed out onto the patio where the Salvation Army would pick it up the following morning. She explained with animation to her guests, "I want it out of my sight! Eddie will sleep in a regular bed as if this never happened. The sight of that bed sickens me and reminds me of the terrible years my parents had to endure."

Progress

Eddie's clear eyes danced with expression when his doctors told him he would be going home the next morning. Vicky was there when they told their improving patient the good news. After only four days awake in a new world, Eddie was able to grunt and twist his pale fingers when he was hungry or thirsty or when he had eliminated in his diaper.

Sister Sara had his bedroom all ready for him. Les was content to sleep on Sara's sofa in her condo while his mother stayed in the guest bedroom. Vicky would be spending five nights a week in Eddie's condo until he was self-sufficient.

Lauren and Les kept extending their visit. During the first few days of Eddie's return home, Les played his music on Eddie's stereo while Lauren sat on Eddie's new king-size bed reading to those slow-blinking eyes that could now sleep for eight hours and then open.

Meanwhile, Sara was on the hunt for a speech therapist who would work with Eddie several times a week. Dr. Marjorie Dundee from the University of Arizona Medical Center came by Sara's condo the same day Lauren and Les were returning to San Diego. She was quickly hired, and Eddie had a top-notch speech specialist willing to work with him on Mondays, Wednesdays, and Fridays from ten in the morning until two in the afternoon at a cost of $1,200 per week.

At first there was progress. Eddie's throat would bob when he tried to move his tongue to speak for Dr. Marge. This went on for two whole weeks. But lack of any further progress frustrated Eddie. Soon his throat stopped moving as he attempted speech, and it seemed as though the patient had given up.

Around the middle of Eddie's third week of therapy, Dr. Marge saw progress in Eddie's eyes. He was crying. The doctor explained to Sara that her brother was frustrated and really cared about speaking. "He hasn't given up. He's fighting. That's progress," she smiled at Sara and her patient.

One night, after six more weeks of nothing from Eddie, Sara showed him an ass-backwards copy of *Blue River* brought up from the salvage dive in Oklahoma. The sight of his book made him gurgle sounds that Sara excitedly shared with Dr. Marge the next session. When the doctor opened the book to a page in front of Eddie, a page that was upside-down, Eddie smiled for the first time and groaned out, "Ass-backwards."

That smile and those two words were big progress for Eddie. It was the first obvious facial movement since he came out of his coma. From then on, Dr. Marge would read from *Blue River,* pointing to certain words that he would repeat for her. Eddie was talking again. Sara was elated.

Next came his physical therapy — getting Eddie to move more and more. Vicky was his physical therapist; she was getting him to move his head off his pillow and from side to side. Sara would sit at his bedside for hours coaxing him to move his hands and feet.

One morning Vicky came into Eddie's room and was shocked to see that Eddie had both of his legs raised and bent at his knees. Vicky screamed such voluble praises in Spanish that Sara could hear her from her condo, thus prompting her to run over and investigate the source of the commotion.

Then came sitting in a wheelchair and going for a ride on the River Walk with Vicky and Sara. At first his head would be slumped forward during these excursions, until one morning on the pedestrian bridge when a rider on horseback came close to them, about to pass under the bridge. Sara lifted her brother's head in order for him to see the horse, yelling, "Eddie! Look at the horsey!"

When they rolled Eddie to the other side of the bridge in order to see the horse again, Sara repeated, "Horsey, Eddie! Look!"

Eddie's neck muscles strained like heck until he held his head up on his own, much to the excitement of the women.

From that moment on, Eddie was wheeled out to the bridge every day to see the horses pass by. Within two more months he was sliding a walker on wheels — all of his own volition. And now he was no longer like a two year old that had to learn syllables with vowels and consonants. Rather, his motor skills for speech from brain to tongue were starting from scratch. Eddie was making real progress.

Lauren and Les visited often — about every two months for a long weekend. Les was proud of the fact that he'd been legally adopted in name by Eddie. Les Edward Dense now had a real father who could see, listen, and sometimes talk to him. This made Lauren very happy, and her love for Eddie grew. Her pure, exultant joy would completely consume her whenever she would visit Eddie. It was real and everyone near her could see it and feel it — even Eddie.

Eddie had his braces removed and thus didn't whistle in his sleep anymore. And he had lost his lisp, which he very much liked. "Mu-sic," Eddie would point to the stereo several times a day. And if Les was visiting, the thirteen-year-old would gladly blare his music off the walls for his recovering father.

Yes, Eddie was making real progress in every area of his rehabilitation. He was gaining weight, even though he had the dexterity of a five year old with a fork and a spoon. Diapers were still mandatory because he soiled them two or three times a day, yet he was making progress with his toilet training because of Vicky's unwavering care and patience.

Oddly, Eddie was using his right hand when he ate or colored or printed words on paper. Sara asked Dr. Marge how this switch of hands could be and if she'd ever heard of such a switch.

"It happens more with left-handed people. Lefties tend to change sometimes to right-handedness more than natural right-handers switch to left. There's no data to prove it, but I believe it's a simple reprogramming of the brain and nothing to be alarmed about."

Overall, Eddie's progress was slow and tedious. Sara wanted her brother back the way he was. Dr. Marge reminded Sara that her brother was still working his way back from being in his early twenties — but his body was now thirty-five and his mind was only about seven years old. He could only get back to who he was when he sank to the bottom of that lake nearly fourteen years ago.

It seemed to Sara to be as good a time as any to get Eddie his own television for his place, since he was driving her nuts with his loud music day and night. She also thought this was the time to tell her brother about the loss of their parents and about his near-drowning in Oklahoma. And business matters would have to be discussed because Eddie was worth a fortune and it was about time he knew it.

One evening after dinner she told him about all of those things. Yet the thing that interested him the most was the fact that he had a now-fifteen-year-old son whom he had legally adopted. Eddie was at last more aware of what that meant. He was also aware that Les Edward Dense made him smile more than anyone else could. He asked his sister if he had really made

Les his official son; Sara explained that their attorney had handled it and it was true.

Over the next few months, Eddie was motivated to mature at a much faster rate. A couple times a week Les would call his dad and read to him passages from his writing — something Eddie really enjoyed. Eddie was happy that Les was a better writer than he used to be. Les was a rebel who found the world to be a rotten place. And since I wasn't filling Eddie's head with negative thoughts, Eddie was now a fantastic listener and observer with zero desire to write again. Reading didn't interest him, either. He loved cable TV. Even though Sara was glad he could walk with her on the River Walk, she always knew he was anxious to get back to his remote control.

Sara's decision to not inform the media and their publisher about Eddie's coming out of his coma was paying off in big ways now that he was ambulatory. He was free to be himself and was now expressing interest to his sister in driving again.

Les Time

About four years later in the late fall, Les decided to drop out of his freshman year in college. His mother was disappointed and asked Eddie to talk to Les about his future. Les had written his dad about his plans to quit school and sent him a copy of a paper he did for his creative writing class titled "The Empty Sole." The story was about how:

> *Passion has been drained out of Americans because of this gaping hole at the very bottom of every one of us. There seems to be this festering rage tormenting American youth today. Up until now, that rage was able to vanish into the ether of music and time until the next generation took its flame of discontent. But now, on the horizon we can see the bad things coming that our parents and grandparents ignored and passed on to us. They have caused us to resent them for not acting on important things and showing us how to live well. Now my generation is forced to plug this hole in the ozone all by ourselves. We must be the youth that cleans up our past transgressions on our blue planet. Like dumb donkeys we are left to carry this heavy burden of neglect. The elderly will not support us. They will prefer to fight for cheaper drugs and never take any responsibility for the massive withholding of funds and energy they believe should have been handled by the same politicians who filled their medicine cabinets with affordable drugs that will numb the pain they have caused.*

Les visited Tucson often, and Les and Eddie always got along well. Lauren and Sara were having coffee on Sara's patio while Les and Eddie went for a walk on the River Walk.

Lauren was telling Sara how worried she was after Les dropped out of school at San Diego State and was smoking pot with his buddies.

"I think Eddie will help him," Sara smiled.

"I hope so. He needs some direction . . . some kind of male bonding."

Sara went on to tell Lauren that she didn't think Eddie would ever write again, and that freed her to write her own romance novel. "I want to write about myself and this guy, Larry, that I knew back in high school. He was my first — and so far my last — love."

"Did you sleep with him?" Lauren wondered out loud.

"Larry would knock on my window late at night, and we'd go to the river and just kind of roll around in his sleeping bag."

Lauren leaned forward as if keenly interested.

"It was before Eddie's friends died at the river, so it was still . . . magical," Sara laughed.

"Go on," Lauren coaxed.

"Well, in the book I end up getting pregnant in high school, and there go my future plans. And then Larry leaves me, I have the kid, and my parents make me give it up to the orphanage. But I secretly visit the kid throughout her life . . ."

"It was a girl?"

"Yeah, Bonnie. Bonnie Ellen. B. E. Dense," Sara laughed with Lauren. "It's all about staying connected to your past mistakes . . . resolving them in order to live well now."

"That sounds like Eddie."

Les was now an inch taller than Eddie, but he was thirty pounds lighter. As they walked along the River Walk Les said, "Do you believe I'm your genetic son?"

"Of course."

"I know we look alike, but how do you really know?"

"When I first saw you, I could feel this electric shock tingle up and down my body from head to toe."

They walked across the pedestrian bridge to the other side of the dry river and onto the desert trail of the River Walk that was littered with thousands of gopher-like holes not far from the organic chicken farm. Roosters would crow off behind them.

"Aunt Sara told us that your parents died when you were asleep. Do you remember them?"

"I remember them. I know I loved them, but it hasn't really hit me yet that they are gone."

"I was thinking how cool it would be to be you. I mean, you woke up rich and you got to sleep through losing your parents and all this B.S. in the world."

The more they walked, the more Eddie noticed how frail Les was; he appeared as if he could be blown away by the slightest wind. And his freckled face was dotted with acne blotches around his mouth and nose. It reminded Eddie of his life in FIKSHEN.

They reached a bridge overpass and stepped within its cool shadow where they saw three young men lying back on the sloping concrete embankment. Les wanted to join them on the slanted pavement as the young men ignored them with wary eyes. On the sidewalk was a freshly spray-painted white graffiti circle with the word "FOOL" printed inside a drawn heart. Eddie thought that whoever put that there was angry and cynical, and it likely could have been one of those three guys.

Looking back, I can recall telling Eddie that Les was communicating silently with those three men about something.

But at the time all Eddie could do was give his son his complete attention, and that kept me quiet. Eddie said to Les, "Maybe you could hang out in Tucson. If you don't have to go back to San Diego, you could stay with me and Sara awhile. I'd like to spend more time with you."

"Yeah . . . that's cool."

Somehow Eddie knew that his son was happy to stay for other reasons — reasons that were here in the shade on the cooler side of the river, where just above them the air was as dry as a cow's tongue, shimmering in places where heat collected and stayed on the sandy river bottom.

It was here, surrounded by cool cement, that Eddie chose to think of his parents, how they had married when young beatniks and waited to have Sara until they were in their late 30s. Forty years they were married, Eddie ruminated as Les sneezed and sniffled from the pollen that bothered him every fall in Tucson.

When they headed for home, Les blew snot out of each nostril onto the desert trail. That's when Eddie could see how Les's fingers were dirty and stained yellow. Things like this Eddie would see and not judge, for he had reached his Blue River — a simple state of Being. It began when he was floating on Sara's foam bed she gave him, while he was unconscious and riding those passive waves on that big lake after the storm. Now Eddie could talk with Les about his drug use in terms that reflected his new state of consciousness. Yes, Eddie didn't use me like he used to. He used me to plan his words carefully.

Meanwhile, back at Sara's condo Lauren was telling Sara about her love life after Eddie. "When Les was about two I met a guy that I really fell for."

"In San Diego?"

"No. He had a house in Orange County. I met him at a store in Pacific Beach with Les. We lived together for six months at his place. We broke up on good terms. He moved us back to San Diego and I got hired as a manager for this restaurant . . ."

On the other side of the river, a carnival was in town again and setting up inside the racetrack. Les recalled the fun he'd had with his mom years ago at the carnival. Against the mountains, Les and Eddie saw the giant yellow and royal-blue ferris wheel spinning along with an orange tilt-a-wheel. They walked over to the carnival to watch the carnies setting up for the weekend.

Vicky sat down and joined Sara and Lauren on Sara's patio. Vicky told Sara she'd found a great nursing job in Phoenix and would move back there since Eddie was now on his own and doing well. Sara agreed with Vicky that she would wait to move over the Christmas break. Then the women got into a discussion about how bad the drug scene was in the Tucson area. "Les has been smoking pot and God-knows-what else," Lauren told Vicky. "He needs a good work ethic now that he doesn't want to go to school. I think it's great that he'll spend some time with Eddie."

Before Lauren headed back for California, Sara told her that she would buy Les some clothes during his extended visit. Les only brought one pair of jeans and a few black t-shirts. Sara had asked Les why he wore black clothes. His answer was alarming. "Because I'm not bright. I'm not going to go around wearing rainbows on my chest when greed and materialism run the planet."

It was dark when Les checked out the carnival. Eddie walked him there on the River Walk and gave his son forty bucks.

"I don't need this much," Les protested.

"You have to have some cash on ya," Eddie smiled.

Eddie watched as his son, wearing black Nikes and a black t-shirt with his faded jeans riding low down his rump, headed for the neon lights across two hundred yards of graveled parking lot. He could see by the way Les carried himself that he was not happy; his head was craned as he loped slowly with his posture silently screaming his uncertainty. His forward-lurching shoulders reminded Eddie of his father and the times he came home late at night after closing the bar. This was before his parents had separated. Now Eddie was seeing the same walk of unhappiness in Les. As Les disappeared into the crowded carnival, Eddie headed for his condo.

Skyler

The lights at the carnival were not neon. There were thousands of colored tubes and bulbs of red, yellow, green, and blue. I was like a boy in a candy store — nineteen going on twelve. My face looked like it was sixteen, dotted with a dozen pimples I'd habitually pick and squeeze at night. But not tonight.

The first carnie I saw wore a black t-shirt like mine, except stenciled on the back was, "If you can read this . . . you're losing." Kids were everywhere. I went to each ride as an observer. I would stand back and study how each ride worked to see if it was worth riding.

While standing in the ferris wheel line, there was a girl in front of me who appeared to be my age. Right away I liked her clothes — tight black shorts, a man's white sleeveless t-shirt, and black sandals. Her hair was red like mine; it was thick and short and spiked wild as if she'd just finger-combed it after a shower. Her shape was thin and without definition. Above her waistline on her back was a red tattoo with "NO" printed in small letters that reminded me of the graffiti on the sidewalk I had seen with my dad earlier today.

She turned to me when the ferris wheel music stopped and said, "I hope I don't hurl."

I laughed and said, "If you do, I hope I'm not below you." She laughed until all we could hear was awkward silence despite all the sounds around us as we watched the passengers off-boarded one double-seat cage at a time.

I finally summoned up nerve enough to ask, "So that you don't hurl on me, may I ride with you?" She shrugged a casual yes as if it were no big deal as we each paid our buck and took our tandem seat.

"What's your name?"

"Skyler."

I asked her to spell her name, which she did. Then after I gave her my name she said, "One S or two?" I laughed and asked if she was from Tucson as the big wheel turned. She told me her folks moved here from Chicago when she was twelve. As we climbed higher and higher, she pointed across the river to her trailer.

"You live by the chicken farm?"

Yeah . . . too close."

When we stopped at the apex of the wheel, swinging slightly as our hands held onto the metal safety bar in front of us, we could see downtown Tucson and the city lights. "I get motion sickness if I don't smoke a joint," she said. Then she asked if I'd mind while she looked deep into my eyes for something. I said I didn't mind as long as she shared. She rummaged inside her stained little buckskin purse for a joint and lighter that was inside a coin purse that she snapped shut like a cap gun.

We hit the joint discreetly as we turned. I could see that Skyler was also bothered by the pollen. I had seen her red eyes and heard her sniffles. I could feel her staring at my profile as

I looked at the purple mountains that were close and lit by a vanilla moon that was full.

Skyler laughed when she thought of something she did earlier in the day. She told me how she took her sister's records and saucered them into the riverbed. I asked her if there was ever water in the river. "Oh, yeah. It can rain hard and I've seen water all the way to the top of the banks. It's a trip."

I told her I was from San Diego and visiting my dad. I wasn't going to talk about Eddie, but my thoughts were racing. I told her I was just getting to know my dad. She wanted to know what I meant. This kind of angry fury came over me to not explain things, so I changed the subject while we turned and shared this puddle of fear caused by the weed. Both of us were paranoid and insecure; this was our common ground, our statement to the world that we've joined them in the same fear that every generation before us has sustained.

I asked if she liked living here. "Sometimes. It gets too hot in the summer, and my allergies bother me now and in the spring."

We talked about indoor air pollution, and I told her about this great air purifier my mom got me. She told me that when she gets rich, she's going to have one of those environmentally safe homes where the air is filtered — with no pets or carpet. Then she said something I'll never forget, "God, at my parents' place there's barking dogs and roosters crowing night and day. Cocka-doodle-do! I figured out they're saying, 'People lie to you! People lie to you! Cocka-doodle-do," she laughed.

"That's funny. How'd you come up with that — people lie to you?"

"Well, they do, don't they?" She put her joint out on the bar in front of us and returned it to her purse as I thought of those words made by a rooster.

We strolled around the carnival, and between us we made fun of the people we thought weird. A few of the kids knew Skyler because she had babysat them. I noticed that her mouth was always scowling like she was ready for combat. That's when it occurred to me that I attract certain negative people who never challenge me to grow up.

We walked toward the River Walk and headed for the other side of the bridge where Eddie and I had been today. We shuffled our feet with this flinty scuff over the track's pebbled parking lot. On the dark River Walk, a distant ambulance wailed which caused packs of coyotes to howl in the darkness in several places. This was a modern suburbia that sounded so alive with nature's prowl all around us.

When the wind was gone, as on this night, the stifling dryness made me wish I had a third nostril to bring fresh oxygen to my pollen-soaked body. I asked Skyler why she had "NO" tattooed on her back. She laughed when she explained that it was "NO WAY" and that the "WAY" was below the "NO."

At First Avenue I followed her turn left onto the narrow sidewalk of the traffic-heavy bridge above the river. I walked behind her. That's when I noticed she had a tattoo on the nape of her neck that was some Gothic symbol that flashed a dangerous and evil image in passing headlights above the desert river some twenty feet below in darkness.

On the south side of the bridge, Skyler made her way after turning a sharp left and down a desert path that led to the same underpass where Eddie and I rested in the shade today. There was that same huddled group of young men with their baggy pants hanging low as they called out to Skyler, "Hey, Sky. We need some weed, man."

She yelled back to them, "I'm out of stash."

I knew she wasn't really out of stash. Soon we left the grumbling trio and headed east on the River Walk toward her trailer. I told her I'd seen her friends earlier when I was with my dad. When she handed me a lit roach I asked her, "Why'd you tell them you were out?"

"They were high on meth. I wouldn't waste my little stash on those freaks. You do drugs?"

"Just pot. They called you Sky."

"That's my nickname."

We walked close to the river's railing without saying much until we got close to Aunt Sara and Eddie's condos directly across the river. Skyler stopped in front of an old lime-green skirted trailer that had covered parking on both sides of it. A fenced dog barked at us until Skyler barked back, "Shut up, Perry!" Perry was a brown cocker spaniel with a white neck and belly. She said that Perry was old — fifteen.

Although her parents and two younger sisters were in bed, Skyler was not concerned about waking them. She banged shut cupboards and drawers when making us iced tea; she even turned on her stereo and played a rock song loud as we sat at the kitchen table and talked above the music. "Don't worry. My parents sleep like logs and my sisters go to sleep wearing headphones."

We went outside and sat under the carport on plastic lawn furniture facing the river as Perry whined from behind the fence to join us.

Both of us were restless and bored with our lives. She asked me how long I would be in Tucson. I told her I wasn't sure, that my dad said something about exploring Arizona.

"Oh, yeah? That's cool."

The pollen was bothering me, so I told Sky goodbye and rubbed my eyes raw until I was nearly blind. While crossing the bridge in the moon's glow, I wasn't sure if I'd see Skyler again.

Fall Hard — Heal Fast

Eddie let Les drive his new car at the outset of their week-long excursion. Father and son would get lost in Arizona while really getting to know each other. They stopped in downtown Phoenix to have lunch because Les had never been to Phoenix. He liked tall buildings — the higher the better.

After lunch they went for a walk in the shade of the city's skyscrapers. It felt to Les like he was spending time with a peer rather than a parent. That's when Les asked Eddie if he could call him Eddie instead of Dad.

Eddie drove them out of Phoenix on Highway 87 to Payson. Payson was cool — some twenty degrees cooler than Phoenix. Pine trees were everywhere, one of the few trees Les wasn't allergic to. Les would keep his window down and breathe in deeply the fresh air.

"I can breathe up here!" he exclaimed to Eddie.

And Eddie would do the same thing, breathe in the air like a kid on his first road trip. Little things like that reminded Les that Eddie was in reality about the same age he was. There would be no pearls of wisdom coming from a man who'd been asleep since his early twenties and who had completely missed those years when a man matures from failure.

It was during their short drive north to Tonto Natural Bridge State Park that Eddie realized they were about to share something neither had ever seen before. The parking lot was nearly empty. On foot they headed down the valley toward the world's largest travertine bridge that stands 183 feet high and just above a massive 400-foot-long wind tunnel that was 150 feet wide at its widest point.

Hundreds of stone and timbered steps led them down like pack mules to the sandstone bottom where pools of cold natural springs invited them in from the Arizona heat. "Caves!" Les blurted while pointing to the shaded holes lining one side of the immense shadowed tunnel.

Along their trek down they stopped at the several observation points and let the awesome wonder of nature fill their entire visual capacity. This bridge of nature had the power to quiet the busy mind, and the two men beheld what nature can do over millions of years.

"This is all so perfect, Eddie."

"'Perfect' is the perfect word for this place. Something like this reminds me that we are all a part of this, related to it all. Imagine how it must have been for that prospector we read about who was running from Apaches when he discovered this place. And how he hid in one of the caves until it was safe, then he came back and lived here. What that must have been like . . . living out here all alone."

"Yeah," Les mumbled in agreement. "Ya know, I've always been alone no matter where I am or who I'm with. Most of the time I'm not liking it. But then every once in a while I'll be really content and okay with it. I'd like to feel that way all the time."

Bursts of light fell around them, made from scudding clouds moving across the sun as Les and Eddie moved along the narrow pathway just above the edge of the quartzite floor that was wet with slick mold and cold water splashings coming from secret places above them. Behind them were shouts from children swimming in cold water.

Les broke away from the trail and made his way down to the floor some thirty yards away from the entrance to the vast tunnel. Eddie followed, though he was wary of the detour as he heeded the warning sign to stay off the slippery bottom. Each removed his shoes to feel the invitingly cool, smooth surface of the rock. Gingerly they stepped across the cool patch of slime mold.

Just then Les fell hard and fast, slapping the heel of his right hand on the rock surface to diminish the impact of his fall. Eddie cringed at the sound of bone hitting rock. Les was in awful pain, having to scoot on his rump to get off the slippery surface. His right hand had purpled fast above a red throbbing swelling that was numb from such a severe smacking.

Eddie had an idea and took them over to the natural springs pool. For an instant Eddie could see the pain in his son's almond-shaped green eyes that reminded him so much of Lauren.

They knew from their reading that this water was loaded with minerals, especially calcium, so they both peeled down to their boxers. Les's hand was really hurting when he inched his way into the ice-cold water ahead of Eddie. They howled from the cold water in the pool that was too deep to touch bottom, so they dog-paddled and laughed and shivered with gasps of air forced out of their lungs by the cold water.

"Just imagine that Natives centuries ago bathed in this very spot," Eddie stammered to his shivering son.

Les could only nod while keeping his pale body afloat in the coldest water he'd ever experienced. Innately he swallowed big gulps of the mineral-rich water.

Some forty minutes later they hurried like nervous squirrels to the sunlight where they donned their clothes.

"How's your hand?"

Les was amazed how the swelling had gone down and the purple had vanished. He inhaled through his clear nostrils deeply all the way through his sinuses. "Eddie, my head isn't clogged. It's always stuffed up with pollen and dust. I can really breathe! This is incredible!"

Eddie looked at Les's eyes and could see that they were clear and lit with a spark of light. "Must be the water. It cleared out all those toxins you're allergic to."

Les looked back at the pool of water when Eddie told him that even his face had cleared up. Les undressed and jumped back into the pool and kept his head submerged most of the time. "I should live here!" Les laughed.

Eddie was amazed that this was his son. I tried to tell Eddie how much of the boy's life he had missed, but Eddie cut me off. Eddie just sat down on a big shaded rock and watched his pale son turning like a seal in the pool. All Eddie could see was a young man with hope in his heart taking in more gulps of water. Yes, Eddie was all there with none of my chatter between his ears. He wondered if Les was in his Blue River, a place he himself had found in Oklahoma. Were he and his son sharing a place of peace that Les would also call his Blue River?

Just then buried emotional waves of guilt surfaced for Eddie. They were about his inner-knowing that Lauren was pregnant and that he consciously chose to stay with his books instead of taking responsibility for the life he knew he'd created with Lauren.

And there in the water before him was this red-faced young man who felt alive in his new body. He dog-paddled close to where Eddie was sitting and confessed that he'd peed in the pool. Eddie laughed with Les as he threatened retribution by tossing Les's clothes into the water.

A bit later when they sat together in the sunlight Eddie said, "Your mother told me you like to write poetry."

"Yeah, a little." Les was feeling good and told Eddie that he should live near the refreshing, healing water.

"Feeling good, huh?"

"Yeah, but I'm afraid it'll wear off." Les inhaled deeply through his clear sinuses. "I don't want to lose this feeling,

Eddie. Why is it hard to hold anything good for long? I mean, that's why I smoke pot and do things that are dumb. If something like water can make me feel this good . . ."

"Hey! I've got a few empty gallon containers in my trunk. Why don't we fill 'em with this water and you can drink some every day. See what happens."

"Great!" Les smiled.

No Plan . . . No Map . . . Lost

Les and Eddie spent the night at a Show Low motel on twin single beds. They'd left the unscreened window cranked open and listened to a thunderstorm for hours. The rolling thunder in the mountain town was so incredibly loud and close that their bodies would shiver from every rumble as they talked.

"When you were writing, when did you write?" Les asked.

"I don't remember things like that."

"Do you remember thinking about what you were going to write?"

"No, I was just learning to let it come to me."

"I haven't learned that," Les sighed.

"Try letting it come out of you. Something will. Of course, that doesn't mean it's any good."

"So don't force it?"

"Right. I might not have waited long enough for the real good stuff to come out, but I tried not to let my mind tell me what to write. I remember that much."

"That's so cool."

"Sara did the cool stuff. She made my book ten times better, and she was incredible to market it the way she did."

"You mean after that creep died and she went to Europe to help those people get their life savings back?"

"Yeah . . . and a bunch of other stuff."

"What I think is cool is, like, you're my age in experience, but you're really forty."

"Yeah, I guess I can say I know what it's like to be your age and mean it. I can remember I had no clue where my life was going. I had no college and no desire to go."

"That's how I feel."

"But I got lucky because I have a sister who made my book into something I couldn't."

They listened to the storm's rumblings and were satisfied to say nothing.

The next morning they had a big breakfast and got directions to Chevelon Lake west of Heber. On the way they saw several deer grazing close to the road. Les had never seen wild deer before, so he asked Eddie to pull over.

The lake was not easy to find until they spotted a truck with a boat in tow and followed it. The blue waters made them wish they had fishing gear, but they decided on a long walk around the lake. Les told Eddie about meeting Skyler at the carnival and writing about her in his journal. He told his dad how he smoked her pot on the ferris wheel and later how they ran into her friends under the overpass.

"They were the same guys we saw there. They wanted weed from her right away. She told them she didn't have any, but she did. The way those guys looked — so disappointed. They didn't talk at all. It was pathetic. And, Eddie, I saw myself in them. Lost. No clue. Aunt Sara's been sending my mom money, so I always have money for things. I think the money makes me lazy. My friends that didn't go to school went into the service. My mom says I don't have to know what I want to do, but she'd like to see me take an interest in something. Eddie, how come you never got married?"

"To your mom?"

"No, just married."

"I don't know much about why I did or didn't do something. It's a blur. I'm like you . . . except I'm not worried about my future."

"Because you're rich?"

"Maybe. I know now that Blue River is a state of mind I control better now."

"But if you weren't rich you might use your mind more and have more worries."

"Yes, but the difference is I'm aware of that now. You can slow things down by knowing that . . . and at least feel better in your skin."

Les's allergies weren't bothering him in this higher elevation, even though Eddie could see that he'd lost the glow on his face he'd gotten at Tonto. They observed more deer on the other side of the lake while a family of ducks floated along the shoreline following them at the same speed. Eddie stopped and showed Les how the ducks stopped with them, their heads and webbed feet turning to the shore to see what the visitors were up to.

They came upon an elderly couple fishing from cushioned aluminum lawn chairs. Their lines were stretched out into the lake with their poles angled and elevated on a red tackle box. The woman was reading a used paperback while the old man puffed on an unlit cigar under a wide-brimmed straw hat that concealed his eyes.

"Catch anything?" Eddie asked the couple.

"Nothin' much," the old man grumbled.

Eddie thought the old man looked like the ferry captain who had nearly cost him his life. Eddie even asked the old man if he had ever run a ferry in Oklahoma.

"Can't say I've ever done that."

They walked on circling the lake. Then they sat on a picnic table facing the lake by Eddie's car.

"I can remember being your age and having no plans . . . no map for the future. I was lost. That old man back there reminded me of that time I was at the bottom of that lake in my van. I can recall for a split second that I was glad my books were ruined and I didn't have to sell them anymore. I'll bet that in everyone's life there's a moment when ya have to decide something really important that tells you what you'll do with your life. Mine was calling your mother to have her visit me in Tulsa. Because of that decision, you are here now. I never had any moments like we're having now with my dad. It's all so incredible, Les.

They drove back down Route 260 to Payson and headed north on 87. It was a perfect day to explore Arizona. They drove like rubber-necking tourists through Prescott and Cottonwood, and then up to the panoramic heights of Jerome, the mining town 7,800 feet up on Mingus Mountain.

Les was impressed with Jerome with its row of businesses squeezed together with gift shops that sold Arizona art. Les kept telling Eddie he felt like he'd been there before. Then Eddie told Les that he'd sold his book there and perhaps that's why he felt a connection.

They spent the afternoon in Jerome going from shop to shop after having lunch. Backtracking to Prescott they picked up 89 and headed north to Williams where they would pick up 64 on their way to the Grand Canyon. They got a motel in Williams where all of a sudden both of them came down with a severe intestinal virus. For two days they stayed in the motel in double beds riding out an awful virus that kept them running to the bathroom several times an hour. It was the kind of awful flu that left from both ends at once, and it would not let them sleep even for a minute.

Being sick together bonded them more than anything else. They stayed in bed watching TV in a stupor. Finally, on the second night they got some sleep.

Late the next morning they left for the Grand Canyon and fasted. The view from the North Rim was new to them. Side by side they took in the view with suspended awe. Eddie told Les that he recalled thinking he'd see this view one day with the woman he loved.

"Sorry to disappoint ya," Les smiled. "It makes me wish I'd brought Skyler with me to see this."

"You think you and Skyler will get to know each other?"

"I hope so, " Les laughed. "But I think she has a bunch of problems."

"She was probably raised with parents who have a bunch of problems . . . like me. You have to learn to live well on your own. But ya have to want that."

I knew what Eddie was telling Les was true, because he never once let me run him like I used to.

North of Flagstaff Eddie and Les tried to learn how to ski. Of course, Eddie rented all their equipment and paid for their lesson. But all they managed to get were gravity lessons and an hour of laughter. Still, they had the best time.

The next morning upon waking up in a Flagstaff motel, their bodies ached from the ski lesson; so they decided to head south back to the Tonto natural springs to soak in the healing waters.

Skyler's Warning

Again the salubrious water at Tonto restored their road-weary bodies to tingling aliveness and sent them back to Tucson feeling fresh and ready for new beginnings. While soaking at Tonto, Les confessed to his dad that he would have to stop putting drugs into his body if he ever wanted to feel good naturally. That's when Eddie told Les that he'd pay for his schooling anywhere. Upon hearing that, Les cried openly — something he'd never done. It's not that he wanted to go to college; rather, it was the fact that someone believed in him enough to support his future. He said he didn't want to burden his mother with school loans since he wasn't sure what he wanted to do with his life.

After recounting their trip with Sara during dinner at her place, Les headed for the bridge that led to Skyler. Her trailer overlooked a twelve-foot-deep cement canal that angled off the main riverbed. When he knocked on her trailer door, behind him wind chimes hanging from the carport tinkled from the ominous wind coming with black storm clouds above the Catalinas. The sun had just vanished below the blue horizon and darkness came fast. No roosters crowed and the racket from barking dogs was missing as powerful distant rumblings of thunder came from behind the mountains and reverberated that something rare was coming.

Sky knew it was coming as she lay wrapped in her blanket. When she heard a faint knock on her door, she figured it was a delivery for her parents. She was shocked to see Les at her door. And he was surprised to see a nose ring piercing her nostril and a smaller one through her lower lip, and her red hair now had broad streaks of purple on one side of her head.

Sky stepped outside in her bare feet with her blanket yet wrapped around her, as if she didn't want him inside. "How was your trip?"

"We had a blast," Les smiled as he watched her light a half-spent cigarette that had been saved in an ashtray on the white plastic patio table. He sat down on one of the four plastic chairs near her and could see that she'd been doing drugs recently. "What've you been up to?" he asked.

"I got a job at this really cool coffeehouse near U of A. I work nights. I have to be there at eight. Want to go with me?"

"Sure."

They sat watching the storm forming above the Catalinas as wind came in furious gusts. "The river might run wild tonight," she warned. "I don't want to miss it if it does."

"I'd like to see it too."

"A friend of mine, Lisa, got me the job. She's got the best weed."

Les was not too excited to have anything her friend might have; he was feeling pretty good without it.

In the falling darkness, Les could see that the desert growth in the Rillito had changed to a golden brittleness from recent cooler nights. He could not imagine water running wild as Sky warned.

"Yeah, I'd like to see that," he affirmed absently.

I Am Les Dense

Skyler drove her dad's Mercury to work. Les rode along after calling Eddie to tell him he'd be home late. Eddie said he'd leave a key under the front doormat.

The Java House was crowded with dozens of college students. Some were clad in casual earth tones, but black was the most popular color. Groups of friends sat at mismatched tables on high-back wooden chairs painted different colors. There was a small stage with a lone light shining down on the miked podium.

These were the young artists of Tucson with their sketch pads poking out of their colorful backpacks that held textbooks, notebooks, and their drug of choice stashed in secret places. This is what Les saw and wrote about in his notebook as he sat at a table for two at the back of the big room.

He could see Sky working behind the tall counter, her red and purple-streaked hair pinned up and scattered with fallen strands without concern for appearance. She was learning the register after being shown how to make coffee. Huge stainless-steel coffee makers towered beside rows of black coffee mugs stacked three high and flanking both sides of the brewing machines. Bean grinders and coffee makers running continually kept the pungent aroma of fresh coffee in the room.

Lisa was Sky's best friend from high school. Les was like Eddie — he'd observe people without labeling them, noting things about them that most would not see. He noticed Lisa's painted fingernails when she brought him a cup of coffee and introduced herself. Her nails were short and chipped in places and had been colored hurriedly with a purplish-pink polish.

Poetry readings began. Young poets lashed out from the podium at an insane world, using dark prose that uttered their fruitless attempts to accept lives of discontentment as seen by their own minds. After hearing a few of the readings, Les decided to put some of his own thoughts on paper.

Sky saw him writing alone at his table and did not bother him when she filled his mug. A short time later Skyler was surprised to hear Les's voice reading to the room.

"I am Les Dense. At last I feel free. Or at least free of enough stuff to call myself Les Dense. A trip with my dad to Tonto. A view of the canyon walls. Made me feel lighter. Craving things unknown. Yes, darkness all around us. Yet we've all made it so. Impossible to see it. When a house is built alone."

Skyler was part of the smattering of applause as Les went back to his table and crumpled his words into a ball. But Sky picked up the ball of paper and put it in her back pocket; she told him she wanted to save it.

"Why save it?" he asked her.

"That's the only way I'll remember it."

Les's mind was busy and he wanted to stop its chatter. He had told Eddie on their trip, "My mind, the way it is, will keep me stuck in low self-esteem and confusion. I really know that."

At her break time, Sky dropped a joint into his shirt pocket. Lisa had given it to her. That's what she told him when he looked at her.

Lisa walked into the back alley with them on their break. They passed the joint between them as the girls chatted about other employees. Les found out later that Lisa had given Sky some pills that she took with a cup of coffee after their break. Lisa didn't even know what the pills were, yet that didn't stop the girls from taking them.

I really don't believe Les would have taken any of those pills. Even though Eddie and I haven't known Les that long, I still believe Les wasn't that dense.

After Sky got off work, she and Les sat on her patio looking at the dark river. Although the storm had stayed in the mountains and hadn't posed a threat to Tucson, the river held some evidence that heavy rain had fallen nearby somewhere and was making its way through the desert.

Skyler told Les the Rillito Race Track would open the next morning. "I've got some free passes. Wanna go bet a couple races?" she asked.

Les remembered he still had most of his forty bucks Eddie had given him. "Sure."

Princess Sky

Eddie and Sara had breakfast without Les. When their guest finally got up it was noon. Sara was concerned about Les sleeping late and about his pot-smoking and how it might mix adversely with his allergy pills. After a shower and no breakfast, Les told his hosts he was going to the races next door with Sky.

From his patio Eddie watched Les meet Sky on the bridge and walk to the track parking lot that was filling fast. Eddie told Sara he was going to the track to watch a few races. He was really concerned about how haggard Les looked when he left. Sara gave him a pair of binoculars that she'd used to watch rabbits in the river. "If he's taking drugs I want him to go home," Sara informed her brother.

Eddie blended into the crowd after buying a program. He finally spotted the couple with the aid of binoculars from his seat high in the grandstand. Eddie could see the free-spirited Sky with her exposed tattooed skin and jewelry on her neck and fingers. Her orange belly t-shirt was easy to find in the crowd. Both wore sunglasses and shared a cigarette from the pack she removed from her waistband as they stood behind the front railing watching the end of the second race.

He could see why his son was attracted to the girl; she had a cute shape and a wild playfulness about her. When Eddie lowered the binoculars, an inexplicable feeling of regret over his own missed youth overcame him — how he'd slept through these formative years his son was now beginning. Eddie realized he'd had to nearly die in order to be here now — and that nobody was going around spying on him.

At the track, surrounded by smells of dust and cologne mixed with beer and popcorn, I was able to tell Eddie he had no business spying on Les when Les was being Les — especially since Eddie had failed at being Eddie when he was young. Believe me, I wanted to press Eddie more and tell him that Les was living his life the only way he knew how with an absent father most of his life. And that now is not the time to try changing the young man when the great E. L. Dense himself had dismissed his son from his consciousness some two decades ago.

There was no denying that Eddie had failed in many ways to live his life — until now. Now he would not listen to me or allow what I was saying to emotionally move him. Instead, Eddie flooded his body with breath and silent space and kept his attention inside his body without any noise from me.

Just as Eddie was watching the beginning of the third race with Sara's glasses, that damn Slow Eddie said, "Fast Eddie wants to live in your head just as Fast Les wants to live in Les's head. Help Les learn to quiet Fast Les as you have learned to quiet Fast Eddie. Eddie, you must give that gift to your son."

Eddie focused the glasses on the young couple at the end of the race. They were excited because Sky had picked the winning horse. She kissed Les on his cheek and hugged him excitedly before leaving to collect her winnings. Eddie opened his racing program and saw that the winning horse in the third race was Princess Sky, and he recalled hearing Les refer to Skyler as "Sky."

River Bed

Later that same night after they left the racetrack, Les and his "Princess Sky" walked down the Rillito's concrete ramp on Sky's side of the river. She warned Les to be careful of the horse dung because equestrians used the ramp to reach the sandy earth on the river bottom.

Princess Sky had a little meth that she wanted to share with her new friend from San Diego. Les was reluctant to try it because he'd never tried it before and was afraid of it. However, Les still had his low self-esteem combined with the fact that his allergies were making him miserable. He'd decided not to take his allergy pills because of the intense paranoia pot gave him when he mixed it with his medication.

As he helped Sky up onto the three-foot-high circular concrete ledge of the power pole base that was near the middle of the river, Les confided to her, "I'm weak . . . from my allergies. I'll try anything that takes away what I feel like now." Then he helped her spread out a dark blue blanket on the ledge that she'd brought from home.

They shared the evil drug and sat Indian style while facing the full moon that was high in the eastern sky. The moon's light illuminated desert shadows of brush and sand and a thirty-foot cottonwood tree some distance away. They were quiet, sitting on the cushioned cement loft staring into the fleeting senses of their drugged minds when a distant ambulance wailed, causing coyotes to howl around them. The desert dogs were hunting rabbit and eerily kept up their own siren song directed at the full vanilla moon that appeared to Les and Sky to be sinking fast.

The next day neither Sky nor Les remembered being together.

Three nights after their numb passion on the power pole ledge, they were going there again — this time without a blanket and no drugs. It was around 11:30 at night, a half-hour after Sky had gotten off work. They had agreed the night before to meet at the "river bed," a name Sky gave their meeting place. She'd left her blanket there and had to retrieve it the next afternoon when she awoke in her bed chilled with cotton mouth and chapped lips from the drugs.

Sky could only recall certain things Les had told her on the "river bed." He talked about religion and politics, two things she deplored; and yet she was mesmerized by his words she recalled after the numb and hazy night on that ledge. "I truly believe our generation has to change the politics of our country by reaching out to every unregistered voter who believes God is the source of all life forms and that God has no interest whatsoever in organized religions. Religion and politics are driven by the male ego and will keep us from being united by using their greedy egos to justify their insane identities with myths — things that can never last."

Now, three nights after their first time on the "river bed," Sky wished she had brought her blue blanket as she waited on the ledge for Les to meet her.

Les woke up abruptly from his nap in Eddie's condo. Looking at the clock he knew that Sky had gotten off work a half-hour earlier and was probably waiting for him on the power pole ledge. His hands were sweating as he walked to their meeting place carrying a copy of *Blue River* to give to her.

Les could see that another storm was brewing above the Catalinas as he turned left after crossing the pedestrian bridge. He could just make out the orange glow from Sky's cigarette on the power pole ledge some three hundred yards off in the black void of the Rillito.

All of Tucson could see that the night sky was ominous with distant rumblings of thunder and monster lightning flashes forming electric spider webs. Of the two of them, only Sky knew of the Rillito flood warning issued by the media.

Down the dark ramp he went, often stepping on dried balls of horse dung with both feet. He joked to Sky that he had scraped a ton of horse crap off his shoes at the bottom of the ramp. Gusts of humid wind blew in his face on his way to the "river bed" as the storm above the mountains dropped an inch of rain every twenty minutes.

Sky was glad to see him, although her greeting contradicted it. "No drugs tonight."

Les told her he didn't care about that and started telling her about *Blue River* when he handed her the copy he'd brought for her. He described vividly how he dreamed of a worldwide Blue River that was a crystal-clear, unpolluted space that would remain unreachable until the majority of human beings became conscious and stopped the insanity of ego and separation that dominated society. Speaking quickly, Les recounted Dave's father's metaphor for Blue River that was in Eddie's book. "Sky, it's like the horizon seen through your windshield while driving on the open road. It's this clear blue space that's so quiet and beautiful . . . it quiets your mind. And if you hold that gap of silence, you get closer and closer to your true inner purpose for being here . . . right now. Do you see it, Sky? Each of us has to find our Blue River — one at a time. Only individuals can clean up the planet."

"That sounds so idealistic. Overpopulation will wipe us out. That's history."

"Sky, if the world was conscious, we'd populate the planet to a living degree that was balanced. The real issue is that people our age are not organized. We delay action because we want to delay growing up . . . because we fear the future."

Sky noticed how Les's eyes were lit with an incredible light when he told her he was changing now, that he was not going to put any drugs in his body, adding, "I'm going to clean up my inner space and see if that brings out my inner purpose that truly makes a difference. Like in my dad's book, I know it has to make a difference for the people who think such endless thoughts that keep running their lives into this collective insanity that rules the world. Religion, politics, corporations, the media, crime, war, poverty . . . they're all ego-driven things born of fear, greed, and a lack of consciousness."

All Sky could do was nod her head. She was thinking how he'd changed since they were last on the "river bed." Her busy mind was telling her that he was losing interest in being with her, and fearful thoughts of doubt and rejection roared through her head.

Another kind of roar was coming from seven miles away, behind the purplish-black Catalinas. Sky told Les that it if started to rain they'd have to leave. For a few minutes she listened for approaching rain, until she heard something she'd only heard a few times since living there. "Listen!" she warned.

"I don't hear anything."

She hushed him as she stood facing east into the darkness of the river channel. Nothing. Nothing. Then only minutes later it came — the sound of water hitting dry vegetation.

"It's coming," she warned as Les stood beside her.

"What's coming?"

"Water," she said without averting her stare.

"Should we get outta here?" he asked.

"You can if you want. I'm staying here."

She also told Les that the water came fast, and that last year the water reached to within a foot of the ledge they were on.

Just then the water came. It flowed with such incredible speed and force that they both stood behind the power pole to avoid the rushing current. It seemed like a safe place at first, but then the water began covering their feet and splashing hard all around them. They huddled together and held the pole tightly. They laughed together for a long time until they were getting soaked and freezing cold.

When the water was rushing up to their waists, they tried swimming for the ramp. They jumped off the ledge together in the dark. Les had yelled for Sky to grab the ramp's railing before they were swept past it by the rushing current. He helped raise Sky to the railing and she grabbed it, but Les was swept on down the river. The last she saw of Les was when he crashed headfirst into the cement embankment, then she saw him go limp as if he were unconscious.

Father to Son

Eddie stood on the pedestrian bridge on the other side of the dry-again Rillito. He was looking down at the wooden white cross that Sky had planted, marking the spot where Eddie found his son's lifeless body floating face-down in six feet of water covered with brush and debris.

The nightmare of losing Les was five days old. Sara was with Lauren in San Diego after Sara flew her nephew's body back to be cremated. Eddie was again recalling the events of that terrible night.

Eddie had been awakened by Sky's pounding on his door the night of the flood. She had hopped to his place on one leg after breaking her ankle when she dropped onto the other side of the ramp. Eddie had carried the soaked Sky back to the ramp where she kept screaming that Les was washed away by the current. From the moon's light, Eddie could see the cuts on Sky's face made by rushing debris as she kept wailing about how Les had saved her life.

Near the end of the bridge Eddie had to put Sky down, for he could see a white figure floating against the embankment where the cross stood now. The next half-hour they were in shock. Eddie was trembling from the cold water and fatigue after swimming some seventy yards from the ramp out to Les, then swimming his dead son back to the ramp, all the while knowing this was going to devastate Lauren.

Sky had called the police while Eddie waited on the ramp with Les's body. That's when Eddie found the copy of his book wedged in Les's waistband. Slow Eddie talked to Les's dead body, "You are too young to die, Les. Just when you saw your life changing for the better, you lost it. This is all so unfair."

Now Sky stood on crutches beside Eddie, her foot and ankle in a cast as she too stared down at the white cross. Eddie noticed that her nose ring was gone and her hair was its natural red color. "Are you okay?" he asked her softly as a rooster crowed "people lie to you." She nodded yes, keeping her eyes on the cross.

While still looking down she told Eddie about the poem Les read at the coffeehouse and how he had really enjoyed their Arizona trip. "He talked about the pool of water at Tonto that healed his hand and made his allergies go away. He told me you helped him not fear growing up."

"I want to know all about Les, everything you can remember. I want to write about him, and you know things I don't."

For two hours she talked about Les. When she had told Eddie everything she knew, she told him she put the cross there to remind herself to live free of drugs, the way Les was headed. They cried together. Eddie put his arm around Sky and told her it was Les's destiny to change them, adding, "I'll always remember he liked you and enjoyed being with you."

He hugged her goodbye and walked away, across the bridge to his side of the river where lime-green palo verde trees shaded half-burrowed desert squirrels and lizards that imitated scorpions by curling their tails when scuttling across the River Walk.

Eddie had never in his life experienced such terrible pain and all-consuming grief. He could not bear the thought of living his life without his son. Before his fateful ferry ride in Oklahoma, he had spent his life hiding behind his fears. Once he awoke from his coma, he spent his life hiding behind his money. Something had to change; somehow he had to go forward, facing reality and living in the moment. "There's no looking back for you, Eddie Dense. You have to move on and live better — somehow."

That was Eddie's voice; not mine. Eddie's mind was not separated from him and running him now. I got to say three final words to him: "Wake up, Eddie."

Now I Know

The old man gingerly bent down to the lake's packed-sand shoreline. He knew this had to be the same van-driving young man who had been a passenger on his ferry. He'd never lost a passenger — let alone a vehicle — in his thirty years as a ferry captain until he saw the van go into the lake during the storm. He tapped his passenger's shoulder. "You okay, young man?"

Eddie's eyes opened lazily, fluttering from sand caked on his lashes. He felt different. There were waves of energy flowing from head to toe with every breath, and it was happening without any effort on his part. He picked and flicked sand off his eyelashes. His clothes were stiff and dried from the sun and the wind, and he had sand caked at his knees, elbows, and ankles. His shoes were still on him and squeaked as he sat up on Sara's gift that had saved his life.

Because of his aching arthritis, the old man couldn't help his passenger get to his feet; yet he hovered close as if willing the young man to come alive.

"How long have I been here?" Eddie asked groggily.

"A couple hours, at least. I thought you drowned. Worst storm I've seen in thirty years on this lake. It turned me around and blew me a thousand yards west," he pointed. "By the time it cleared, I wasn't sure what happened to you. Never seen anything like it in all my years. I was just about to call the law when I saw you here."

Every tree and blade of grass glowed an aliveness that was new to Eddie. Jenna had told him that this would be his first sign he had reached his Blue River.

"Can I give you a lift? I can take ya to Joplin. There's a hospital there."

Eddie got to his feet on shaky legs after folding his mattress in half and tucking it against his side and under his arm. *I dreamed it all,* Eddie kept telling himself on the way to Joplin in the old man's truck. The ferry captain asked his passenger if he had any money to get home. Eddie found twenty-three wet dollars in his pocket.

"Yeah, I got enough to get home," which meant to him that it was all perfect because he was home right now, living in the moment for the very first time in his young life.

There were moments when Eddie waited to hear what I had to say now; however, I wasn't the same mind Eddie had before he hit the bottom of that lake. There was nothing I could say. I only knew what Eddie was doing from moment to moment. He was no longer being run by his past.

In Joplin Eddie finger-combed his hair in the mirror after washing his face in a truck stop restroom. He was relieved that his face had not aged, and he didn't mind at all that his Dense teeth were still bucked. As with Dave and Jenna, he could see that he also had a luminous light emanating from his eyes. He smiled at the new light, picked up his mattress, and exited the restroom.

In the truck stop convenience store, he was drawn to a rack of paperbacks. It reminded him of his book and those ass-backwards copies at the bottom of the lake. He thought of his briefcase that held his writing and his list of customers — all gone. He felt nothing as he stood there slowly spinning that rack of books. "This is good," he told himself with a new grin on his face that strangers appeared to like. Eddie was truly grateful and he felt so — another first for him.

Within ten minutes Eddie was getting a free ride from a trucker who told Eddie he was headed for Omaha. Eddie listened to his loquacious driver for most of the five-hour drive up I-29. For the first time in his life, he was listening without the endless mind chatter Jenna had talked about. Things were definitely different since he woke up on the shore of that lake in Oklahoma. Before I would have told Eddie that this guy was boring me with his talk about how he had to pay child support for his three kids even though his ex-wife had remarried a guy "with a squat pot full of money."

Something strange happened. As Eddie truly listened to the man gripe about his problems and how "the country had gone to hell," the trucker seemed to get less agitated and ended his diatribe on a positive note, adding, "Well, I guess since they're my kids, I gotta help support 'em. It's a way to stay in their lives since I'm on the road so much."

Not long after they left Missouri and crossed the Iowa state line, Eddie told his driver that he always took for granted all those truckers on the road and how lonely the job is. "Now I know you are part of a system that keeps us supplied with all the things we use year-round. I want you to know I appreciate what you do and how most men couldn't do what you do."

It was near sunset on Sunday evening when Eddie had the trucker drop him and his mattress at the I-29 exit nearest to FIKSHEN. Instead of walking east to see his family, he went west toward the river to the very spot where he had found Dave and Jenna. There was no thinking back, no remembering the loss of life here; it was as if the destiny Jenna had talked about was here — right now.

His back was to the flowing river. He could hear it moving south mixed with the sounds of birds in song all around him. At no other time in his young life could he recall "Being" where he was. He was content and giving no thoughts to the future or the past. He was now here for the first time. He was cold and his body shivered.

The way to FIKSHEN was new to him, though everything along this path had always been there. This was the double-tired trail that Dave took when he drove Jenna to the river. How odd it seemed to be here now, closing in on FIKSHEN after escaping from the bottom of that lake. He had sold his book to the point that it had nearly killed him, and now he was here.

The green trailer was gone, now an empty lot. Three vehicles parked outside FIKSHEN meant his parents and Sara were home. When Eddie walked in the door with his mattress under his arm, they were surprised to see him. They were even more stunned when he told them about his ferry ride in Oklahoma and how Sara's gift had saved his life. Ike let his son know that he should call his insurance company the next morning and file a claim.

Right after Eddie had his first home-cooked meal in months, he called Lauren in San Diego to find out if she was pregnant. She wasn't. This threw Eddie, for he was certain his dream at the lake was pointing him to certain fatherhood. Lauren told Eddie she had met a nice guy on the plane when returning from Tulsa.

"And you're sure you didn't get pregnant in Tulsa?" Eddie asked again.

"Eddie, I should know whether or not I'm pregnant," she laughed.

They had a long chat, ending the call wishing each other the best. They expressed their love for one another and that was that. Eddie had no problem whatsoever accepting that Lauren was in love with another man. How strange this new reality was!

It was funny to Eddie how his family had heard every word he'd said to Lauren, for they were quietly seated in the living room waiting for him. He was compelled to let them know about Lauren's visit to Tulsa and how relieved he was that she wasn't pregnant.

Ike and Mary offered their son twenty hours of work per week for cleaning the bar after hours at ten bucks an hour, plus room and board at FIKSHEN. "Until you get on your feet . . . and want to do something else," Mary nodded.

To their surprise, Eddie accepted their offer, explaining, "That would be perfect for me now. I don't know what I'm going to do next. And thank you."

Ike, who had sold the house in Council Bluffs to pay for a remodeling and expansion project at the bar, gladly gave Eddie his old room back; although Mary was not looking forward to her husband's endless snoring and sharing her bed. Now Mary worked days and Ike closed the bar. This schedule allowed Mary to be asleep by the time Ike came home. One of Mary's new house rules, she informed Ike when Eddie went to bed, was that he had to take a shower when he came home after closing. "I don't want to smell the bar in my bed all night," she told him.

Ike complained that a shower would wake him up and he wouldn't get to sleep. They compromised: Ike didn't have to shower if he slept on the couch.

Later that night, lying in his old bed with the window cracked open and his foam mattress stowed under his bed, Eddie listened to the cold wind howling. His back was sore from his ordeal at the lake, and he was grateful to be here now. I was unable to pester Eddie about his past or future or the fact that he had no material possessions, only a few dollars and the clothes he could hear tumbling dry on the other side of his closet.

Eddie slept for twelve hours. Ever since he opened his eyes on the shore of the lake, I have been still. Now I know those invisible lyrics to Jenna's sweet harp music that crossed that space between their windows. They were notes that told Eddie we will not always be together to help each other live in this fear-dominated world run by the mind's addictions. All we can really do is help each other live well by showing each other that we must learn to live in new ways in a new world that runs on conscious presence. Yes, I am also new now.

I could list a thousand negatives about the world today, but Eddie won't let me. He's sleeping. And when he wakes up tomorrow I will serve him, because now he uses me when he wants to. He's in charge now. Before his long dream, and just before he hit the bottom of that big lake, I was like a mongrel dog that was allowed to bark day and night, coming and going as I pleased. Now I know who the master is: Eddie Dense. I'm happy to wait until he calls for me. Now I know it's time for me to serve Eddie.

Not the Last Chapter

Ever since Eddie awoke on the shore of the Grand Lake O' The Cherokees in Oklahoma, he has paid more attention to his breathing and to all nature around him. A stone, a tree, a bird — all things alive and sustained without man's intervention — are all respected for their eternal silence.

One day Eddie left home again with enough money to travel the country. He was scouting for what he wanted to do and where he'd do it. Every place he liked, yet no place suited him enough to settle there. From the hard sandy beaches of Corpus Christi to the very bottom of Key West, nothing in between in the South showed him what he was ready for.

He drove the Atlantic coastline all the way up to Maine in the spring, but he was chased out by black flies. Canada was explored from Nova Scotia to Manitoba until the weather turned cold and his money ran low, forcing him to leave Winnipeg and roll south on I-29 all the way home to Council Bluffs.

That's when he read the mysterious letter that had arrived months earlier from a gentleman in Minnesota. He was an elderly, self-published author who had a proposal for Eddie:

> *Dear Mr. Dense:*
>
> *I am an old man — too old to write my next book, my 18th novel. Someone sent me a copy of your book,* Blue River, *and I must say your marketing approach is similar to mine in many ways. I want you to help me write and sell my next book. I will give you one hundred thousand dollars to write my book from my notes — sort of a ghostwritten work with my name as the author. You will also get another one hundred thousand dollars to sell and deliver my last novel to my*

five thousand readers in roughly twelve hundred small Midwest towns.

It will take you about two years until the last book is gone. I have the best route to these towns on easy maps to follow. For each book, you will sell and collect twenty dollars rather easily I know, for they have bought my first seventeen novels this way. All my customers were women who owned small beauty shops in these twelve hundred towns. Some will yet be there; others will be gone, but you can find most of them or friends and relatives of them who will buy the book from you on behalf of my readers, or they will direct you to them if they are still in town.

Mr. Dense, I want you to keep every twenty dollars you collect from my five thousand copies for my select readers. That's the one hundred thousand dollars for selling and delivering my book, which should more than cover your expenses for the entire venture. You will gross two hundred thousand dollars in approximately twenty-seven months.

It should take you about three months to type my book from my notes. I prefer you work from my home and live here. Not bad for a hundred thousand, I should say!

I will explain to you while you are ghostwriting with me in my home why I have to get my last book into the hands of my readers before I die. You are probably asking yourself why I don't just mail these books to my readers. The answer to that is in my last book that you will help me write and distribute.

Please call me and let me know when to expect you, E. L. Dense.

Sincerely yours,
Wallis Pond
Kenwick, Minnesota

Frozen Moment

It took Eddie Dense several years and a chance encounter before answering the old writer's mysterious letter. The only novel Eddie had ever written was *Blue River.* The ordeal of writing, self-publishing, and selling his book door to door had so burned him out that he hadn't taken pen to paper since waking up at the edge of that massive lake in Oklahoma. He had let his father convince him that "there's no way to break into the literary mainstream without an agent and publisher to back ya," so he settled into a life of complacency, joining the manswarm and earning a living.

Eddie had taken over running Ike & Mary's after his father dropped dead while tending his bar and his mother had become nearly crippled with arthritis and unable to work. Sara had married and moved to Lincoln, Nebraska, where she was raising her two red-headed boys with Dense horse teeth; and Eddie continued to live in FIKSHEN, convincing himself that he could better care for his mother by living with her.

Ike & Mary's was a negative for Eddie. Not only was the stifling second-hand smoke bothering him to no end, the selling of alcohol to the rheumy-eyed regulars was killing his soul. After over four years of managing the affairs of Ike & Mary's, Eddie convinced his mother to sell the bar and he got a job driving a cab in Omaha. Driving a cab had been the best job for Eddie since he was now awake and seeing things clearly. He was able to stay independent and work on his own with no boss looking over his shoulder. He also liked observing the characters he'd chauffeur during the night.

Then one night Eddie had a chance encounter with fate. Arriving at the seedy little motel he'd been dispatched to, an old man gingerly climbed into the back of his cab.

"Where to?" Eddie asked, eyeing the man who was unmistakably familiar.

"Nearest liquor store. Not real particular," the old man said.

Although Eddie couldn't clearly see the face of his passenger in the dark cab's rearview mirror, he knew that voice and was nearly certain he was carrying the same old man who had ferried him across the lake on what turned out to be the ride of his life. In a rush, everything came back to Eddie — the thrill of putting pen to paper, the passion for telling the story, the sense of fulfillment when the words finally came together and the concept was made clear. Like a man who studies his face in the mirror then walks away and forgets what he looks like, Eddie realized he had forgotten who he really was. He had forgotten his first love — writing.

That night, for the first time in over five years, he started a new journal and wrote under his cab's dome light:

> *The real me was not at all in my book,* Blue River. *I was not even "here" when I wrote the damn thing. Now, I've quieted my mind long enough to know this is my "frozen moment" — that time in a young man's life when he must sink or swim in the unforgiving manswarm and find the way he truly wants to live. I must fly out of the nest and take this offer, writing about the experience along the way instead of observing life from a cab, talking to people in the mirror, and rushing back and forth over the same roads, shuttling the same regulars to their predictable destinations.*

Eddie decided to call the old man in Minnesota. He admitted to himself that his number-one reason for taking the old man's mysterious offer was because he wanted to finally break away from his mother and throw himself into a project that would keep him away from home and force him to grow up. Although Eddie had experienced five years of contentment since having reached his own Blue River, he realized that no river is stationary. Rivers flow and travel through the landscape in its various terrains until reaching their destination. NOW was the time for Eddie to ride his Blue River.

Until next time . . .

BIO — MICHAEL FREDERICK

Michael Frederick graduated from high school in 1970 with a busy mind. Despite attending four colleges, he managed to come away with zero college credits. It was after his tour in the Navy that he decided to be a writer. "I've lived in a hundred places in America, but I validate my gypsy lifestyle by writing about my travels in my novels. I ascribe to Tennessee Williams's philosophy that 'writing is my ideal reality; life is not.'"

In 1979 Michael self-published his first novel, *White Shoulders*. He personally sold ten thousand copies door to door over a two-year period, giving him a Masters-level education in salesmanship, perseverance, and handling rejection.

He is currently working on his tenth novel in the Sioux Falls, South Dakota, area where much of his new story takes place.

To my loyal readers and librarians, I want to thank all of you; you allow me to live my life as a writer. Where would I be without you?

To the young men in high school reading my books, I want to encourage you to keep reading and expanding your horizons through books. I encourage you to read my book *Autumn Letters* if you have not yet done so. Although by its cover it may appear to be a book for girls, it is a story of a young man's coming of age and his quest to establish himself and realize his true identity. I think you will be greatly rewarded by reading that story.

To the readers who like my books, please tell your librarian or media specialist that you would like to keep reading my books, so I can place my next book in your library. I call all of my 7,000 librarians one at a time, and every good report helps so much. I could write a book about it!

In the Fall of '08 I plan on coming out with two titles. One will be a mainline reissue of my third novel, *The Paper Man* (which needs editing for high school readers). I will also have completed my tenth novel and sincerely hope you will want to read it as well.

Thanks again for making it possible for me to live my life as an independent American writer.

For Feedback & Ordering:

Michael Frederick
P.O. Box 657
Sioux Falls, SD 57101

email: mfrederick310@aol.com

WGRL-HQ FIC
31057100257362
FIC FREDE
Frederick, Michael.
Blue River

6/01